Ghosts

OF THE SUPERSTITIONS

Dot Jay Gomez

"Fiction is real life with a twist."

GHOSTS OF THE SUPERSTITIONS is a work of fiction. Names, characters, places and incidents are the products of the author's imagination or are used fictitiously. Any resemblance to actual events, locales, or persons, living or dead is entirely coincidental.

Published in the United States of America.
Quail Harbor Productions
P.O. Box 8185
Cave Creek, AZ 85327

ISBN

978-0-578-14690-4

Printed in the United States of America.

Library of Congress Cataloging applied for.

Cover design by Shaun Wawro.

A special thanks to
Grant the Great,
and 'Marketeer'- Andy.

ALSO by Dot Jay Gomez:

Blakely High PHOTO PLAY

A young teacher, Gina McHenry, becomes entangled with danger as she searches for answers to a kidnapping, a terrorizing car chase, and a mountain trail ride shooting. Qwest for answers to hidden secrets take you from the CAVE CREEK desert to the high country of the RIM and into the BLUE RIDGE forest.

Blakely High and the VOODOO PHANTOM

The principal, Dr. Shieter, wishes he could rescind the order of "African Studies Across the Curriculum" when a VOODOO PHANTOM causes havoc all over the town of Cave Creek, Arizona. As body parts start showing up everywhere, some of the miscreants start taking bets as to where the next one will appear…Where is the body? Who are the saboteurs?

The VOODOO PHANTOM is especially vengeful toward Gina the young preppy high school teacher and harasses her almost daily. Who is the VOODOO PHANTOM? Is it her current crush, the handsome titan, RICK DEL RIO? Maybe it's one of the FAMILY FARM cycle group members.

Could it be one of the two eccentrics who came to town….the affluent and flamboyant MR.HOLLYWOOD who flaunts his riches driving a different prized convertible roadster weekly… or BERTI the gigantic Russian dog groomer who brags to be "cleaning up the town" as she fills her truck with the garbage of others?

Gina's family and friends, Pop, Dixie, Nancy Lopez and Richard/Raquel spin around in circles solving the mystery of… THE VOODOO PHANTOM!

Mystery - Romance - Action

About the Author:

- Dot Jay Gomez
- Retired high school teacher.
- 24 years at Paradise Valley High School.
- B.A. and M.A. from Arizona State University.

Favorite Mottos:

- It's not what you know; it's what you do with it.
- He who is bored, is boring.

"If you get lost in the Superstitions, you will never be found."

-Melvin M. Jay, pilot

"Superstitious mountains are haunted by spirits"

-APACHE

SUPERSTITION WILDERNESS—158,345 Acres of DESERT, is an urban park of FOREST, RIPERIAN, and WOODLAND territory. Due to the close proximity of local towns, hikers are in abundance on any one day. Hundreds get lost each year. Few never get found.

Scattered among the dusty-dirty-wide-open desert spaces are miles of FOLIAGE, an abundance of WILDLIFE and REMNANTS OF STUFF a hiker may encounter.

FOLIAGE: Arizona Black Walnut, Arizona Rosewood, Arizona Sycamore, Catclaw, Cottonwood, Honey Mesquite, Jumping Cholla, Juniper, Manzanita, Mimosa, Mountain Mahogany, Netleaf Hackberry, Palo Verde, Prickly Pear, Redberry Buckhorn, Saguaro, Shrub Oak, Single Leaf Pinyon, Sonoran Cacti, Sugar Sumac, Tomatillo, Willow Trees, and Yucca.

WILDLIFE: Black Bear, Bobcats, Coatimundi, Deer, Fox, Javalina, Mountain Lion, Ringtail Cats, and various birds.

REMNANTS OF STUFF a hiker may encounter in addition to Bones of old miners: Barbed wire fencing, Bucket pieces, Closed mine chutes, Concrete slabs, New caves, Old cattle corrals, Petroglyphs, Pottery Sherds left by Salado Indians dating between 1100 and 1400, Prehistoric caves, Rock cairns, Stone corrals, Windmill towers, Wooden trail signs and an occasional scattering of Gold Nuggets.

CHAPTER 1

APACHE CAMP
Massacre Grounds
December 22, 1848

The whining wind captured icy sleet and threw it into the shallow cave where a motley group of SIX campers were stumbling about in a varied range of activities unaware of the Southwest cold. Sheets of windblown sleet trying to become fuzzy snow slithered down the north side of Superstition Mountain, approximately three miles away from Apache Camp. Peaking at a little over five thousand feet, the mountain is already white at its promontory. The first storm in months brings unknown silence and serenity.

Then:

"APACHE! Get that gal-dern thing out of your mouth!" DUTCHY sat on a small boulder low to the ground, his knees above his rounded belly, his ready-made boots planted in the damp sandy gravel. Taking the Weiss Harmonica he had brought from Germany from his whiskered mouth, he slapped the spit and sleet out of it against his new canvas Nankeen yellow-pants. His scratchy voice barely audible he ranted. "That snake'll bite cha!" He continued playing while keeping one squinty eye on the hunched, nearly naked APACHE covered only by a loin cloth, contorting in a corkscrew before falling down flat on his back never releasing the bow in his left fist and arrow in his right. Long black hair scattered thickly about his face unattended by a braided headband.

His whooping and screaming decreased to a moan as slippery snowflakes fell blurring his face paint. He rested.

Oblivious, the five foot Diamondback anxiously slithered unnoticed to the nearest thicket of Prickly Pear arousing a half dozed Jack Rabbit that quickly hopped away in a blur leaving the snake uncontested.

DUTCHY stared at APACHE now lying there silent, shook his head a negative and continued on his harmonica.

One handed MEXICAN MANO grumbled in Spanish, got up and carried a pot of soaked beans to a circle of rocks, a fire camp outside the shallow cave chiseled from a cliff where they were hunkered.

After carefully setting the pot on a special circle of rocks around a pit, he adjusted his wide sombrero shoving it down further to keep snow out of his eyes. Brushing sleet from his handmade solid leather boots unhurriedly, he decided to check on APACHE.

Using his right boot, he toed the Indian lifting one foot at the ankle then dropping it. APACHE lay quietly, knuckles still clutching a weapon. In a flinging half-second MEXICAN MANO took his knife from the tooled leather case anchored at his hip and threw it hard at APACHES'S chest. It went through and stuck in the wet desert sand. APACHE jumped with a piercing whoop and in a blink, notched his arrow and let it go fast into MEXICAN MANO'S heart traveling through and into the surrounding thicket where the Diamondback rattled menacingly.

MEXICAN MANO, taking a slow breath in and out, cursed in Spanish, a language well known to APACHE. He continued to fix the campfire to cook the pot of Pintos, gathering the bundle of stubby Mesquite sticks he previously prepared.

APACHE lowered his weapons, ducked his head in despair and sat squat on the dampening earth with shoulders slumped and head resting on wrists.

DAVEY, the young foot soldier from General Cook's Camp McDowell miles away, sat leaning in the shallow cave, his back against the edge of the chiseled cliff watching MEXICAN MANO. He took off his wool Army hat, ran his hand through his long yellow hair, slapped dust out of the hat and put it on again. Next he played with the few hairs now growing on his face smoothing them down.

"Ain't got no Lucifers," he called out to MEXICAN MANO who was now searching his pockets with his one hand for the phosphorous match with the poisonous heads.

DUTCHY pocketed his harmonica, retrieved MEXICAN MANO'S knife from the ground where it spiked deep to the end, picked up a piece of wood where he was sitting and began to whittle. All the while he never took eyes off APACHE who now stood silently slumping.

GAMBLER MOONEY, the latest member of the group of six, scrutinized the scene from the far end of the chiseled notch of a cave, shifted his canvas bag closer under his legs where he sat silently watching from a small boulder. His beaver slouch hat pulled tightly down against the wind secured long dark hair that hindered his view as he ducked to avoid the beginnings of soft white flakes of snow blowing slow motion inside the cave. A long black broadcloth frock coat hung low to his boney ankles. He secured the collar tightly around his neck with one hand. With the other, he dusted small pieces of dried debris from his matching broadcloth pantaloons that were 'lumply' tucked into his ready-made boots secured from the store at Camp McDowell for three dollars.

Across his black vest was a gold watch hanging from a long chain, eyed and envied by the other five. A large hook on one end fastened into a button hole while a funny looking key for winding the watch, attached to a toggle bar at the end of the chain. He wound his watch extending the key to the slot and turning it.

"Time for a smoke!" he said looking out at the group. "APACHE! Decease this discombobulated nonsense and start MANO'S fire."

After ordering loudly, he opened his bag and pulled out six 'long-nines' super cigars with a pig tailed twist at the end to hold them together. They were a specialty. "No—these we save for Christmas." He put them back in their paper wrapping and from his bag grabbed a handful of bitter tasting 'stogies', cheap 'short-sixes' that he had bought from Camp McDowell, two for one cent. These were the cheapest of cigars named after the drivers of the Conestoga wagons who smoked them regularly.

At the sight of the cigars, APACHE got busy with his fire drill—a crude bow with a loose string that rotated a wooden drill on a flat piece of wood until friction created tiny glowing coals.

Large rocks provided a crude tent shelter for the fire and after a few attempts, it was glowing.

CHINA ROSE, a tag-along from an entertainment venue somewhere, came running over from where she had been sitting next to FOOT SOLDIER DAVY, and held her long faded green velvet skirt in a semi-circle to fan the fire and shield away the wind and snow. Holding her skirt wide and almost over the flames exposed her faded pink tights fitting snugly on her huge frame. She was as wide as she was short. She too wore ready-made store bought boots like the men. These were the norm for this area of dirt, rocks, snakes, cacti, scorpions and other menaces.

Five gold mongers hovered over APACHE who provided the fire—all momentarily oblivious of the on-coming snow, cold and wind.

It was early afternoon as the sky darkened quickly.

No animals stirred while white began to settle on the tops of Saguaros, packing arm pits that extended like crooked fork prongs, handles firmly attached deep below the surface.

Forming a circle around the fire, each silently chewed on a stogie. It was a togetherness of overwhelming discontent.

Then an interruption!

****

Suppliers from the valley hauled a strange looking wagon pulled by a wheeled contraption unlike any they had seen before and left tall posts pounded in the ground. It was an invasion of their area. A party was coming. They stood gaping at the group of four newcomers strangely dressed in dark blue canvas pants and thick vests. Black hats and leather gloves completed their attire. They stood close and stared at the invaders…..listening.

"Let's hurry and git the hell out a here," said one.

"I feel someone breathing down my back," said another.

They stared around them. It was a strange quietness, a wilderness kind before attack. No rabbits scattered. No coyotes howled. No red-winged hawks hovered above.

The four newcomers stood together and looked around. From a chiseled ledge about one hundred yards away, the sound of a tin cup clanked.

"Squirrels! You ready? I'm gone," said one.

"There's a faint smell of smoke."

"Why anyone wants to ride here is beyond me."

They shivered.

"It's haunted!"

Lightening struck a Saguaro splitting an arm where it stood tall on the crest of Flat Iron Mountain a half mile away. The blowing wind chased the men into their trucks.

CHAPTER 2

CAVE CREEK, ARIZONA

December 17, 2014

"TRAILRIDE mandatory meeting Monday after school" was taped to the outside of my door all last week. "Miss McHenry's Room—4 p.m."—completed the sign pure and simple and although I expected the twenty-one students to be there on time, I was in doubt about the adults. The nine adults would do anything to miss a meeting—including me. "Just give me a handout," each said. "In case I can't make it."

Now sitting on the tall stool at my podium, my back against the wall and my handy desk on my right, I faced all the trail riders who were busy reading the handout with the do's and don'ts. Teens cuddled together with their pals—all excited—all talking.

"Are you taking your horse?"

"No, we're not supposed to."

I had told them that parking was a problem and that the mountain horses were ridden daily and knew the mountains.

"Stock horses are well-heeled to the fluctuating terrain of twisting trails and sloping canyons"

Of the adults, there were five of us at the meeting so far. Nancy Lopez—AKA my partner in crime, or better known as "little red" by the faculty, was a helpful rider and we rode on week-ends all over the Cave Creek desert.

Heleena Dunkin, in charge of the English Department, was smiling while wiggling in a student desk, tapping her tennis shoes on the carpet to a tune in her head. Too old to teach but too young to retire she begged to go on the all day ride. "I've never been on a horse before," she hesitantly said last August, "but I am now taking riding lessons from a friend's English riding stable."

"One problem," I warned her, "make sure you learn Western style, your butt firmly planted in the saddle."

Sitting in the far back corner of the classroom were the Principal, Dr. Shieter being his flamboyant self, and our pal Becky Painter the Commercial Arts teacher.

We chummed. She, Nancy and I ditched unnecessary after school faculty meetings. Once we got caught by the Principal's main secretary as we three were standing in the ticket line for an early afternoon movie. "Popcorn anyone?" she asked with a devious grin as she sneaked behind us. "I'm buying!" No words were further needed as the four of us sat tiredly together and watched the best afternoon comedy ever. We four agreed that all Principals must be assigned to teach one difficult class for a full year. For sure, frequent meetings would soon stop.

Now, Dr. Shieter scooted his desk closer to Becky's touching her elbow with his. "Have you done this before?"

"Gina, is this my fourth ride or my fifth?" Directing her question loudly to me she scooted her desk a few inches away from the purveyor. Too late! He put his arms around her shoulders and said, "We're riding together."

She squirmed.

He squeezed.

Dandy! I'm glad that they're sitting far back away from the chatty kids.

"Becky, he likes you." We had always told her.

"Yeah!" she would reply over and over. "He likes skirts, plural."

Thinking I heard noises in the hallway, I looked up from my podium of notes towards the open door at the back of my classroom. Swaying in the open doorway was an indistinct figure. I stared, scrunched my eyes and blinked several times thinking phlegm from persistent allergies was blurring my vision. I ducked my head, closed my eyes and ran my fingers through my springy mess of Shirley Temple curls which habitually made things go away. One swipe and I was usually better. I counted to five before looking again. I took a deep breath and sighed loudly.

Clear.

No one noticed.

I reached over at my desk an arm's length away and refilled my coffee cup, a blend of Christmas spices from my thermos. Immediate renewal!

Others too had drinks allowed for this special meeting on a tired Monday one week before Christmas vacation. I had planned the meeting one week prior to the ride so everyone would focus and seriously prepare necessities. The pre-paid sign up was last August and all had been coached to ride-ride-ride in preparation for this Saturday's all day event.

"You don't want to ruin your day with saddle sores or stiffness." I was a broken record for the past four months. Also, the students in my Western Literature classes voted at sign up time for the all day event to take place the twenty-second before Christmas because many were going out of town on or after the twenty-fifth.

Some of the riders who were repeaters begged for a longer than the usual four hours ride---with an hour break in the middle. They were exuberant with the new change for longer hours.

"Ok. A new troop of Wranglers has mapped a different route for us—a longer ride—six hours total round trip, split in the middle for recreation and eats." They were ready. I thought I was.

I handed out maps to eager hands as I walked around the room still talking. "We bring our own snacks and drinks which we'll keep in our horse's large saddle bag. Bagel sandwiches work best. Don't smash."

Now the kids were really chatty while talking about food. Heleena Dunkin had brought colorful Christmas hard candy, and started waddling through the rows offering the special dessert. I chose my favorite round orange one with a juicy tart center, and continued.

"'Shince' there are exactly thirty of us," I slurped, "twenty-one students and nine adults, the Wranglers are splitting us in three groups."

Oops! Among the now griping and groaning group, I told them, "Those are the rules. Makes sense! However, we will be split apart by only five minutes. As we ride up and down hills like a roller coaster, you can wave at each other." I smiled while illustrating the princess wave. Of course, this prompted some students to turn around while seated in their desks mocking me. It's Christmas!

Next, I pointed to the board which had three separate groups numbered one through ten. "Adults are listed already, three to a group---plus a Wrangler in the lead. Write your name wherever."

"Do we have to ride in a line?"

"Yeah, like a string?" Jamie Mink rolled her baby blues and Kim Rose pouted. They loudly swished ice around in their vanishing drinks and poked straws up-and-down in the containers.

"Don't worry," I said. "When you get to the vastness of the Superstition Wilderness you'll be thankful for collective grouping. And at times we'll get in a circle as we encounter bears, long bearded old prospectors with wooden shotguns, and Indians with bows and arrows." I paused between each grouping for special affects and didn't look up for awhile as I stood reading my notes. When I did, all was quiet as a room full of gapers stared back.

"What?" I asked dumb faced.

"She's smart mouthing us," said Kim sitting in the middle of the room swiveling around to others. "Get used to it!" She wrinkled her freckled nose and the two of them laughed.

I intervened. "Actually, this is a good plan because each person is responsible for the one riding directly in front. No one gets lost."

"Have you ever lost a rider in the group?" This of course came from two freshmen boys. Good riders, but young.

CHAPTER 3

"Let me think!" I leaned forward on my big square podium and rested my heels on the bottom rung of my tall metal stool.

"No! But almost! It all depends on the weather and you the rider. STICK CLOSE!" I pointed my finger for emphasis. "If it's windy, give the horse its rein and let it lead. It'll follow others. Don't try to duck behind a large boulder. You'll get left behind. This happened once in my five years of trail riding with students."

Time to pause for dramatic affect and let them know I meant business. After a good gulp of coffee, I continued to a totally silence group. I'm such a drama queen!

All eyes looked at me except for Dr. Shieter sitting back in the corner busy writing…or playing tic-tac-toe…I don't know.

"We had to stop, wait, and go back for a small group of three trying to huddle out of the wind behind a large boulder down in a small ravine…a snake curled at their feet. They didn't even see the snake." I hope I scared them.

Loud laughter from the empty hallway echoed into the room from the open door shattering the serious mood as all eyes riveted in that direction.

Dr. Mallory, AKA Delilah-movie-star-gorgeous, wiggled into the room with a big smiley face----the one left over from laughter---the one that accompanies a great delight of some sort, like a rosy pink school girl crush. And she was wearing her painted-on faded blue jeans topped with a clinging fuzzy red holiday sweater.

At her heels was the regal Rick Del Rio. MY Rick with the emerald green eyes, wavy dark hair and black shirt belted in just right.

I snarled, clenched my teeth, sighed deeply and blew smoke out of my ears. Feeling flush, I quickly turned around, grabbed a tissue feigning a cough. No one noticed except Kim and Jamie who were whispering. I shook it off.

Discombobulated, I motioned toward the board with numbered spaces on the three groups and said, “sign-up”.

Rick tried to look serious now, and to Delilah’s dismay, didn’t sit next to her but wandered towards the one empty seat in the front, took two handouts from my desk and sat reading.

Simultaneously, desks scooted, bumped, and toppled as the riders ran to the board.

“Don’t panic. You can switch places later if someone agrees to it!” Above the din, I think they heard.

“Don’t change the adults’ places. I have them at the lead and at the rear of each line.” It was important that friends rode with friends….teachers included.

I watched Delilah contemplate the three lists, foolishly erase her name off one and add it to Rick’s list who now stayed seated and kept looking at his watch.

To my chagrin, Delilah had begged to go along when she had learned that a couple students had to cancel. She met me one tired afternoon in the hallway and said, "Besides being a forensic anthropologist, I have basic medical training for emergencies." She played with the silver charm bracelet dangling from her slim wrist as she pointed her long enameled fingernails in the air so the chain would spiral up-and-down. Occasionally she put her hands on her hips as she spoke, accenting the fact that they could almost encase her twenty-two inch waist. Of course, she never made eye contact. I'll have to stare her down later in my slinky dress with Rick on my arm---like candy.

Well, damn I was stuck. Instead of spitting fire, I stammered and stomped, checked my broken-down nails and said, "We'll see. Check with me next week." This gave me the edge until next week came and there were no replacements.

Now here we are, and I refuse to let her ruin MY trail ride.

To make things worse, I learned that she had been queen of the Horseman's Gymkhana her earlier years. She did the fancy stuff, bobbing up and down on the saddle with her hair in a bun and butt in the air. When I told Pop all this, he said, "She can't be better than you, Queen of the Desert!" What does he know? He's my dad.

My best friend Nancy Lopez, who teaches in the room next to mine for the same amount of five years, told me to "quit fumin' and fussin'. Del Rio is yours. His eyes are only on you. But, if it'll make you feel better, keep her at the end of the line. Like, in front of Dr. Shieter." She raised her eyebrows up and down multiple times and we laughed at the thought of an elated Mr. Flirty.

From where I was standing, I could see Delilah's beautiful long nails envelope the handout as she purposely read with both elbows on the desk top and paper in the air. I looked at mine. Nuts! Handling and grading masses of papers daily did wonders for my nails of different sizes and hidden cuticles. I grabbed a tube of lotion-paste and creamed my hands pushing back cuticles before everyone sat down again.

Jamie waved "give-me" fingers so I threw the tube to her. She shared with Kim who passed it on to friends. They love me.

Looking at the clock on the wall, I realized we had thirty minutes remaining of the meeting and hurried on. The group was content, eating and drinking, so no pressure here. I too had my cup in hand and snacks within reach.

"Now, back to the weather and essentials. Pay attention and make notes. Temperatures for next Saturday should be in the low sixties, which is quite chilly when sitting on a horse out in the open. Since my legs get cold fast, I bring a small blanket to throw over my lap and I tuck it under my legs. It works for me. The temperature could dip. Tied to the back of the saddle is a yellow trench coat with big attached hood in case it rains. The hood will fit over your hat or cap."

"A storm is comin'!" All heads turned to the far side of the room where a small clique of boys sat. Coyotee had spoken. Very rare! In the past when he talked, everyone stopped whatever they were doing and listened. His voice was gruff, his speech staccato and his face always expressionless.

He was Apache, a senior having arrived last year from the rim country in northern Arizona, near Pinetop. Boys accepted him, but girls feared him except for one, Catora Bell, known as Cat by the student body. She was on the ride and would want to stay close to Coyotee. "Hey," she would always brag to her friends loudly. "We are on the same cross country team and he is really nice. Besides, being fourth generation Arizonan, I know that I have some Indian blood in me too!" She thumped an empty palm on her chest.

She was freckly, white as a sheet and looked Irish.

To answer Coyotee I said, "Yes. A storm is supposed to roll in late Sunday and arrive full force on Christmas Eve."

"Yeah. I love snow!" Someone said, as the group became robust.

Super! I had opened a can of worms. Continuing now in a hurry since I was the only one watching the clock on the wall and Rick was half out of his seat continually looking at his watch. I said, "We will take our chances. You know Arizona weather. What they say doesn't always happen!" I tried to be optimistic but an icy-desert-snow storm—a photographer's dream—would be a disaster for us.

"Dress warm! Dig out old ski jackets if necessary. No 'cutesy' dress jackets will work. Remember, there are rawhide ties on the saddles for such things."

"We don't have any boots." Two girls sitting together complained after reading about protective foot wear.

"Doesn't matter. Wear tennis shoes, hikers, anything but sandals. No open toed shoes of any kind. Also, for pants, choose what's comfortable. Warm sweats or loose denims will work."

Going down the handout's list, head gear was self-explanatory. Caps, visors or Western hats must fit tightly.

"Any questions about head gear? Remember, no one wants to retrieve your hat if it gets blown away. Ask Roy, our star retriever!"

"Yeah." Roy the hunky senior spoke for the first time and brought his desk down on all fours for emphasis from its position of a two legged lean on the wall. "This year I'm charging one dollar for every hat I retrieve…two dollars if it lands in cactus." He smiled. They laughed. He continued since he had an audience of admirers. "Girls, wear your Dale Evan's tie downs and boys, your Pancho Villas." He was done and leaned back again against the wall.

Smooth.

"Snacks. Next item on the list."

Round faced Russell whose long tee shirt always expanded loosely at his middle, questioned before I could continue. “What can we bring?”

“The saddles are equipped with large canvas saddle-bags for things like candy, combs, chips, sun-screen, lotion, hand wipes and whatever else.”

“Butt wipes.” Sparky Kim candidly remarked. She giggled.

I simply raised my brows and shrugged my shoulders with no comment other than, “What we carry in—we carry out. No big green dump truck will be around to carry your garbage off the mountain.”

With my left ear I heard Coyotee from across the room where he too had been leaning against the wall. “Hit the can before we leave;” and with my right ear I heard Rick quietly say, “They have facilities spotted here and there. We’ll find one.”

Concerning such a serious matter, the room became very quiet. Even Dr. Shieter, the Principal, quit writing and looked towards me.

Suddenly, my heavy classroom door slammed shut with a loud bang and everyone jumped.

CHAPTER 4

"Must be wind suction from outside in the hallway!" Rick said quietly as he got out of his desk, opened the heavy wooden door and shoved the rubber contoured peg firmly under it. He looked down both ends of the long hallway, each containing double doors that open to the outside. They were closed.

I said, "Someone must have entered the hallway to cause the wind suction to slam the door shut." It was more a question than a statement.

Rick looked puzzled as he stood in the open doorway. Then looking at his watch he mouthed "I have to leave," threw me a kiss and stepped back into the hall.

I did a short business wave, nodded, then snuck a peek towards Delilah whose cat eyes never missed a trick. She was half out of her desk when I hurriedly said to her—"There's a bit more!" She sat back down.

After six cell phones rang almost simultaneously, I said, "Take ten—then we'll finish the list." All got up to chat, snack, or go to the campus bathroom.

"Miss Mac, what are you wearing?" A circle of girls who were discussing their clothes for the ride wanted to know.

"My stretchy, thick riding-pants with the foot stirrups to prevent crotch-cramming!" I smirked.

A couple girls were expressionless until Cat and another said that is what they were wearing and explained where they could be purchased.

I continued. "Comfort is number one if you're sitting in the saddle for a total of six hours. Also, I'm wearing a long sleeve turtle neck under a thick sweatshirt. I'll have a hat with ties and a neck scarf like the ones I'm offering to everyone next."

Everyone returned and settled in their seats. Again, Heleena passed around her bag of hard Christmas candy with the chewy centers.

"Now, I have a bag of colorful western neck scarves, the old Western type, only these come in bright colors. Please wear one around your neck so we will know that you're part of our ride. We won't be the only ones on the trails you know—and there are thirty of us. What if one of you gets lost?"

Everyone was quiet again.

"A horse could bolt and take off. A ghost could come and lead you astray! It's haunted you know." I didn't crack a smile but spoke seriously while looking down at my podium.

Kim interrupted. "There she goes again!"

No one laughed. Considering all the television shows about ghosts lately, this is the era.

I added, "We're riding through Massacre Grounds where Apaches and Mexicans fought in the early 1800's. Many skeleton bones and skulls were found there much later. It IS supposed to be haunted." I didn't smile.

That invited a heavy conversation of all the popular ghost stories shown currently throughout the week. Roy, the stout senior football player sitting in the back of the room by the door, scooted over to the light switch and turned the lights off and on a couple times.

"Ok special effects. Tell us about past weather conditions. You've been riding with us since your freshman year."

"Dress warm. It's always cold. One time the weather man predicted the middle seventies—it sleeted. And it's always windy." Done, he stopped sharply and leaned his desk back against the wall—a Mister Cool.

"Like I said, you're exposed on horseback so be prepared." I thought Roy had done a good job getting out the message. Student to student 'info' was always the best tool.

"Back to bandanas: Black, red, yellow, purple, pink, green,--choose a color and don't fight." I grinned and saved two black ones for Rick and me.

Delilah came forward first and selected red. "I'm leaving," she said abruptly and walked out.

This prompted others to select from the batch that I passed around. They were in a good mood. "I'll trade you a pink for a red." They tied them around their necks with a bow in the front. Someone said, "cavalry style". They helped each other. Was it Christmas yet?

All were jubilant except for Coyotee, the Apache kid. He sat quietly, his chair leaning against the side wall, his expression un-readable. Tanned, lean and thin from Cross Country, he seemed more worldly than his classmates most of the time with his closed attitude and cynical demeanor.

"Catora," I whispered. "Help Coyotee!" She grabbed three colors and went over to him. Choosing a yellow like hers, she tied it around his neck. How could he resist. I held my breath. He did his half smile and shyly turned his head sideways to check out those around him. She settled next to him to chat.

"Good news," I continued. "Mr. Cloud will accompany us on the bus and will give details on the legends and lore of the Superstition area and the Lost Dutchman Mine."

Kids reacted favorably to this. Richard Cloud, the teacher in the room next to Nancy's, was quite popular as a tutor for the teens on any subject. He was like an encyclopedia of knowledge and a go-fer-info for both Nancy Lopez and me. He often stayed late after school offering free tutoring for students, always with parents' permission and always with his door open. Because of his looks with his little bow tie and mannerisms, kids at first nicknamed him R & R for Richard/Raquel. After they saw him helping at football practice and throwing the ball twice as far as any one of them could, they quickly referred to him as Mr. Cloud.

Go figure! Nancy and I call him Cloud.

"Are we finished at the board?" All eyes studied the three lists quietly. All of a sudden, the door slammed shut again; too loudly this time, echoing a bit in the quiet room.

We all jumped a few inches in some direction from the reverberation.

"What the hellishness!" Kim was loud.

Roy moved quickly to the heavy door to open it. "The rubber wedge is gone," he announced loudly.

Two to three students now helped him look for it in both directions of the hallway. They came back with palms up—"It's gone."

"Very weird," said one.

"Ghosts," Coyotee offered too flatly.

"One more minute and we're done for the day. Put a desk in the hall to prop the door open," I said to the kids at the doorway. "For the remainder of the week, come see me if you have questions about Saturday's ride—five days to go!"

CHAPTER 5

Grabbing backpacks, everybody milled around chattering away about the ride and sharing their preparations. Dr. Shieter had been quiet the entire time while sitting next to Becky Painter, the Commercial Arts teacher. Enamored as usual, he acted too professional which was out of character for him as the two conversed quietly about items on the handout of "Trail Ride Do's and Don'ts." Shieter shadowed her out of the room with no goodbye to me or questions about the ride. As he was out the door and in the hallway, Becky turned back at the door and did her usual raised-brow-eye-roll kind of thing and waved her purple bandana at me. "See you soon."

Mental note to self. Put Shieter with Delilah's group.

Last to leave were Jamie and Kim. "Ok, Miss Mac. Be sure Roy is in our line," said Jamie. They emphasized the fact by underlining the three names on the board.

"Put him between us," said Kim.

"What are you going to pay me?" It was my turn.

"How about your favorite candy bar?"

"Dark chocolate?"

"Dark chocolate!"

You have a deal. I'll sandwich him between you two so you'll stay out of trouble."

"That'll work" They high fived, slapped hands a little too hard and hurried out.

Nancy Lopez and I stood at the chalk board studying the three lists. We made sure that three adults were in each line of seven kids. "Adults in the front and rear," we said as we moved a few names, making sure to keep the same friends in the same line as signed.

"Rick will be the leader of his group and Delilah and Shieter will be at the very end." I said in contemplation while examining it all.

Nancy added, "Becky wants to be in the same group as Guy Wagner. Being Athletic Director, he's good at giving orders that might be needed."

"Done," I said. "And let's put your cop friend Colt at the front of their group."

We checked-off names on the board before writing them on paper. Group 1: Gina McHenry, Nancy Lopez and Heleena Dunkin. Group2: Rick Del Rio, Delilah Mallory and Principal Shieter. Group 3: Colt, Becky Painter and Guy Wagner. Seven students will be in the middle of each line with a Wrangler at each lead.

"Since I'm worried about Heleena, let's make sure she's with us. She can ride tail and help keep order. I have her following Cat and Coyotee." I continued explaining to Nancy my problems dealing with Heleena.

"Last August she begged to go with us even though she had never been on a horse and vowed to take lessons from her neighbor plus ride daily to get ready."

Nancy said, "I'm sure the Wranglers will be ready for all types of riders. That's their job."

Nancy and I were on the same page when it came to analyzing Heleena. As head of the English Department she was such a pain in the ass.—Yakity-yak: "Be sure to lock your doors at the end of the day; If you lose your key, you won't get another; No cups of coffee in the classroom—we have to set a good example for the students." Yakity-yak—as she thundered through the long hallway in tennis shoes, her gathered skirt down to her ankles swaying to and fro....always in a hurry to her break room, the custodian's office for a smoke.

"She is confused. We are the adults and not the kids." This we repeated numerously.

Frequently during our lunch time we would console each other with progressive ideas. "Every 'head-cheese' on this campus needs at least one large classroom of students to teach daily—all year long," I always told Nancy and Becky.

"Yes," and Nancy would add, "That would cut back on the unnecessary after school meetings and other superficial activities that limit our grading time."

Becky insisted, "They should each have a class of thirty-eight freshman all year long."

We were a broken record as we ate our sandwiches. However, we not only had coffee or tea drinks on our desks, but also kept a small fridge of snacks nearby.

Stepping back, Nancy and I looked at the three lists. "This is a good start!" I said.

"It'll work," she sighed while bundling a stack of papers that she had been grading during the meeting. "See you tonight for Celebrity Ghosts Stories," she left smiling while waving her pink bandana. Good match for red hair, I thought.

A heavy Rap on the wood frame of my classroom door introduced the shy, lean Coyotee Raintree who was on List One of his first trail ride with us.

He didn't look at me while entering but unfolded the map that I had handed out a few minutes ago. His staccato speech matched the heaviness of his boots clomping on the thin carpet.

"It's cursed!" He shoved the map in my face, laid it on my desk and thudded it loudly with the back of his hand. With thick fingers he tapped the area of Massacre Grounds, pulled his navy wind-breaker a little tighter around his middle and zipped it half-way. Putting his hands in his jacket pockets, he shuffled back a few steps, stood stone still and looked at me eye to eye waiting for an answer.

I sighed, dropped my shoulders and leaned back in my chair. "It's not alone," I said. "Many places are supposed to be haunted in the Superstitions." I tried to fake a matter-of-fact attitude towards a well-heeled Indian runner who knew more than I did about the matter.

"It'll be day light and we're having an hour picnic there before turning around." I leaned back in my chair nonchalantly and put both hands behind my head staring at him trying to read what he knew that I didn't. He was savvy, no mistake about it!

"My family say, it's dangerous. Not good to stay there. We go quickly through." His faltering speech re-emphasized his mission of confronting me and I realized its seriousness. When nervous, his English became sterile.

"I'll work on it," was all I could think to say.

He turned on his heels quickly and left. He was unreadable. I decided that I needed to call his mother for good measure and make sure that he was prepared for a change in the weather.

Sitting at my desk, I proceeded with my end of the day ritual by putting my head down on my folded arms to relax and think uninterrupted. Mentally, this was my time to reflect on what I had or had not accomplished today, to think of my lesson plans for my five classes tomorrow and decide what papers to grade for tonight.

A heavy cool breeze swirled across the back of my neck.

"Rick," I said loudly and looked up. There was no one in the room, but within my immediate sight at the back, and standing in the doorway was a man. This was the same stocky person I had seen earlier, dressed in faded denim overalls, with long arms drooping close to his side. An angry face, fully bearded with shrunken eyes stared a few seconds before disappearing.

Gasping, and sputtering, I did a crunchy blink and sat straight in my chair wide awake. "Hey," I yelled as loudly as possible. I walked quickly to my door and looked down both directions of the hall. Gone!

Nancy came running out of her room to the open hall.

"I have a story to tell tonight!" My heart thumped as I stood with both hands on my hips.

CHAPTER 6

"Malarkee!" exclaimed Pop loudly while flipping a cheese crisp in the hot flat iron skillet.

"I saw what I saw when I saw it!" I loudly questioned the fact myself in disbelief, waving both hands in the air.

"Who's on first?" asked Pop slicing his face in half with his huge grin. Waving his spatula he asked, "Jalapenos or not?"

"Why ask," I said. "Double it."

He continued. "When's the last time you had your eyes examined? And, I suspect you've been too busy and too tired lately—grading papers until midnight, preparing for your trail ride, and the excitement of Christmas." His listing persisted while putting finishing touches on his homemade salsa, pouring olive oil through the top of the blender as he spoke.

I went to the beverage bar counter-top and poured myself the last cup of morning left-over coffee as he ranted on. I needed to stay awake for tonight's Celebrity Ghost show.

"I'll believe in ghosts and the entire gamut of paranormal"—he stuck a long teaspoon in the blender for taste—"needs more cumin—when I see one first hand." Of course, his ear to ear grin accommodated his next statement. "I could use some extra free help at the bakery!"

Dixie, Pop's live in girlfriend for twenty years, had changed out of her fashionable school garb to a comfortable large-boob covering baggy dress. She hastily threw the salad goods together and placed the bowl on our big round table in the kitchen. "Show starts in twenty minutes."

I followed her speed and threw green place mats on the table, the ones embroidered with red poinsettias, and a thick towel to protect the wood from a steaming glass casserole of beef enchiladas that I would soon take out of the oven. "Nancy Lopez is coming to dinner and to watch Celebrity Ghost Stories. Pop, you should watch it with us. It's phenomenal!"

"Cheap entertainment," he said. "They're great actors you know. I'll watch the news in the den. That's about as Sci Fi as I want to get." He met Nancy at the door with a big hug.

"I brought our favorite garlic-onion chip dip," she excitedly hollered petting Nellie the Greyhound who was jumping around.

"Hah! That's why you girls believe in that stuff. It's the garlic."

Nellie the rescued Greyhound turned circles a couple times, laughed as dogs do, tongue out, drool and all. She waited until Pop sat down before she did her usual curl under the table, lying her head on his feet. Eternally grateful to him who found her dying in a South Phoenix River Bed, she now never left his side.

Conversation was quick. Television was turned on and we left to settle on the couch after Pop mentioned that he would 'clean-up' the kitchen. Before doing so he decided to light the fireplace to eliminate the chill from our stucco framed four bedroom home.

"We have ten more minutes," I said. "Hand me the wood." I stood by the doorway in the darkening night ready for an armful. I watched and waited as a colder than usual December wind slapped at my face. I reminded Pop that his baggy elastic-at-the–waist shorts needed to go. "Tis the Season!"

Security lights framed the wood pile of neatly stacked cut pieces in the long breezeway between our carport and the tool shed near the barn. As he headed toward the pile, a totally unexpected cold wind, a twister of some sort, almost knocked him over and he stumbled to his knees. Simultaneously at the corrals, a spiral of whirling dust lifted a pitchfork near the haystack and in a hurdling force, catapulted it toward him, missing by inches.

"Unbelievable," he gasped after it landed prongs down a few yards from his feet.

I yelled, "How could that happen?"

"Impossible." Wild eyed, he grabbed the tool by the handle and hurried it to the area from where it was supposed to be stored, on a peg firmly between a shovel and rake. He looked around expecting to find a devious culprit. "Nothing," he said. "No one."

The funnel of wind continued away, dancing toward the desert below in the adjoining wide wash, convulsing between Brittle Bushes and Catsclaw all the while lifting heavy sand over rocks and boulders.

Shaking, we put half the wood in the fireplace and stored the remainder in a large metal bucket nearby.

"What was that?" I looked at Pop's ghostly white face.

"Watch out for wind funnels," he said as he started the kitchen clean-up. "Go watch your show!"

"Hey," I said to Dixie and Nancy loudly after sitting by the television to accompany them and anxious to tell about the traveling pitchfork.

They jumped. "Shhh," said Dixie. "Wait until commercials. It's starting."

Enticing music and shadowy figures began the introduction.-------PEEKING INTO THE KITCHEN I SAW AN OLD VERY THIN GRAY HAIRED LADY, LOOKING STRAIGHT AT ME WITH LARGE HAUNTING EYES-----

Commercials began and we muted the television. Nancy asked, "What happened to you?" My hair was all over my face.

I told them about the ordeal I saw when Pop went for wood. He joined me while running his fingers through his thick dark hair to flatten it and said, "I could turn gray over night with the unexplainable."

"Ghostly," I added.

Pop said, "You all better be prepared for a windy day Saturday regardless of weather predictions."

"You're still not going with us on our fifty passenger bus? You know that your biker pals, the four B's are going." I arose, put a kettle of water on high heat for a pot of tea, and selected tea cups from the cupboard. The half cup of coffee before dinner wasn't enough whatsoever. "They're hiking—not biking. You could get rid of that middle your building. Or you could shop with Dixie in Apache Junction."

Now he laughed hard. "I'd rather rake rocks. No, I'm staying home to run the bakery. I have some special Orange-cranberry loaves to bake. With my helpers gone hiking, I'd have to close down and it's too close to the holidays."

The four B's--AKA-- THE FAMILY FARM-- is a retired cycle group of professionals---Bing-Bob-Brad and Blake. New to Arizona and quite anxious to hike the infamous and dangerous Superstition Mountain range, they pleaded to go along last September. "We could hike behind the horses and pretty much stay on the same trail. We'll pay our bus fare."

How could I refuse a group of pudgy, balding, bearded retired professionals? "Just stay in shape." I warned them. Since then, they walked one hour daily all over Cave Creek.

Dixie said, "The bus driver is taking me to Apache Junction for shopping while everyone's riding. I'll have a whole day to myself." She sighed almost deviously.

I took the whistling tea kettle off the stove and poured water into a tea pot of three Earl Grey bags in time for them to seep until the next set of commercials.

The same vision grabber pre-empted the show again for emphasis and continuity....SHE STARTED WALKING TOWARDS ME WITH OPEN ARMS. I STOOD AND STARED, TOO AWESTRUCK TO MOVE. AS SHE REACHED OUT, SHE FADED--------

CHAPTER 7

Commercials began about "Silly Bars"-- full of oats and nuts. Among death and the damned, we have silly bars. I poured three cups of hot tea for us girls warning that they were extra hot.

"Hog wash," stated Pop who had been busy in the kitchen listening. "How can you watch that stuff?" He hung towels in their spaces after finishing.

I shrugged. "Well, they make it seem so real."

Dixie added while shaking her finger at the T.V, "Angelica Jane Marlow is my favorite actress and I believe that she speaks with great credibility."

"Pop," I whined. "If you watch it with us, you'll soon discover who the old lady was and why she's haunting the place!"

"Malarkee! I'm going to the den to watch the news."

I watched him stoke the fire some more, then stand by the window staring toward the tool shed searching for an explanation.

Cupping my tea with both hands, I joined him. "That pitchfork thing was unexplainable."

He said nothing until the security lights came on again out back. “Rabbits,” he quietly muttered. “The security lights are extra sensitive tonight. I’ll reset the dial in the morning.”

I reminded him to look for deer tracks. “You know how they travel down the wide wash and jump the fence to attack our hay stack when they’re hungry.”

I looked at him standing there wild eyed. Was it tiredness or fright? We both were thinking the same thing…the pitchfork was a heavy-duty one.

We watched the end of the show with all its special highlights for emphasis. The heightened music, the grayer than gray shadows, all acted to perfection with muted sounds.

We got up and stretched. Dixie started. “So, the old woman that haunted the house had been pushed down the flight of stairs by somebody.” She finished her tea.

I yawned, rinsed out my tea cup and set it by the sink.

“And,” Nancy began, “she comes back to warn others as she greets them at the bottom of the steps. So, that is what they want us to believe. Places of traumatic violence ending in death seem to be haunted.” Grabbing her purse and keys she continued. “Ok, walk me to my car. I’m still shaking.”

Three miles north of the town of Cave Creek was considered desert wilderness to most everyone. Here, the moon shone brighter, breezes blew cooler and Coyotes howled louder. So it was as we three looked at the slice of moon, the jillion stars and heard the howling. Rodents and cotton tails scampered through thick Desert Broom, Creosote, and Jojoba noisily at our feet as a cold wind swirled ominously in the too quiet night. Moving dark clouds quickly blanketed the moon and stars.

“I fear it’s going to be a cold ride this Saturday,” I mumbled while hugging my large sweatshirt tightly.

Dixie stated, “Let’s hope that’s all you have to fear. I’m always reading about haunted places in the Superstitions.”

"I hope we run into one." I flatly said.

Nancy looked at me as she opened her car door. "What?"

I continued. "It'll be day time. What's there to fear? Besides, we'll be with a large group of people."

"Yes, but if we're on horses for six hours with a one hour break in the middle—and December days are short—we better all mount-up early," warned practical Nancy.

I assured her that we have always been back at the bus way before dark."We'll just start out earlier. It'll be fine."

Nancy drove off with a wave of her arm. "See ya tomorrow," then quickly powered her window shut.

We hurried out of the darkness to the security of the porch lights. A night Owl hooted somewhere close.

Five more days.

CHAPTER 8

In my bedroom I turned off the lights, opened the curtains to the large picture window next to my bed on the south wall, and looked forward to the warmth and comfort of the covers.

The crazy moon fanned a glow that softly brightened the room with hues of gray and darkness from traveling clouds.

As was my nightly ritual, I called Del Rio from the land line on the adjoining night stand. By ten p.m., if we hadn't talked, than one needed to call the other.

"It's about time." His voice manly soft added to the tranquility of bedtime. "I heard about the fuzzy apparition that visited your room."

Ok. Noting a change in his voice, I frowned not knowing which way this was going. "Who'd you talk to?"

"Does it make a difference?" His voice this late, a whisper.

"Yep, it does. If you talked to Dixie, she's on my side. If you talked to my dad, than you're a skunk!"

"Well,"—pause and a couple beats later—"I'm in the middle. People I highly respect are believers with what they thought they saw and heard. Myself, I'm like Pop. I need my own experience."

"You're not making fun of me?"

"Course not! You're a rational person. You'll figure it out."

So now I needed to be rational. "It's never happened to me before. I wasn't tired. I had no caffeine earlier in the day—only the Hazelnut Decaf from my thermos."

"It's that damned flavored coffee!" His breath was deep.

I pictured the gleam in his eye and felt his honeyed smile. Since our pauses were getting longer, it was time to sign off, except there was something I needed to clarify. "I'm jealous of Delilah you know. She's so movie-star-gorgeous and hangs on your every word." Now I felt like a computer flashing a WARNING signal.

"Hey, you're my only snap-dragon. Besides, I have a giant plan. Let's put her in front of Principal Shieter. Mr. flirty can't keep his hands to himself."

And," I added, "she can give him pointers on how to stay in the saddle." Although Nancy and I had decided this earlier, I made him think it was his original.

I signed off with the usual since our conversation de-formalized to nonsensical mumbling.

"Kisses."

"Kisses."

I cuddled facing the window with curtains pulled all the way back to the edges. Tucking my blue denim coverlet close under my chin, I hugged my red silky-cased pillow and stared wide eyed for a short moment at slow moving Mesquite branches waving out in the distance, stirred by a cold breeze. I loved the illumination of a night sky and often counted helicopters hovering high in the far distances.

What was that? I raised my upper body with my elbow to stare. A rolling translucent shadow sculpted a convulsive image outside the window—tapping for a short five seconds.

I slammed down, closed my eyes and hugged the pillow more tightly refusing to believe it was anything other than a windy swirl of heavy dry sand.

Spooked, I questioned why I had decided to stay home. Del Rio is only five minutes down the road. Our usual week-ends together end on Monday considering the work week ahead. This has to change!

CHAPTER 9

APACHE CAMP
Massacre Grounds
December 22, 1848

Purple thick clouds obscure the afternoon sun as the darkening camp now introduces a soon to be heavy rain, washing a dusting of snow from the cliffs down into the many crevices below. Whether light or heavy, the campers are oblivious as they argue and fight in roguish dissent, each bound and tormented by mysterious spirits. They scurry about, frantically hoarding unique gear with tormented attitudes.

Camped on the south edge of Massacre Grounds and within two miles from the slope of the Superstition Mountain which marks the entrance to the Superstition Wilderness, they unknowingly feel the grandeur of its peak. Cresting over five thousand feet, its huge lop-sided square changes colors from purplish-gray to hues of slate and dark indigo—manned by sun and clouds.

Hoodoo pinnacles, like the squared rock monoliths of Easter Island, mark the territory near the six gold seekers stripped of chances. Harbored now in their shallow cave, an alcove chiseled from a crest of rock, they hovered in and out impatiently fretting over their demise.

FOOT SOLDIER DAVY rocked back and forth as he sat on a small boulder under the shallow eave, sipping coffee from a metal cup he always carried in his canvas shoulder bag. MEXICAN MANO had filled it for him earlier from the old black kettle.

One three inch yellowed suspender drooped low off his shoulder to his elbow. He readjusted his woolen army cap to protect his eyes from the wind, tucking his rusty colored, shoulder length hair behind his ears as he did so. Now cupping his drink with two hands, he glared at the trail and its zig-zag pattern, the path that led him here from Camp McDowell.

Now and then he patted the dried blood on the gaping gun-shot wound three inches down from his left shoulder and winced at DUTCHY. His spent Army revolver lay in the dirt by his side. On a hard flattened spot of soil, he set his cup so carefully and continued stuffing crushed dry grass into his right boot, the more heavily worn of the two.

CHINA ROSE had stood over him all the while, watching his task. She soon plumped down next to him in a splat, fanning out her faded green puffy skirt to cover pink stocking legs. She was now feeling the cold and bumped into Davy while settling in close. With her fingers, she swept his grass pieces into a neat little pile.

FOOT SOLDIER DAVY moved only a few inches giving her room enough. She was twice his size but the nearness of her was inviting.

"How about some chaw?" She insisted as she handed him a short piece of tobacco hewed from a plug of wine sap. "Stole it from the GAMBLER while he slept." She wiggled her booted feet in mischievous merriment.

FOOT SOLDIER DAVY licked the casing with pleasure, inhaling the combined flavors of licorice, molasses and fruit syrup before placing the piece in his mouth, knowing he would savor it for a long while.

"Thank ya." He nodded woefully and continued his task.

Settling in closer, CHINA ROSE shifted to bent knees sitting Indian style. Taking a woefully looking boot from his side, she too stuffed grass and soft weeds into its interior slowly while making conversation.

FOOT SOLDIER DAVY began, his spirits lifted from the tobacco. "You ain't Chinese. Why the name CHINA ROSE?"

Eyes twinkled and lips puffed. "Cause I was headed for California seeking gold with a group of China men and others. When we all camped together, I was the entertainment."

"What d'ya do?" DAVY spat far to his left.

"I dance, I sing!" She youthfully rose, twirled about whirling dirt and damp sand around as she rotated kicking her knees high.

Mischievously, she rushed over to DUTCHY who was sitting with his back turned about ten yards away at the perimeter of the chiseled notch of a cave, and grabbed the Germany made Weis Harmonica from his hand. He had it at his mouth playing a tune she didn't recognize, so she slapped the spit out of it on her hip and began. DUTCHY grabbed nearby sticks and rocks to throw at her from where he sat, not rising. He was tired from his recent excursions to the valley.

GAMBLER MOODY nearby, sharply viewed the altercations with a twisted mouth and squinty eyes. He rubbed his crooked neck as he spoke.

"I say, tub! Stop that hullaballoo. My cards are shuffling about from all that twirling and twisting, you crazy loon." Lying on a flat but tipsy rock were cards of various types for Solitaire. After re-arranging the cards, he opened his black frock coat revealing the watch attached to his matching vest. It was pertinent to check the time on his new machine-made-Waltham watch with the interchangeable parts. Secured to a Dicken's chain running across the vest, a toggle bar and funny looking key dangled from the watch. Every five minutes, he patted the entire bit for security and played with the chain.

MEXICAN MANO and APACHE wanted the watch for different reasons. To MEXICAN MANO it told time. To APACHE, it was evil and didn't belong on his superstitious mountain.

GAMBLER MOODY was tall and skinny, the opposite of stocky MEXICAN MANO. He wore creaseless tailor-made broadcloth pantaloons tucked in tall Wellington boots. Dropped off—or kicked out—of the new four wheeled wagon, he too eyed the trail—always waiting. He checked the time frequently as he pranced around while rubbing his sore neck. He shuffled his cards five more times before laying them out on the damp rock table. Because of the ever blowing wind, he meticulously anchored each card with a small pebble in the middle.

DUTCHY, without his harmonica, got busy doing his next favorite thing—whittling with the knife he took from MEXICAN MANO. Finding a piece of Mesquite wood, he whittled it to a sharp point, all the while squinting at APACHE, never looking away, waiting for the repetitive scenario.

Soon and on time, APACHE and MEXICAN MANO attacked each other while shouting words in Spanish. Dirt flew, a lone long eared Jackrabbit scurried away in leaps, and lightening introduced a heavy down pour from the malevolent clouds.

They wrestled and stabbed at each other with whatever weapon was handy. APACHE knocked ruthlessly on MEXICAN MANO'S skull with a perfectly fist fitting rock. With his one hand and stump of the other, MEXICAN MANO punched away at APACHE'S mid frame until they both collapsed on the ground. They lay there licking the raindrops that fell on their forlorn faces.

FOOT SOLDIER DAVY ducked his head, tired of the repetitive scenario. Stressed, he pushed his back against the wall of the shallow cave hardly noticing when a small stick punctured through his shirt and skin and a drop of blood now seeped through his faded shirt.

CHINA ROSE, clasping two fat pink hands around one arm, buried her face in his shoulder. Sitting near, she saw the puncture and removed the stick as a late afternoon rain pounded harder sending rivulets snaking a few feet beyond. They cuddled and scrunched in the enclave with knees up. She pulled her huge skirt over the both of them like a blanket. DAVY hugged his mid section and rocked.

DUTCHY hurried over to GAMBLER MOODY and socked him hard on the shoulder. "Gimme that." He grabbed at the watch from the stunned man, getting a handful of heavy gold chain pulling one end out of the buttonhole releasing the hook from the vest.

Slim fingered GAMBLER MOODY whipped out a Southern Derringer from a hidden brace near his wrist, the one used for unfortunate card games, and plugged DUTCHY a couple shots in the chest at close range.

They both crashed on the soaking ground in anger.

DUTCHY stuffed the watch and chain into the large pockets of his heavy canvas pantaloons. Still in a rage, he went over to CHINA ROSE and grabbed his harmonica. She saw him coming and handed it to him without a fuss. She could retaliate later.

APACHE formed a mountain lion's stance, watching on all fours ready to pounce. He grabbed the harmonica from DUTCHY and they tousled and rolled. APACHE stopped, sat squat and howled several coyote calls. DUTCHY just sat there grieving in the rain.

With clenched teeth, GAMBLER MOODY stiffened, clutched his valise more tightly to his chest and stood tall staring down the evil narrow road from whence he came. He rubbed his sore crooked neck, oblivious of rain cascading off the edges of his beaver made slouch hat, walked over to MEXICAN MANO and extended his hand.

"Give me the map."

"No—it's mine. I bought it off APACHE with whiskey and tobacco." He took the map out of his back pocket and with his one hand, shoved it deep inside an expensive hand-made boot.

GAMBLER MOODY grabbed at his boot dumping him from his sitting position, pulling him anxiously forward and down the muddy trail—pumping the boot from heel to toe yanking until it slid off.

APACHE howled in Spanish. "Map no good. Only APACHE know where is gold mine."

As MEXICAN MANO attempted to reclaim the map, he landed on GAMBLER MOODY forcing him face down in the mud, moustache and all. A dog pile ensued with DUTCHY on top, GAMBLER MOODY on the bottom, MEXICAN MANO and APACHE sandwiched in. APACHE pounded everyone with a large rock.

Thunder cracked simultaneously as lightening flashed splitting a huge boulder a hundred yards away.

Like spiders, each man crawled hurriedly to the long shallow notch of a cave.

FOOT SOLDIER DAVY and CHINA ROSE sat quietly staring out at the rain, stunned with the realization of their dilemma.

Rain poured.

DUTCHY sniffed and coughed from the ruckus then fingered the new rubber piece deep in a pocket—a wedge of some sort. He must keep it a secret and vowed to show it to no one. It was his treasure from the valley.

Soon, all melted away.

CHAPTER 10

CAVE CREEK, ARIZONA

December 18, 2014

Early Tuesday morning, Dixie and Pop were still at it as I popped four slices of potato bread in the toaster oven.

Dixie began. “My cousin’s nephew hears noises at night.” She stood by the toaster oven with a plate and a butter knife.

“Rats,” Pop answered while whipping a freshly chopped green jalapeno into a bowl of four eggs.

“And wooshing sounds!” She continued while grabbing three plates from the shelf.

“Rats!” Pop was adamant.

“How about ghostly wooshing sounds?” I had to intervene.

Pop scrambled the eggs and chili in the hot skillet then served each of the three plates turning the skillet sideways using a rubber spatula to slide each steaming morsel out. “Be sure to call me when you see a ghost. You have my number.” His laugh was contagious this early.

I was hoping to prove him wrong—someway, somehow.

Without sitting, we ate, filled thermoses, rinsed dishes and loaded the dish washer.

"But, what about reputable people who insist that they've seen ghosts or that a place is haunted?" I grabbed my purse and keys hanging from a wooden peg by the door and waited for an answer.

"Hog wash! It's either rats, other vagrant critters, or human vagrants."

"Good grief." I gave him my best downward negative hand wave, than with a quick hug, reminded him to bring home a few chocolate éclairs from the bakery today. One must always be gracious when asking for free goodies, you know.

Dixie Hoot was out the door ahead, clicking her boots on the paved walkway towards out carport. Her rounded figure was always dressed Western "vogue". Today she was all brown—long pleated cashmere skirt below the knees, matching v-neck sweater with a soft Christmas red scarf wrapped around the neck, all tucked into a short coat. Dazzling red lipstick was ninety-five percent of her make-up. Dripping with Western silver jewelry, her trademark, she sparkled in the darkness of early morning. Her gob of keys matched securities'. One of them would open the front office door for all personnel including Principal Dr. Shieter who never carried keys.

She was head secretary and "go-fur" extraordinaire. A maze of duties awaited her as she filled teachers' mailboxes, readied the attendance bin, and most importantly, matched file folders of absent teachers with teaching plans for today's substitutes.

I followed behind her in my Wrangler on our three mile trip to school, a usual ten minute drive depending on the rain-filled washes.

She met me at the door to the front office. "Hey! Friday night a clairvoyant is coming over....more details later." She hurried away avoiding my twenty questions of excitement.

After gathering my multi-colored handouts from the bin in the front office as fast as Dixie shoved them in, I felt I had a peacock by the tail when looking at the fist full of red-gold-purple-and most importantly, golden rod papers of to-do info.

Quick stepping to the English Department, I blew early morning fog from my mouth in the semi-darkness---thirty-five degrees was my guess. Outside steps lead to the second floor, the English Department rooms of multi subjects. On the first floor is the Business Department whose teachers always accused us of plugging the toilet above. Periodically, the head of the Business Department, Mr. Zee, would attack us.

"What's going on up there?" What did they expect from us eighteen teachers with only one toilet, and five minute breaks between classes all-day-long?

Our extensive hallway includes double doors at each end with a tunnel between. Rooms on each side of the wide hallway are large and adequate. Students can conveniently enter from each end, eliminating congestion on the two stairwells. Security has to remember to open each end very early during cold mornings.

I shuffled up the steps in my gray fashion boots—no heels, just walkers. And since the highest temperature for today was supposed to be in the low fifties—cold for us bloodless desert people—I was smartly dressed in my warm navy leggings and matching long sleeve dress. I too wore a red scarf tied in a loose double knot.

As I pushed open the heavy door to the hallway, I heard a student running before I saw him hit the door on the far end of the empty hall. A loud slam followed.

My room was in the middle of the hall between my best pals Nancy Lopez, and Richard Cloud. Hearing the noise since their doors were never shut, they popped out of their rooms and looked down the hall. We three met in the middle.

I was first. "What was that hoopla all about?"

Nancy replied, "I thought I heard a noise at your door a while ago."

"Coyotee was here about ten minutes ago asking for you," said Cloud looking fresh in his bow tie and jacket even though I knew that he has been here since his usual five a.m. to grade papers. He thumped a pencil several times in his palm…eraser down.

"What would he want? Maybe it's about our trail ride Saturday." I told them how ruffled he was when he saw the trail ride map. "He insists the site is haunted."

"Delightful!" Cloud exclaimed with a smile. "We need excitement! I'm ready for haunted." And he meant it.

"Not me. You know what a chicken I am!" Nancy ran her hand around her neck, pulling her long red hair from the confines of her Kelly green sweater before shaking her head making it feel perfect.

I told them, "Be prepared for conflicts on the trail. Love always seems to blossom"

"I'm on the bus and shopping with Dixie." Cloud smartly ducked back in his room.

Nancy said, "I hope it's a good ratio of boy students—more boys than girls. They're the better caregivers if we get in a jam. Remember last year? What's the count of each?"

"Nine girls and twelve boys. I mixed them together in the three lines." A quick flash to last year's major mishap was the trail through the Garden of seven foot tall Chollas. The lead horse was new to Cholla and flicked his tail at the wrong time. Two quick thinking Wranglers put a clamp on the horse's nose as a distraction while one combed out the deathly Cholla. The young rider had to get off the horse and walk about to keep from fainting.

"This year's route is different. I told the Wranglers that we are definitely not going through the Garden of Chollas."

We walked back to our rooms. "What the heck is this?"

Taped on my door was a small rubber tomahawk, the kind found at Western gift shops. Well secured with duct tape, it would be difficult to remove. Under the fake rubber blade of the tomahawk was a folded note of student paper with the crinkly edge still attached.

"FRUM THE GHOATS OV THE SUPERSTITIOUS."

Coyotee's distinct printing was evident, and so was his sense of humor. It was both funny and not funny.

"This makes my day," I said.

Nancy shouted, "Cloud, come out here and look at this."

Of course, he didn't think it was the least bit funny. "This could be serious. Be careful with Coyotee. He's full blooded Apache. They dance to a different drummer." Cloud's voice, serious and deep, gave the matter an undertone of fear.

I said, "An on-going conflict perhaps."

Nancy removed the sticky tape off the door with her spray bottle of vinegar water. She sprayed, I scrubbed with zest since the morning hours were escaping fast and the hallway was filling with students sitting on the carpet, leaning against the wall finishing last night's home work.

Thankful it was fresh tape, we were able to remove all the goo. Of course my first hour students were 'agog'.

"What's that smell?"

"Yuk!"

"I'm going to be sick," said a measly-mouthy-trouble maker as she held her double pierced infested nose.

"No you're not!" I said hotly with boots planted firmly for emphasis and my shoulders' squared. "It's just healthy vinegar. They use it on babies." I made that up. I'm good at it after five years of teaching.

"Oh!" They sniffed as they started to get to work.

I wrote on my Tuesday note pad a "to-do" list for today. Number one, find Science Fiction book of Paranormal.

CHAPTER 11

CAVE CREEK, ARIZONA

December 19, 2014

The day started with the most important reminder on my list---Get the phone number of Coyotee Raintree's mother. I wanted to make sure that Coyotee was prepared for our ride and in good spirits about it. Most importantly, I also wanted her opinion about yesterday's tomahawk episode.

The semester is ending this week before Christmas so I handed out their final exam and answer sheet. It is a particular schedule, a juggling of classes different from the regular school day. Exams are all day Wednesday and half a day Thursday.

Teachers have half a day Thursday and all day Friday to grade exams. Grades are due Friday. This schedule allows for a fresh start next semester with the new year. We liked it.

Since we each have about one hundred and seventy tests to grade, we use computer bubble sheets—pencil fill-ins that we feed through a machine. Modern Miracles!

I walked around between the rows well aware of which roaming eyes to watch. I hate times like this that turn me into a truant officer. Where is the merriment? Where is the fun? A teacher has to do what a teacher has to do or get fired.

Each held up a hand when finished so I could snatch the answer sheet—before it got copied by another desk occupant.

"Five minutes left!"

The bell rang and everyone rushed out but one kid trying to finish.

"Miss Mac," Larry asked. "Who is Puck?"

"Only the main character," I laughed.

"Oh yeah! Now I've got it." He erased a couple answers and bubbled in new ones.

"This is an 'A'," he said handing me the test and gathering his stuff to leave.

"Good luck," and I meant it. He was such a pleasure in class. My favorite.

The classes before lunch went as usual. Students were quiet while taking their tests. I didn't have to lecture or overly man the room. I like test days.

My thermos of Hazelnut went empty, so in between classes I attacked the little fridge behind my desk for a sip from an open bottle of Mexican Coca Cola, the kind with real sugar.

The last class left before my lunch time. I hid the test papers in a desk drawer for after school grading and rushed to the door in a hurry to lock and get out.

Hemming me at my door was the forever-smiley, forever-handsome Guy Wagner, Athletic Director. Smiley face entered closing the door behind which was a "no no", and handed me a small gorgeously store wrapped Christmas present.

"For you—for our trail ride! Which list am I on?" This was him, quick talking charisma. Looking toward the chalk board from yesterday's meeting, he walked over, erased a few names changing the list, and was pleased to see his name next to Becky Painter's.

"Sorry I missed the mandatory meeting—wrestling tryouts."

I stood stunned, helpless as always by his usual aggressiveness. It must be the sports.

"What am I? A worm? You have the audacity to change names on lists that the students selected." I folded my arms, only half mad and looked at the changes. "That'll work," I said.

His twinkling smile was so boyish. He put his hands on his hips making his chest pop-out a few more miles when his wind breaker opened. Compacted well in his sports uniform, he ran his hand through his sandy hair, one of his manly habits of flirting.

I looked at the package and coyly twisted my head eyeing him. "Is this from Santa?" I can flirt too!

"From Santa! Hurry, I have a short lunch today." He rubbed his hands together in haste and added his bigger than life smile.

"Super. Now I really feel special." I ripped the red and white ribbon and matching paper to the floor in one sweep. A little black velveteen box sat in my palm. Lifting the lid, I found a shiny, expensive looking silver whistle on a red cord.

"Pretty!" I held it high before me.

"Use it for the trail ride." Taking it from my hand, he put it around my neck than planted a kiss on my lips, all in one blushing motion.

Turning he said, "See you later." After pointing to the board, "Keep in touch."

Dazzled, I teetered a bit, and felt flush. Grabbing the sack lunch from my fridge, I locked the door and hustled out. Although Del Rio was special, Guy had a welcoming demeanor. Friends?!?

Del Rio was on my right, but I kept Guy on my left for safe keeping….just in case….whatever that means.

The English Department was packed with action. Teachers were in line for the bubble-test-grading machine which graded about forty tests in thirty seconds.

Laughter is abundant while lunching. We are happy-happy a few days before vacation, probably more so than the students.

Heleena was at the Office board, the one we kept for important notes, text messaging us as usual. Mry Xmas and Hpy-n-yr. Bouncing around half frowning and half smiling she babbled directions about this and that, than waved me over. Today's outfit was a long sleeve red shirt partly tucked into a sweeping-to-the floor red tiered skirt, all accented with a short green vest. Her usual drab tennis shoes were now sequined. While talking to me, Nancy Lopez stood behind her and finished tucking in her shirt. Heleena didn't notice.

"Just to let you know, Dr. Shieter and I have been taking riding lessons together." She was hard to read about this. Was it a secret? Was she being coy?

"Goood," I drooled. Her giggle was very unusual.

Before leaving for the day, I double checked that my book about Paranormal activity was still on my desk for take home and referencing. Dixie, Nancy and I were getting together again Friday for some more spooky telecasts. Also, we were trying to find a psychic around town to come over.

My book was there where I had left it, and so was another tomahawk lying on top…..with specks of red paint on the blade.

CHAPTER 12

APACHE CAMP
Massacre Grounds
December 22, 1848

CHINA ROSE, AKA ROSALEE, sat under the shallow overhang, her small two-cup-silver tea pot now wrapped in the large fluid folds of faded velvet-green skirt. Secured earlier from a hidden cache, she polished it lovingly as it rested on her lap unblemished. Rubbing her fingers over and around the silver's coldness, she caressed its loveliness as would a child with a doll. "Been in my family a long time," she said sorrowfully.

FOOT SOLDIER DAVY watched her while he mechanically packed his tired worn out boots with more dry grass, becoming harder to find with the pounding rain. Most was gone from the small shelter. Still rocking back and forth, or side to side, he stopped now and then to lean his back on the wall of the shallow cave, thankful for the lip overhang. Heavy rain now curtained the overhang, almost obscuring the robust activity in the courtyard of a camp. As always, he numbly patted the large gaping hole in his chest and sneered at DUTCHY.

DUTCHY and APACHE were again groveling in a wrestling match, pitifully smearing mud everywhere. APACHE insisted on ownership of the magical harmonica and grabbed at it viciously. DUTCHY kept it at arm's length. MEXICAN MANO got involved with a plan to steal away APACHE'S knife which he kept tightly secured in a raw looking leather case strapped to the outside of his thigh, out of sight beneath his loin cloth.

GAMBLER MOODY watched all three hit, kick, and stab at one another again. Hate reeked from them like a smoking tower of dry manure---never burning down. Grimacing, he again shot all three at close range with his new 1848 Colt Dragoon revolver, pulled from his canvas valise. Hell upon earth stopped. Stunned, they looked up at him before quickly crawling away. The interloper was no one to reckon with.

Chill eyed GAMBLER MOODY, disgusted with the calamity of events, squinted in the rain where the three men had been fighting and retrieved his three un-spent bullets. Loading them meticulously again into the chamber, he secured all his belongings and made his own little camp, a short distance away from the others where he could think of a plan. Empty faced, he stared in duress long and hard down the single road remembering how he was rolled out of the new four wheeled wagon and dropped on the hard rocky ground. Now his head was getting heavier on his crooked-sore neck and he leaned back against the wall of the long extended chiseled notch of a cave. Shallow but secure, he thought it would suffice and felt added comfort in this alcove.

One hand MEXICAN MANO shuffled like a three legged toad to a dry spot and put a blackened two quart pot on his lap. From a pouch tied to his waist, he pulled out a handful of dry pinto beans again and counted them as they 'pinged' into the pot one by one…slowly.

APACHE re-adjusted the knife in its case tied to his thigh and sat far away, out of the rain. Chanting to himself the song from his tribal forefather about this place called the haunted superstitious mountain, gave him hope. Hanging his head with chin on chest, he chanted lowly the Legend of the Apache Chieftain.

DUTCHY cursed loudly in Spanish at all who could hear him and put the harmonica back in his pantaloon pocket. Finding the knife he had stuck previously in the cave wall, he began to whittle again on another piece of hardwood, a rudimentary design, a flawed figure of a young woman. Again he secretly fingered the strange wedge of wood and rubber he hid in his pocket. Secretly, he would make more trips to the valley.

GAMBLER MOODY, sick of the rigmarole and realizing peace was unreachable, decided what he needed to do—a first for him. To appease the vile torment of the raging camp occupants, he unlocked his canvas valise and headed towards APACHE.

CHAPTER 13

CAVE CREEK, ARIZONA

December 20, 2014

Number one goal today was to confront Coyotee and get to the bottom of his anger….if that was even what it was. Also, I needed to check with Catora Bell and Guy Wagner to get some feed-back on his Cross Country performance. Apaches were historically noted for being the fastest runners. I read in a history book that they were able to run seventy-five miles in one day while our cavalry could only run twenty-five. How in the world did they document that anyway?

Coyotee came in, took his test and left before I could talk to him. I had told him to see me after class but he didn't. So much for the power of my influence!

Late Thursday afternoon all my grades were calculated and turned in to the front office. Now my worries shifted to a real nail biter—the weather. Projection is "slow storm from California should hit Sunday night."

Nancy, Cloud and I met in the hall.

Nancy said, "Don't worry. Everyone has been told to be prepared."

"And the saddles have large ponchos attached." Cloud added. Then he smiled knowing that he would be shopping in Apache Junction with Dixie—warm and dry.

I said, "We need to remind the four B's to carry ponchos in their packs."

"Those old 'coots' are retirees from the snow country. Go dancing tonight and don't worry." Cloud always made a person feel better with a state of the art analysis. With a wave, he ducked into his room to work. "See you Saturday morning at eight in the front parking lot."

Tumbleweeds is having a "special" early Christmas dance tonight, but to us it is an end of the semester celebration. The whole gang is coming. Walking to the faculty parking lot, Nancy and I discussed our mode of dress for the dance.

She said, "My new long red dress with matching ankle boots."

"Me too! Let's wear our matching concho belts, the ones with pearls…and out special pearl bracelets with the safety hooks; they won't come off while dancing. We high-fived with great pleasure and left. Another semester under our belt. Done!

Driving home, the weather was a balmy seventy degrees with not a cloud in the sky. I powered the windows down on my Jeep Wrangler, letting my curls tangle, feeling good and anxious to see Rick tonight. During lunch he had called. "I'll meet you there later. I'm working on a case."

I sighed. He's chasing criminals and I'm grading papers. Subconsciously, I visualized my sexy red velvet outfit during the entire three mile drive home and added accessories at each mile.

Arriving at Tumbleweeds a little later than I anticipated—because of my pass-out power-nap earlier, I was delighted to see my table of friends wave me over. Our reserved large round table in the corner, away from the noise, but easily accessible to the dance floor, was crowded. Someone from behind started to lift my white woolen coat off my shoulders.

"Hey, you're here!" My smile lifted my face two inches. Rats! I'm such a sucker. Slowly, he unbuttoned the pearl latches. Rick's warm hands and long arms wrapped around my back as he drew me close. I throbbed. How does he do it? Red was his shirt and green were his eyes. He played with my pearl bracelet as we walked to the dance floor.

The band started. I did a Princess wave to those at the table and we swayed to the music of the live band "Jingle Mania." Traditional and timely Christmas tunes never sounded so sweet, so merry.

Bing, Bob, Brad and Blake were in Holiday garb—brightly colored plaid Cowboy Hardware shirts and matching vests. Since they were busy passing around bundles of ribbon tied mistletoe with their new found girlfriends, I didn't chat with them much. But, I had to ask. "Are you guys all playing Santa?" The heavily whiskered group smiled in unison and hand combed their six weeks of beards.

Bing said, "It's all coming off when the heats on, and it'll be follow the leader."

Our piles of nachos vanished too quickly, sour cream, guacamole and all. Steaks were the highlight of the evening served sizzling on thick plates.

We all nibbled, sipped, danced and chatted about Saturday's big ride with added reminders. Nancy and Colt were the leaders.

"Sunday's storm might hit us on Saturday," Colt warned.

"Huh!" started Bing. "You've never seen a nor'easter."

"Yes," added Bob while cutting his steak in small bites. "In Indiana we get Canadian Clippers from the Great Lakes while you're sun bathing here."

"You talk about cold!" Brad joined in. "I was an active young Marine during the end of the Viet Nam war."

"And that's why we all moved here," a final statement from baker Blake. "We'll be ready. Question is," and he pointed at me with his fork, "will you?"

Of course this prompted another round of "pass the mistletoe."

Towards the end of the evening, Rick's cell rang. "Can't someone else handle it?" He talked low, frowned, "Emergency, gotta go. Coming by later?" He looked at my disgusted frown.

"I'll think about it," I said.

He pretended not to hear. "Don't forget the hidden key." He knew I lost the personal one he gave me. A perfunctory kiss with warm hands surrounding my face, a wave to all and he was out the door.

From the corner of my eye I saw Delilah, movie-star-gorgeous, get up quickly and head out. Flashy long silver drop earrings were swinging in cadence with her hips, flashing above a tightly wrapped silver-sheath dress.

"What the hell!" Of course I was too loud.

"Forget it," said Nancy. "Remember she's with forensics and there could be a cadaver somewhere."

"Yeah, she's dressed for it!"

CHAPTER 14

The evening wore on and I didn't worry. Tomorrow would be a sleep-late morning. So, we all shared long tales of life's experiences—mine being the shortest, the four B's the longest.

We girls all danced together in a circle; the guys laughed hard, clapped to the music than danced with their dates. The men did a good job of faking the fact they couldn't dance-- just picked up their feet and did some arm swings.

Near midnight, Guy Wagner walked in with his happy face.

"What a rowdy group!" Taking off his jacket hurriedly, he put it on the back of a chair to join us. Coincidentally, it was the one Rick Del Rio vacated. "Your jingle-belling can be heard out in the parking lot."

"Join us," the ladies said as they pushed a pile of mistletoe in his direction. He weeded through them, picked out the fattest bunch and looked at me.

"Why are you walking in here this late and looking so fresh?" I had to ask while avoiding his flirty smile. A sprig of sandy blond hair fell on his forehead and his scent was always beguiling. Enticing!

"The high school dance needed chaperoning. Now, I need to be with adults. So refreshing."

"Merry Christmas," said the teetering bunch clanging the heavy mugs of beer together. Boy, were we getting happy!

Blake poured a mug for Guy from one of the four pitchers on the table and he joined us, turning the chair around to straddle it.

"Let's dance," he said to me and tucked the thick mistletoe in his shirt pocket.

"Absolutely!" My tone was happy or defiant, I don't know. I was pissed at Rick. I caressed my pearl bracelet like a security blanket.

"Whoa." Guy led me to the dance floor and insisted on eye contact. "Had a little rift with the big guy?" He held me at arm's length.

"Not telling."

'Silver Bells', my favorite slow one was next and we swayed to the music, after which he mistletoed me. Our kiss was quick, sort of manufactured.

Guy didn't care. Anyway, Nancy and I were secretly trying to match him with Becky, the director of Commercial Arts. I was impressed that he wanted to ride next to her out at the Superstitions.

At one a.m. pitchers of beer were replaced with complimentary water and coffee.

By one-thirty we were dragging and heading out. Guy had joined the retired, whiskered group in loud laughter and craziness, still telling tall tales of cycle riding.

As everyone headed toward the main entrance, I headed to the bathroom. After all, home was a three mile journey and maybe…just maybe…another mile to Rick's place. "Go on. I'll catch up." I waved them on.

Now, five minutes later walking toward the main entrance I noticed the place was dark. The dance floor was vacant, and most of the lights were off or dimmed. One girl was at the cash register, her back turned away, and my loud outside crowd of friends were being rowdy. This place could win a contest for shutting down the fastest. Chairs were turned upside down on some tables allowing for an early morning sweep.

The entrance was surrounded by dark shadows with a lone red light above the door spelling EXIT. Before I reached the door, there was movement to my right, and out of the darkness a dry heavy hand grabbed my right wrist. I gasped for air, tongue tied. Before I could pull away I heard from the shadows, "*You get in—You don't git out. Buzzards and critters will eat ya before you git found.*"

His desperate voice was whispery and slurred, gruff and slow. Not able to pull away from his heavy grasp, he pulled me closer with a firm hold of my wrist. Forced to face him, left me with nightmares for days! Heavy eyebrows bushed above squinty dark eyes. A descending thin nose pointed downward to missing front teeth. His dusty hat and faded yellowed shirt looked foreign and frayed. Was he sitting on an upturned old barrel? I couldn't tell.

Desperate, I jerked my wrist down causing his hand to open, and ran out the door in a panic. Some of my group were gone, while Guy, Nancy and Colt stood yards away talking.

"Hey." My tone frightfully loud, caused the three to stare.

"What happened to you?" Guy asked. "You look like you've seen a ghost.

"Maybe I have." I explained.

Colt and Guy tried to re-enter Tumbleweeds but the door was locked.

Nancy said, "We'll follow you home."

"No, I'm ok. I have my cell. I'll be home in ten minutes."

"We'll keep ours on and you have our numbers." They almost spoke in unison.

Guy continued, "Call Nancy when you get home. If she doesn't hear from you in fifteen minutes, she calls one of us." He was shaking a finger like a demanding instructor.

"Ok! Ok!" Trembling, I climbed into my Jeep and drove off into the darkness. Three miles of twisting turns and low dips seemed ominous in my beaming lights. Slow, slow, I always tell myself because of deer, and javalina crossing. It was tough. I was in a hurry.

Lights from an oncoming car on my right, at the Fleming Springs Crossroad worried me. I looked at the time on the dash—two a.m. Scary. I didn't want to run into a weirdo this early in the morning—or late at night—hard to tell. Besides, I had already met one earlier.

I zipped over the crossroad ahead of the other car and pressed down on the accelerator. Soon the other car was close to my tail, only with flashing cop lights.

Pulling over on the slim right shoulder of the pavement, I stopped and powered down my window. Rick came rushing over and slammed two hands on the window frame, a little too heavy I thought.

"Colt called. Why do I always have to hear about your predicaments from others?" He was too demanding. Was he mad? Was he tired? I couldn't tell.

I sighed, played "it" coy and looked at him blankly with my best little orphan expression.

He put a hand under my chin and convincingly said, "Come to my place. I'll tell you where I've been and you tell me all about the old man."

"Deal." How could I refuse such an offer at two in the morning…from my boyfriend!!!

Pulling off the side and onto the pavement, I put two hands on the wheel. "WHAT," I yelled in disgust. My right wrist was bare of my beautiful pearl bracelet with the butterfly amulet---the one with the safety hook, never to be lost.

My cell rang and I jumped a mile in my seat. Pop was loud and clear. "Mrs Raintree called our house asking for you. Coyotee has disappeared."

CHAPTER 15

Pulling into Rick's three acre desert place was easy. Small solar lights were planted here and there along the driveway and especially close to boulders that dotted everywhere, too heavy to move. The patio light was on and I parked under the carport—my usual. He pulled in next to me, and grabbed my hand as we walked in.

Tiredness overtook us as we undressed for bed and flopped down with its heaviness. Forget a slow romantic interlude although he did light an unscented candle with a long flame glowing on top of his dresser, dancing on the wall and creeping up the ceiling.

He pulled the warm brown corduroy covers under our chins and we faced each other. After I described the dirty looking man in the shadows I added, "He was actually dressed like a prospector, using suspenders instead of a belt. Maybe he was a 'prop' for Tumbleweeds...like regular décor."

"Never have seen him before."

"And he swiped my favorite bracelet."

"Are you sure you didn't lose it while dancing with Guy?" He smiled and his eyes gleamed in the candle light.

Ok. It was his turn. "How did you know?"

"Satellite." He pulled me close and we shared a pillow.

Delightful. He was a bit jealous. "And your night?"

"Too ugly to discuss. Not bedtime chit chat."

My eyelids got heavy. "Coyotee Raintree ran away.

"We'll handle it tomorrow."

I threw one leg over his. We both passed out.

It was a late Friday morning before we rolled out of bed and showered together. He slathered soap all over me and I washed his back. Since he was finished in half the time, and too splashy, I waited for him to get out of the wrap-around-stall before I washed my hair.

Purposely, all phones were still shut down and we were able to get seven hours of sleep...plus take showers. This was nice. Now wrapped in a towel, I sat on the edge of his bed writing notes and rambling about my Friday to-do-list going over it once, twice, thrice. Was I nervous about tomorrow? I thumped the eraser end loudly on my note pad like a drum stick. This seemed to get my brain in motion.

"What tune are you playing?" asked Rick combing his dark brown hair over and over, looking at me slyly, a towel wrapped at his waist like a sarong.

"I forgot to make extra copies of the line-up of riders. I'm going into town to make a bunch of copies so each person can have one to learn the names of others."

"You're so thoughtful." He had slowly finished drying with an oversized creamy beach towel. "I'll double check at Tumbleweeds this morning about your bracelet."

Sitting next to me, he pulled me down. We both lost our towels.

Later that day, Mrs. Raintree and I decided to meet inside Screamin' Ice Cream concerning the 'where-abouts' of Coyotee. Although I had met her briefly before, I was still impressed with her style of orderliness. Eyes matched dark brown hair that brushed softly on her shoulders, every hair in place. Slender framed, she wore a faded soft plaid Western blouse tucked in skinny jeans. Authentic earrings matched her bracelet and belt buckle---all petite, not gaudy. Softly, she exuded a regal countenance.

We each ordered grilled hamburgers and filled our iced cups with tea. I bought a large stack of French-fries to share. Togetherness, I thought. The Native Americans I have met in my short lifetime have a way of obscuring their emotions. She was a good actress and didn't appear to be overly concerned or worried at this point.

Not until she spoke did I see fright in her brown eyes. They became larger and the pupils seemed to vibrate as they turned from brown to black. The calm elegance disappeared.

"I called the family in McNary where we are from. They know nothing." Her speech was perfect but spacing between words was different---staccato Indian language.

"He was here for his semester final and I'm proud to say he got a B-."

No reaction. Stone faced now she looked down than swiped a French fry in catsup. I followed.

"I was fifteen when he was born." She looked at me squarely and I knew this information had to be of importance. "His uncles helped raise him." She continued.

Did she know where she was going with this? I sat still and ate slowly---very out of the ordinary for me, the 'Snapdragon', according to Rick. I tried to Indian myself and absorb her quiet countenance.

"They are obsessed with the Indian Spirits---the old ways."

Her stare was 'freeze-frame' and I knew what was coming.

"They told him many times that Apache lives have been wasted in the 'superstitious mountains' and that they are haunted in certain places....evil places." She arose and cordially refilled our cups with ice and tea. "They are good story tellers."

I stiffened where I sat, my mind revisiting haunting ghost stories from television shows.

"Hundreds of years ago, the mountain area was referred to as "superstitious" in our language. It is said that spirits---ghosts---from Indians before the Apache, are still there.

I said, "The history books refer to them as Solado Indians because they housed around the Rio Solado---or Salt River that ran fluently through this entire county before all of our dams."

She lowered her eyes and shook her head of acknowledgement. "Coyotee believes in the Medicine Man."

"Is that a negative or a positive?" I needed to know.

"Could be both," she said, taking the last bite of un-wasted hamburger.

Heck, she probably knew miles more than I did. She was about eight years older, but I felt terribly young next to her and what she represented---her families' history of the Arizona Apache, a group that lived for thousands of years in the area.

"Would he be with friends around here; you know, the Cross Country team members?" My thoughts were of Catora, the girl he cared for, and of Guy Wagner the coach.

"I called each of them. They know nothing but will be watching for him." She cleaned our mess at the table, throwing away napkins and stacking the little plastic trays on top of the garbage container. She sat and stared at me for an answer. "I have called every relative and friend. No one has seen him. He has disappeared." For the first time, her eyes pooled.

The tomahawk—the tomahawk—although I feared bad timing, I had to tell her what Coyotee had done. Question—what was the significance?

Her eyes flickered as she crossed her arms in front of her. She said that she didn't know but would contact the elders in McNary and get back to me with the information.

I suggested to her that she needs to contact Rick Del Rio immediately and gave her his card.

"I will do this. I am scared that he will go to the mountain alone to seek advice from past spirits at Massacre Grounds where the ancient relatives of his grandfather were killed. His grandfather told him the stories many times through dance and song……it is a dangerous place."

CHAPTER 16

Friday, December 21

We said goodbye and I told her not to worry, assuring her of Del Rio's skills. She left with the card in her hand and a formal nod.

I looked at my long "To-Do" list and started at the top---"make copies of three teams." The business office in town could spit out copies ten times faster than the school's antiquated machine, so this was my starting place.

The Town Center Business Office was crowded with Christmas buyers so I waited in line impatiently reviewing my list again. The girl in charge wore her thick, brown hair short-short with bangs that bobbed below her eyelashes. How could she see? Side swaths chin length touched the corners of her mouth. How could she eat?

I handed her my order and smiled. She didn't. She was so snappy that when she finished I almost saluted. Instead, I rolled my eyes and turned to leave bumping chest to chest with people hovering too closely. For sure, the long line behind me was respectful of her efficiency.

I looked at my notepad containing my list and scratched that off. SNACKS in big letters was the next most important item.

Stepping outside, I was ready to call Nancy just as she rang. "Hey! ESP!" I said.

"SNACKS," she said.

"We think alike," and decided to meet at The Coffee Cup for this serious discussion where we could stumble over friends....but only after we attacked Pop's Bakery for take-along. It was a difficult choice but after viewing his wide assortment of rolls, éclairs, and pies, we selected his new red-devil's cake snowballs—round cupcakes pitted with sweetened whipped cream and rolled in a coconut-pecan mixture.

"Too bad these would smash in our saddle bags," said Nancy licking cream off her fingers after attacking the small box.

The four B's were helping Pop today, so I reminded them to pack rain slickers for their hike tomorrow....and a little brandy in a thermos. They nodded; they smiled. Since everyone was rushing around stirring pots, frosting goodies, pouring ingredients, and lifting pans, we decided to get out of there quickly......but not soon enough.

"You here to help?" Pop's voice came from behind a counter.

"No! Too much havoc and we would only add to the chaos. We have an important meeting."

"Hah, you'll have your own chaos tomorrow."

We hurried out, drove down Cave Creek Road and found a table at The Coffee Cup next to the window overlooking a large Mesquite with arms covering tables situated on a patio of pavers. Everyone was inside due to the chill in the air.

We opened our bakery box, bought mugs of coffee, ate and chatted then decided on the inevitable dried fruit and nuts for saddle bags.

"Boring," I moaned, "but the best choice."

"A hot lunch at Massacre Grounds will be inviting." Nancy added, "If it rains, then what?" Gripping her mug with both hands she looked at me for an answer although she knew I didn't have one.

"We'll find a ledge to hover under.....and get lucky like previous rides." I cocked my head stupid like. "It'll be fun."

She continued, "Change of subject! My neighbor's cousin claims to be a clairvoyant a believer in the afterlife... a medium able to make contacts."

"How'd you learn this?"

"We were talking about the number of Paranormal shows on T.V. that you and I watch, and she just told me."

We stared at each other and our wires did a matrix---a crisscross of ideas---sorta bat-like echolocation. This was getting interesting.

"Where does her cousin live and is it a man or woman?"

"A man, and he's a frequent lecturer at Arizona State University."

We both lifted our cups to our lips and ESP'D. We never texted each other...ESP was faster. She was first. "We need to talk to him."

"Wow! A psychic in our neighborhood. Wait 'till I tell Dixie."

"Ok, let's do this. Go home, get totally ready for the ride tomorrow and I'll see if my neighbor's cousin is available to watch a couple ghost stories with us tonight."

"Good idea. My house so I can show him the traveling pitch fork."

"And, don't forget the ghostly sightings near the door of your class room." When she said this, I shivered.

We both shouldered our purses and prepared to leave. "And the slamming of my door," I said. "Everyone in the room jumped a mile with that one."

"See you at seven." Nancy left in a hurry just as my cell rang. Rick's voice seemed tense until I realized it was his working voice.

"No one has any idea of Coyotee's whereabouts. Catora seems anxious and said that Coyotee was extremely upset when he left school yesterday.....not even telling her his usual goodbye."

"And his friends?"

"She insisted that his loyal friends would secretly side with him on anything and would take him anywhere."

"I wish you had good news for his mother. Perhaps he'll be at the bus early in the morning." This doubtful statement followed my after thoughts of wishing that I had talked to him longer about our trail riding plans, and the significance of the tomahawk.

Rick continued. "I checked with a number of people working at Tumbleweeds and your bracelet has not been seen. Also, the girl closing the restaurant said that she saw you leave, and there was no old man near the door!"

"It was dark and he was in the shadows." My voice pitched. Was I mad or desperate?

"Strange."

"Weird."

He signed off with, "Get some rest. I'll see you in the morning."

Next, I called Guy Wagner who seemed thoroughly surprised about the news. "Very unlike Coyotee. He's been dedicated to Cross Country and preparing for an important meet coming soon."

I told Guy how concerned and irate he was about our chosen route and was insistent about changing it.

To this he added, "Apaches are sensitive and spiritual because they lived as one with the land for hundreds of years. But, you know American history as well as I do. Plus, they're extra sensitive to areas of past mortality. Talk to me! What are you not telling me about our route?"

"Well---we're riding through Massacre Grounds which he claims is haunted and dangerous."

Silence on the other end.

"As a matter of fact, we plan to picnic there." I continued; "Cloud is going to give us a little lecture while on the bus ride about the legends and lore of the Superstitions. A little history about the area."

"I'm bringing an extra large bag for gathering gold."

I shook my head and saw his smart-ass smile. "Goodbye, find Coyotee; go to bed early!" I clicked off.

With only two items crossed off my To-Do list, I decided to work on it later and jammed it into my purse. Next up was a power nap, desperately needed in case a psychic comes over tonight. I need to stay awake. Not to mention our all day ride tomorrow.

Nancy rang as I flopped down on my bed and before I hugged my silky pillow.

"We're on for tonight."

CHAPTER 17

APACHE CAMP
Massacre Grounds
December 22, 1848

GAMBLER MOODY'S emotional discontent of the group's dire situation was second only to the love he had for the contents in his valise which he hugged tightly and kept close to him at all times. Yet, he knew he needed to appease the torment of the two most vile canyon-camp occupants—APACHE and DUTCHY.

He knew DUTCHY'S discontent was one of love for material goods and all the things he remembered from Germany, the country he left behind. These were all the things he had talked about repetitively to the others, now stuck in this mountainous area. There were orchestras of violins, lounge chairs of silk and velvet, polished wood dining tables with matching glass cabinets. Buildings were grand and the forests were green. All these things he left behind, but could have again if he found G-O-L-D, his one and only obsession.

Then there was APACHE. GAMBLER believed him to be a victim of his inheritance, that of fear of the unknown and surreal respect for the mysteries of the natural earth. Stories were invented for the unexplained and these stories became APACHE'S way of life, his education. Emotions were raw, combined as one with the land and its many changes. APACHE reeked with feelings for spiritual things—to explain death. Was there joy? GAMBLER wanted answers as he approached him with trepidation.

And GAMBLER knew that APACHE was hiding the gold mine and its treasures. This was the fierce fight between APACHE and DUTCHY. The Apache had to fight fearlessly the Mexican prospectors who were here stealing gold from the Apache people's mine much earlier. DUTCHY was another intruder.

GAMBLER didn't want gold and material things. He wanted peace. He rubbed his sore twisted neck and remembered the rope, and how he and his belongings were thrown out of the new four wheel wagon drawn by two mules. It was a rough ride from a tough life. Contentment was unreachable, but he must find peace from all the havoc and turmoil this place represented.

He stood a few yards away from APACHE sitting half out of the rain with his back turned away and his head on his knees. Hands played in the rocks next to him. The rain turned to sleet. What did it matter!? "APACHE," he called out.

Disturbed, APACHE pivoted around while sitting on his loin cloth. Colorful pebbles entwined with rawhide adorned his ankle. A tomahawk of encased rock was near his feet and a lone knife tied to his thigh with rawhide looked dangerously menacing.

Looking in his eyes for the first time, GAMBLER felt pity for a gone youth when the too young face looked up at him in fear. APACHE flinched when GAMBLER slowly opened his canvas bag---closed and opened it several times and watched APACHE'S reaction to the magical clasp near the buckle. APACHE did not move but stared, void of emotion.

GAMBLE handed him the closed bag to take as a present and nodded his head an affirmative---slowly---over and over.

DUTCHY had been watching from where he sat whittling away, chin down, eyes slanted sideways. Yelling something evil in Spanish, he jumped up ready to make trouble. GAMBLER didn't know the language but CHINA ROSE did. Paying no mind to her heftiness, she quickly arose and like the approaching storm, attacked DUTCHY with foreign expletives while throwing rocks, hitting him everywhere. She continued in Spanish with hands on the rolls of her hips, verbalizing loudly, causing him to withdraw more tightly into the niche of rock cave and turn his back to everyone. What did he care---he played with a new silver and pearl trinket.

CHINA ROSE retreated to FOOT SOLDIER DAVY and cuddled close, caressing her small silver tea pot again in the folds of her worn velvet green skirt.

All the while, MEXICAN MANO kept the small fire going under the pot of beans. Rain and wind did not faze him as he fathered over the little camp fire, stacking rocks in a circle, piling them higher with the mud mortar he concocted with his one hand and the stub of a wrist.

All was quiet.

APACHE hesitantly reached out for the valise.

CHAPTER 18

CAVE CREEK, ARIZONA
December 21, 2014

By 6:30 I was antsy, flying around the kitchen, melting butter for popcorn, making ice tea, preparing plates and glasses of ice—setting individual tables in front of the television.

Nancy had ordered two large fully loaded pizzas as her contribution for tonight. "My turn," she said.

I wondered what skeptical Pop was doing while I whirled around prepping for company? After fluffing cushion pillows, I barked a few orders his way. He said nothing but re-kindled the fire, almost in slow motion.

Nellie the greyhound read my mind and sat still like a long legged stature turning her face this way and that watching my every move in case I dipped into her treat box.

"She knows company's coming," I said to Pop. "Dogs have a sixth sense you know."

"The hell you say!" He laughed still poking fun.

Dixie came from the bedroom in a loose magenta shift with matching rhinestone flip flops. She scratched her belly. "I'm hungry. I think I need a beer instead of ice tea. What time did the clairvoyant say he was coming? What are we going to ask him?

Be sure to tell him that you're riding in haunted places at the Superstitions."

She babbled and listed when nervous, usually answering her own questions. After opening her favorite lite beer, she offered me half. "Split?"

"Oh yeah." Pop handed us a saucer of lime wedges.

"This is going to be fun," he sarcastically said with his huge smart-ass smile, as he and Nellie went to the den. "ESP me when the pizza arrives."

Nancy, her neighbor Betty, and Betty's cousin Butch the clairvoyant arrived on time; after introductions we all settled down to pizza, tea, beer, or coffee. Dixie had made a full pot of decaf.

Betty and Butch didn't look like cousins but their size told it all. Both were huge, over six feet, squarely built and could have been receivers for the 49'ers.

"Wow! How tall are you?" I asked Butch trying to sound positive. Most tall-tall people love the attention.

"Almost seven feet. Just an inch shy."

Funny, I always pictured psychics as measly-little people with teeny-meek voices. That's television for you.

When sitting, his knees touched his chin, so he turned them sideways. He kept his eyes half shut as if he were practicing a trance….or analyzing something.

Betty had short, stylish dark brown hair, brown skin, twinkling blue eyes and a ready smile. The sky-blue eyes were the cousins' only similarity besides tallness. She and Nancy were happy-camper neighbors.

We quickly finished the two extra large deliciously-greasy-cheesy-pizzas and settled in front of the television.

Tonight's celebrity show was about a famous singer who had bought an old Hollywood mansion that was being haunted by a woman dressed as a flapper from the Roaring Twenties; she appeared frequently at night.

After the singer and other members of her family had been visited by the same apparition, she decided to have the mansion demolished and a new one built on the land. End of visiting ghost.

During commercials I muted the television and we each pumped Butch with questions.

"Is this possible or fake?"

"Why is the woman there?"

"How do psychic's work?"

"Slow," he said friendly like. Leaning back, he put two huge hands around one knee and quietly began his explanation. "Evidently the woman's spirit was still there because of some kind of trauma. They'll probably tell us at the end of the show. To answer your question of how psychics work"---He looked at me, "It's magical. Sometimes it's called channeling--- A gift we have in order to connect with the spiritual world. It's an energy we know is there and can tap into. Sometimes, we don't know how we do it."

Scary! Sounded innocent enough to me. Then the show returned. The celebrity researched the past history of the house and discovered the woman had been pushed off the top balcony to the patio and perished tragically. The description of the woman was identical to the spirit or entity that had been appearing late at night to the family. She never returned to the reconstructed house.

"Malarkey!" Pop had been standing in the back watching. Waving his hand a downward negative added, "I'll believe it when I see it!"

Butch was unfazed. "You and everyone else." It was simply said with impact. "I heard that you had a pitch fork hurled at you."

"The wind!" Pop cleared his throat.

"Too heavy. And a figure appeared at your daughter's trail ride meeting."

"She needs her eyes examined!"

We laughed at his excuse.

"There are many spirits swirling around the Superstition Mountains. Since old times were seriously dangerous, I suspect someone is trying to send a message. Why? I need more information." His eyes became squinty, and he maintained an aloofness as he stood and re-filled his cup of decaf adding two lumps.

"The Superstitions is a Paranormal hot spot of bizarre sightings and unexplained encounters. Tell me," he looked at me and I shrank—maybe he's reading my mind—I'll keep it blank, should be easy. "How is this trail ride any different from your four others? On the drive over, Nancy had filled me in about the uneventful previous rides."

"We're going a different route---a longer one through Massacre Grounds" That was it! Nancy and I ESP'D fear as we stared at each other.

Butch paused and indicated with one finger for us to be silent. After about three long breaths—in and out—he started. "Dangerous. Research the history. Ghostly participants could be caught in a warped time displacement of a scene from the past played over and over….a Residual Haunting."

"Why would they fear us?" Am I a believer?

"Maybe it's not fear they are showing, but they could be seeking peace from a traumatic past….seeking help? The situation needs to be assessed, evaluated."

Betty sat silently, not smiling.

Nancy and I were speechless.

"Very dangerous," were his last words.

Bedtime call to Rick was a replay of the entire evening. "We'll be fine," he said after listening patiently to my rambling. Before signing off, his last words were the most comforting of the entire day----"I'm prepared…..kisses."

CHAPTER 19

December 22, 2014

It was an early, dark Saturday morning when I met the bus humming with lights as the driver opened the big door with a "whoosh" for me to climb in. Wearing a cap with the bus line logo, he looked well-seasoned and told me his name was Coop for Cooper. "Been doing this for thirty years," he said as we shook hands. "I understand that I'm to take you to the trail head and then go to the town of Apache Junction with a few others to park and shop." He lifted his clip board with notes and a map as a reference of confidence than slapped it back down on the ample dash.

"That's right," I said nervously, "as long as you come back to gather what is left of us after the all day ride."

"I've done this before. This isn't my first rodeo you know." He pulled the rim of his cap down in acknowledgement and chuckled.

"Well, I'm impressed." Not really with this old worn out cliché. But, he seemed friendly, innocent and eager to impress. What else is there?

"Now," he continued with info' I didn't like, "there is a fast moving storm headed this way pre-maturely."

"Everyone was warned and should be prepared."

"Good luck with that one!"

He got that right.....new respect for his old cliché. "I'll get my things," and scrambled down the steps of the warm bus into the cold. To save front seats for a few of us, I needed to place items on them. Homing in before the group arrives is important, and like a pack rat, my seat was almost filled with my belongings....clip board, snacks, afghan to cover legs for ride, more snacks and thick vest with pockets for extra snacks of candy coated chocolate.

I figured the first four seats would be saved for Rick and me, Nancy and Colt, Becky and Guy, Dixie and Cloud. All others could sit wherever. Seats were plush with ample leg space between....opposite of rambling school buses.

Hopefully, the elusive Dr. Shieter and Miss Movie-Star-Gorgeous Delilah would sit way-way in the back. The four B's, Bing, Bob, Brad, and Blake were easy to please, liked kids, and had told me previously they didn't care where they sat. Gabby Heleena will sit anywhere. For sure I needed Cloud up front to use the bus's microphone system for his brief lecture on the area of the Superstitions for the one hour drive there.

I reviewed my clip board over and over, made sure all the attached insurance waivers were properly signed by parents...again...and went over my count...again.

"I have a total of thirty-six people," Coop said while looking at an official paper.

"Maybe thirty-five." I briefly explained about Coyotee running off. He just shook his head.

Cars started pulling into the parking lot with kids climbing out carrying their gear. Whatever their gear was—pillows for the ride, snacks, music packs, and more snacks.

"Can they eat on the bus?" I asked Coop loudly so the kids could hear the answer.

"As long as they share with the bus driver." He smiled, got out two black trash bags and distributed them here and there.

I checked off names as the students bounded into the bus, planned immediately where they were going to sit and with whom.

It was seven-fifteen a.m. We had another forty five minutes to leave as scheduled.

Coop and I reviewed his map, more for me than him. I mumbled as I read aloud.

"Take the Old West Highway to the town of Apache Junction. Find the Apache Trail (Highway 88). Drive passed Superstition Mountain Museum and passed the turn off to the Goldfield Ghost Town. Drive passed the turn off to the Lost Dutchman State Park Trailhead. Soon on the south-east side will be a turn off to Crescent Trailhead (Highway 78) and First Water Horse Road. Take this east for two and a half miles to the end of First Water Horse Trailhead and park."

At this location, I showed him the big X on the map. "The horse ride begins here and we will get mounted. The actual trailhead begins one-fourth mile in."

"You've done this before?"

"Not this particular route. We're doing a new one for variety and some kids wanted a longer ride," I explained.

"Sounds reasonable," he said as he saluted to the old guys, the four retirees boarding, each wearing a different football team's cap and sporting a matching logoed sweatshirt. Under each arm was a bright yellow slicker rolled like a bedroll.

The students got louder and the bus got happier….it seemed to shimmer while idling.

The adults gathered out in the parking lot letting the kids board first. I had already called Nancy about the saved seats in the front so no one out there was in a hurry.

Students switched seats here and there as they bounced around sharing music. And these are juniors and seniors? They had heeded my earlier warning and were dressed appropriately for the weather, hat gear and all. Most wore Blakely High's grass green hooded sweatshirts….and no flip flops. They carried another jacket or vest under an arm.

While looking out the door and standing on the bottom step, I watched the arrivals. A chunky girl's chunky mom handed her a tall grocery bag of snacks with chip packaging peeking out at the top. Figures!

"Yippee Kye O Kye Aye! We're here." Kim Rose and Jamie Mink announced with grinning faces while hand slapping others as they strutted down the aisle. They settled as close to Roy as possible. He noticed and nodded with a pleasurable grin.

I stayed anchored on the steps by the driver and surveyed the happenings. Delilah arrived in her top-up yellow corvette. Where's her Jeep? I squinted as I watched her get out and bounce over to Rick.

Hey! She was wearing the same thick black riding pants that I slithered into earlier.

Rick smiled at her too long as he stood THE man's stance—arms folded, legs spread apart—rocking from toe to heel, all in black.

And hey! Why was she dressed all in black too?

"Miss Mac," a freshman boy anxiously yelled. "I forgot my neck scarf."

"I have more." I came supplied and offered him a handful of colors from which to choose.

"Where's mine?" asked Coop.

"Take your pick." He chose orange and tied it around his neck. What a group!

Coop asked, "Everybody horseback riding?" After noticing the age of the four B's he was curious.

"No. We have riders, hikers, and shoppers. Which one are you?" I teased.

"Not a rider. I broke a leg from a fall off a horse. Lightning struck and the horse bolted."

Definitely not a good thought before a ride.

The adults were last to board. It was seven fifty-five.

"Who's missing," asked Nancy.

"Two. Coyotee Raintree and Catora Bell."

At the mention of their names a small truck arrived and Mrs. Raintree and Catora got out.

Simultaneously, a loud thunder roared from somewhere and lightning struck a half mile away.

All silence in the bus.

CHAPTER 20

After the thunder I looked at the driver and said loudly in the too quiet bus, "They promised us horses, rain or shine."

The sun peeked intermittently like a rapidly moving old black and white film---fading in and out with the fast moving clouds.

"They're high," someone said.

"And not cumulous thick," said another.

Quiet on the bus.

I walked out to greet Mrs. Raintree and Catora. One looked tired and disheveled while the other was bouncing and anxious.

"Coyotee called Catora last night," mom said.

"All he said were two words, before hanging up." Catora repeated them, "'Don't worry,' was all he said."

Mrs. Raintree began, "His uncles are looking everywhere for him." She jiggled keys nervously from one hand to the other.

"They'll find him," I said encouragingly. It was eight on the dot and time to leave so we hugged goodbye. She turned and got into her truck.

Catora loaded quickly, found a spot next to friends and joined the now chatty bus.

I settled in my seat behind the driver with Rick next to the window. Earlier we agree that I should have the aisle since I would be popping up and down now and then. "Glue your bum down," he remarked on previous trips. Impossible!

"We're off," said Coop. "I'm taking the back road to hit one of my favorite fast food restaurants out of town, between Tempe and Mesa. We won't lose time."

"Oh boy," I said worried. "Did you tell them this loaded bus might stop? It'll empty when they smell food."

"I did. They're ready."

My stomach grumbled at the mention of food, as always. "Just as long as we're on horses and moving out by ten, it'll work."

Rick did a side glance at me and said, "You didn't eat breakfast?"

Rats! "I forgot!" Amazing even to me.

We headed south on Scottsdale Road, then east on the 101 Freeway which turned south again.

"Ok, listen up." It was Cloud beginning his notes. He took off his thick zip-up sweatshirt, laid it on his seat, picked up the mic and began after leaning a knee on the seat for steadiness. "After a few notes, ask me some questions. Buds out of ears please for a few minutes." He waited as all eyes turned toward him.

"The Superstition Mountains are world famous because of all the legends and lore about gold mines and miners. The Lost Dutchman Gold Mine is the most famous of all and approximately one hundred people get lost each year looking for it. These miners pretend to be hikers when actually they're gold seekers. You might run into a few long-bearded ones on today's ride."

Students were now listening and some chuckled.

"It's true. Ask your teachers later about previous encounters on rides." After sipping from a thermos he continued. "A few notes about the Superstitions before I talk about the Dutchman. The area was named the Superstitions by the Apache who believed in spirits back then, which we might call ghosts. And they believed that these spirits were dangerous. They called the mountains the superstitious mountains from which the name Superstitions was coined. Keep in mind the vastness of one hundred and sixty thousand acres of mountains and all the different Indian tribes that have lived there. For thousands of years there were the Solado and the Hohokam. You can imagine all of the lost people before the Apache and the surrealistic ancient tales about them that persisted. The un-found dead become the lost spirits in an Apache's mind." He stopped and drank some more coffee.

Noticing a few had lost interest he continued with some drama. "Old timers say---'Once you get in, you won't get out'-- Thousands of prospectors have been lost there."

Students were quiet. Cloud was fast when he spoke and made great eye contact.

"Hundreds of non-fiction books have been written about the search for the Lost Dutchman Gold Mine and the failed results. But, I believe it is there," He stopped for emphasis and pointed his finger upward, "and that the Apaches know where it is and have it hidden well disguised."

All eyes were riveted as he talked like an authoritarian. Now I'm really impressed and hope that Guy remembered to bring his grab bag.

"It is strongly believed that a gold mine with top grade ore was found by groups from Mexico back in the early 1800's when Apache raids were numerous in the entire area, and before the Mexican-American War of 1846-1848. Hundreds of bones were found in the late 1800's at Massacre Grounds, where most of the Mexican and Apache fought."

A hand rose, "Who found them?"

"It's documented that the foot soldiers from Fort McDowell in 1861 found masses of bones." He continued. "Legendary history tells us that Apaches attacked the Mexicans who had saddle bags filled with gold they thought came from their mine, so they cut the bags scattering nuggets everywhere. And as late as 1912, gold was found scattered at Massacre Grounds."

A hand rose in the bus of listeners. Catora asked, "But, how did the Lost Dutchman Mine become so popular and where is it?"

This brought laughter.

"Good question." Cloud never smiled so wide before.

"Food time," yelled Coop as he began to slow the bus.

CHAPTER 21

We all scrambled out of the bus with mumblings of facts about the area. Interest was high.

"We hiked there once." A student pointed to a nearby mountainous area.

"On last year's ride, we saw bearded prospectors. They looked lost," I said.

"I hope we see some today." Girls giggled.

"Miners Cave In" was ready for us and provided quick service.

Amazing. We were all back in the bus in minutes with egg burritos, fries, coffee, juice, hot cocoa, apple turnovers and my onion rings.

"Who the heck orders onion rings for breakfast?" Rick laughed before biting into his chili and eggs burrito.

"Make fun of me, I don't share."

Dixie did a quick student count before the bus slowly pulled out….Coop was eating a green chili burrito.

The sun was in our faces and the storm was at our tail, now becoming ominously dark with no wind, sort of pushing us from behind.

No one noticed as happy faces filled with breakfast food, snacks and drinks. The bus smelled like a moving restaurant of sausage, eggs and coffee. Wonderful!

Since Cloud had already eaten and was only drinking coffee he began. "I better continue before we get there. Now to answer Catora's million dollar question." Laughter.

The Lost Dutchman Gold Mine was named much later in life by gold hunters in the early 1900's. The Dutchman was a man named Jacob Waltz who was German….most of the Germans in the early 1800's were dairymen called "Deutchs"—which sounds like Dutch. He was one of many prospectors at that time and as legend has it, the only one who came upon gold supposedly where the Mexican miners were moving their ore from a mystery mine."

The students were excited and silly from the food and on-coming rare storm that Arizonans never see. They interrupted:

"I'm Dutch."

"I'm German."

"I'm Mexican."

Laughter…….

Cloud smiled and continued a little louder. "He killed a couple Mexican miners, and when he went back to gather more nuggets, he killed a foot soldier walking through on a journey from Camp McDowell."

"You mean Fort McDowell," offered a student.

"It wasn't called that until much later toward the 1860's when General Crook commanded armies during the Apache wars. In the beginning, it was commanded by Colonel Cooke in the 1840's. Just remember, Cooke before Crook."

This started a little rhyme ditty with a few students repeating the two names.

"For the ride home, I expect to hear an original rap about the history and today's adventure." I threatened.

He continued. "It's interesting to note that travel in the 1840's was by horseback and four wheeled wagons. Or by foot, and river boats. There were no dams so the Salt River and Gila were flowing. The stagecoach didn't come about until the late 1850's. In a nutshell, since the middle 1800's, thousands have searched for the Lost Dutchman Gold Mine and hundreds have lost their lives."

Roy interrupted, "Remember when the long bearded prospector walked through our camp leading a donkey?"

Previous riders remembered and added, "I was scared."

"He pretended we weren't even there!"

"Now here's the spooky part." Cloud continued. "Since bones were scattered everywhere in the area called Massacre Grounds, it's supposed to be haunted."

Pause.

"So?" asked Jamie Mink.

"Duh!" Added Kim. "It's where we're going."

"Actually, we'll have our lunch break there and get off horses to walk around." My voice echoed loudly through the quiet bus as everyone was thinking about the word 'haunted'.

Cloud whispered in the mic---"You can't pick up anything unless its dry bone or gold....gold you turn over to your teachers---bones you keep!"

Someone frantically asked, "Where's Heleena?"

"Dixie, did you do the count?"

"Humph," she almost choked on her last bite of burro and looked wild eyed.

"Hey, I think that's Miss Dunkin waving out there---sorta chasing us." An observant student in the last seat yelled.

Coop immediately slowed to a stop and asked, "How far is she. Shall I turn around?"

"Yep you better. She's just a speck!" This now came from Dr. Shieter who had been overly engrossed with Delilah and non-communicative to the rest of us.

The four B's sitting in the middle of the bus blamed themselves. "She had been sitting by us earlier. I thought something was amiss, too quiet," said Bing.

Bob said, "I'm to blame. She had been sitting next to me before the stop."

Blake added, "We were all too engrossed with our Chili Burros."

Coop the pro had turned the bus around on a dime and soon opened the doors for Heleena.

She huffed and puffed walking up the steps pulling on the arm bars for help then good naturally said, "I expected a horse to buck me off---not a bus!"

Secretly, I had seen her smoking behind a dumpster bin at the restaurant. She didn't see us leave.

Bob tenderly adjusted her twisted neck scarf while the students began "For she's a jolly good fellow……." And we all joined in to sing the full chorus.

Dixie apologized to Heleena profusely as the sky suddenly darkened north of us. Far off to the left towards the Goldfield Mountains and Saguaro Lake, a trio of lightning flashes distinctly noticeable, aroused the interest of all and the possibility of a pending storm.

Quiet on the bus.

Coop's voice echoed, "It's far to the left and you know this Arizona desert and its spotty storms---it may not come this way, just circle around. Let's hope it moves on to the east of us near Globe."

"We're prepared," offered Roy, quickly seconded by the group of hardy boys.

"What a hunk!" Kim Rose said loudly so the entire bus could hear.

I smiled and said to Rick, "Good collective enthusiasm."

"They're gonna need it." He sighed and hissed while looking out the window. "Remember, we had sleet last year."

"I'm prepared. Are you?" My turn to be sarcastic. I had phoned Nancy and Becky last night and told them to pack ski underwear for leg warmth. We decided on changing in the bus after everyone gets off. Why freeze?

He said, "This trip, I packed fur chaps for my legs. That's the only part that got cold last year."

"I can hardly wait to see them." I raised my left eye brow a couple times to be cool, a trick I learned in seventh grade. My right one doesn't work.

He tickled me just below my ribs.

I continued. "I called Jamie Mink and told her to start a phone chain reminding everyone to pack whatever they had that was thermo."

Suddenly, the sky darkened all around us and so did our bus.

CHAPTER 22

SUPERSTITION MOUNTAINS

The storm was circling a mile ahead where streaks of white on indigo blue introduced rain about to fall near the Superstitions east of us. Everyone was quiet as we headed east on Highway 88, the Apache Trail. The awesomeness of the Superstition Wilderness ahead promoted a silence in the bus as all eyes gawked out windows breathing in the vastness of the emerging mountains, always endlessly impressive.

One can easily become purged of self-grandeur and haughtiness allowing the feelings of humility and humbleness to prevail like a snail in a pond. Historical legends associated with forgotten people impress me the most. In the old days, the Apache considered gold mines their heritage and anyone coming near, mysteriously disappeared.

One legend concerns an Apache kid who was paid money by a group of wealthy prospectors to lead them to a known cave of gold. Mysteriously, he died of poison before he met the group a second time.

It is times like these that I question my authority and the brash decisions I can sometimes make. We could have—should have had a plan B or alternate date to consider during the two week holiday break. After all, December temperatures can fluctuate between a high seventy and high forty in only a few days. This is the crazy Sonoran Desert.

Secretly now, when I think of all the perilous occasions of near death that can occur, I re-work over and over Rick's comforting words of encouragement from last night, "We'll be fine---I'm prepared."

What does all that mean? Everyone needs a hero.

During the past week we discussed the misfortunate accidents from the last couple rides. Have I known Rick Del Rio that long? We vowed to avoid the Garden Valley Loop and cursed the Wranglers who took us through the narrow pathway of seven foot tall chain-fruit-cholla cacti. We held our breaths as did the horses when we walked through, almost brushing the jumping balls of fire on to our legs. No horses flicked a tail. No need; a wind could have stirred these small balls of fish hooks to thrust themselves like magnets under the horses' tender bellies or into our sides as we rode captive.

I lost sleep that night replaying in my mind the horror of what could have happened and glued my body next to Rick's, back then.

When I asked the Wranglers about it afterward and brought up several "what if's"---they simply laughed and displayed comb picks.

"We always carry these. They easily pick-off the chollas; and we have small pliers too. Don't worry so much!"

Wranglers love to tell tall tales to those listeners stuck on horseback like captured audiences.

One told me that he had been bitten by a rattler when he was "way-out" in the wilderness. He said he quickly lay still, stayed on the ground and tried not to move much for one week while his body fought the flu-like symptoms.

I put on my worried face and sighed.

Rick looked at me and read my up-tight attitude. “Look on the bright side. On a winter ride, we face the possibility of a storm, and we come prepared. In the springtime, rattlesnakes are everywhere, and we are unprepared.”

“Good comparison,” said Coop listening in the quiet bus. ‘I’m from Wisconsin. Your Arizona winter storms are like spring showers to me.”

I brightened.

Next, Coop asked Dixie why she wasn’t dressed for the ride like the group of us. “Surely you’re not going riding in that silk blouse and flashy western jewelry?” He chuckled.

“I’m like a delicate bone-China doll; skin getting thinner by the hour as we speak. If I break, there’s not enough glue! I’m the one you’re taking back to the town of Apache Junction for shopping.” She finger punched him in the shoulder then played with her necklace.

“And, I have to baby-sit her so she won’t get lost,” added Richard Cloud. “Pop told me to keep tabs on her spending.”

“Well, that makes three of us,” said Coop. “We’ll be back in plenty of time to gather the worn out crooked-legged riders.”

Cloud grabbed the mic and began again. “To our right is the entrance to Lost Dutchman State Park---hiking only. It’s about two hundred and fifty acres with seventy sights for camping and open every day of the year---no horses allowed nor motorized vehicles.

“No fun there,” someone said.

Coop announced as if talking to himself. “Ok, Crosscut Trailhead is here.” Turning right on an improved dirt road, everyone held on as if subconsciously riding in a stagecoach.

“Where are the horses?” Dixie asked.

"About two miles ahead," I said "At the First Water Horse Trailhead. We mount-up there, then ride about a quarter mile to the beginning of the trail called, First Water Trailhead."

Confusing? The babble began from the students.

"I want a fast walker."

"Not me. The slower the better."

"I don't want no pony." This from a freshman.

"I want a big one."

"I want a short one."

"I want a tall one."

"I want a small one."

I'm glad the kids are acting goofy and in good spirits.....we should bottle it for later.

The four B's were shaking their heads and gathering their walking sticks strewn in the aisle.

"Hey," I interrupted. "Just remember your horse's name as part of a future descriptive essay."

"Yeah, right!"

Coop parked near a turn around a short distance from a corral of saddled and tethered horses. Wranglers were waiting. Three of them.

As planned, I handed them the list of our three separate groups.

They introduced themselves as Pete, Dick and Jack. Each was thin, whiskered, weathered and wrinkled, but looked hard as a rock. Bundled in thick long sleeves, thermo vests, leathered chaps, and spurs attached to worn out cowboy boots, they were ready for the ride. Their black hats looked stomped on which I figured probably happened a dozen times and their names were simple enough to remember, especially Pete's because he had a pickled looking red nose....Pickled Pete!

Three insignificant looking horses were tethered separately off to the end of the corral, well packed with extra gear. They were ready.

About two hundred yards away and dressed in a hooded black slicker sat a man on a large black quarter horse. Black gloved hands rested on the saddle horn. He sat tall and still, wore dark sun glasses watching our every move, and I assumed he was some kind of lead.

We all gathered around, including Dixie, Cloud and Coop.

Pete was in charge. "Walkers—or hikers it seems ya'll prefer to be called—here's a map of the trail and where we're goin' for lunch." Talking loudly with authority as if he had done this act many times, he played with a leather quirt, slapping it on his side once and awhile for emphasis.

Bing, Bob, Brad and Blake lively stepped forward.

"Now don't try to keep pace with us. Won't happen—unless you've got horse legs." He grinned widely and twisted the leather piece in his hand.

"Meet us at the "X" on the map—Massacre Grounds, fer coffee, hot chocolate, and smores."

Bing said, "We're counting on our Marine expert to take care of us." Brad smiled and fiddled with his bandana while Blake snapped pictures of everyone. "I'm the historian on this momentous occasion."

"And if it rains?" Roy the senior wanted to know.

"We've a chuck wagon prepared for food accommodations—and there's a shallow ledge, a chiseled notch of a cave that'll keep ya'll sheltered if the weather gits nasty." For emotional affect, he looked up at the sky and spun around on one heel.

He continued, "I see that everyone's dressed warm 'cept you Miss Petunia in the silk blouse." He looked at Dixie real hard.

"I'm not riding; I'm busing." Putting her hands on her hips she stepped back between Cloud and Coop.

"Good thing. You're wearing enough silver to cause a lightning strike." Pete laughed.

No one else did….it began to sprinkle.

CHAPTER 23

9:30 AM

Pete leaned a hand on a horse's rump like a pro, crossed his ankles and began….This was his comfort zone. "The first thing ya do when you git on your horse is git the yellow slicker that's tied on back of the saddle, and put it on. Be sure to cover yer hats too. We're goin' far and ya don't want to spoil yer fun." He sounded rote, like he was talking to the air around him. Also, the more he talked the more his corny, but interesting accent became evident.

"Before discuss'n the do's and don'ts, I need to separate the pros from the sissies. Don't be offended. It's the only way I kin put cha on the right horse."

Dick and Jack the two Wranglers raised their hands.

"I'm a sissy."

"I'm a sissy."

"Yeah," said Pete, "that's why ye're leading us."

Laughter was a good release of the kids' nerves and they absorbed every piece of corn the Wranglers threw at them.

The three Wranglers in good spirits wasted no time getting everyone mounted. The horses had particular names for particular reasons---or not. The least spirited horses had the wildest names which of course made the sissies feel important. And of course after a while, Nancy and I realized Pete was jiving us, originating names fitted to the riders.

First, the plump-potato-chip girl mounted "Tornado" and as Pete held the reins, he used her as a model for his demonstrations.

"All these horses are well seasoned." On cue, Tornado yawned. "You novice riders, all you have to do is hang on and let your horse lead."

Dick added, "Most importantly, give your horse its rein. Don't pull back as you hold on. Rest your hands on the saddle horn and let the reins loop a bit."--- Demonstration.

I looked at my watch. We had fifteen minutes remaining to mount-up, so hurry with the demonstrations. And, I crossed my fingers hoping Heleena would not interrupt with twenty questions. She had to stand in front of the group, soaking it all in, boots planted in dirt while shaking her split-denim-fringed-riding skirt to a tune in her head. Bob stood behind her.

Please Pete, don't ask if there are any questions; I was getting anxious because of the dripping sky.

Heleena raised her hand. The Wranglers read my mind, didn't dilly-dally and avoided her. I have ESP after all. I'm going to work it while on this ride. Butch, the psychic, gave me instructions…RELAX and CONCENTRATE…

Farther out in the distance, sat the black rider motionless like a statue, watching our every move. Concentrate, concentrate…who is he? What is his job or motive? I nudged Nancy. She shook her head like, 'don't bother me'. I felt alone in my quest.

All the riders had a copy of the three groups which would be spaced eight minutes apart because small groups are easier to manage. Park rules insist on no more than fifteen to a group with ten minutes spacing between. They accommodated our three split groups of ten with eight minutes spacing, so we could be within sight of each other as we headed towards mountain tops and canyons. The overused princess wave becomes popular among the students in this setting, and they will be using it excessively.

Pete asked, "Why the list in this order?" He frowned and wiggled his pickled nose. He was starting to annoy me.

I stiffened and said, "The students chose to ride with friends."

"What ever happened to making new ones?" He slapped the list with the back of his hand and continued matching riders and horses after handing his leather quirt to Dick who I assumed would be in the very front. I ESP'D it.

The three Wranglers joked about horses names as the riders mounted. I realized they were having fun originating names as they saw fit. "These two horses can't be split…Bacon and Eggs are their names." Becky was selected for a stocky dark bay named Bacon and Guy for Eggs…a piebald horse with large patches of white and black. Of course, Guy laughed so hard I thought he would fall out of the saddle. That's my friend!

Next, Pickled Pete looked at Nancy and me and said, "I 'spect you two want to be in the lead of the three groups."

I pointed to his list at our names in Group One, at the top.

"You need the two fastest horses…Boogie and Woogie."

My hand went to my mouth as I swallowed a giggle.

Nancy looked at me, rolled her eyes and shrugged her shoulders. Our usual non-verbal connection always works.

"Again, we have here two horses totally inseparable. Boogie always leads with Woogie at his tale. If separated, one will break down a wall to git to the other."

They were two Strawberry Roans—chestnut bodies in which white hairs were mixed. Nancy said, "I always wanted to ride a horse named Woogie" as she put her foot in the stirrup."

Pete added, "Just keep your red hair covered. He goes wild you know." Before he could help her, she was sitting in the saddle. I too was on Boogie in seconds. "Pros," Pete scoffed.

Courteously, the men and boys waited while the remaining girls' horses were selected and they were in the saddles.

Pete selected Donut for Heleena Dunkin…after reading her name from the list. Donut, a black and white paint, was standing there half asleep. "He's a good walker when awake."

Heleena waved away help as she tried to get on the horse with her left foot in the stirrup and the right one doing a dance on the ground. After watching the unsuccessful third try, Dick and Jack politely helped her with one hand on her upper arm and the other on her waist. "Oomph," she almost fell off the front as she flopped over the saddle horn. "I'm on," she jokingly waved…the princess wave.

"Last year we had a sturdy ladder from which to mount the horses," I said.

"Lost it!" Pete shrugged.

Dr. Shieter and Delilah were next and since they were standing together, Pete assumed they were a couple also.

"We're pros," Dr. Shieter mistakenly bragged. Pete swiftly analyzed the Principal's attire of a freshly pressed collared blue shirt, and expertly creased denim pants with matching vest. Tipped back, an expensive Stetson straw allowed brown hair to wave across his forehead.

"I want that one with the star on his face," said Shieter. "I bet his name is Star."

"No, that's Butter, smooth as silk." Pete brought a brown Mustang forward for him. "Nice fast walker," he said.

Butter my ass! That horse looks like a blind bucker to me. Nancy and I knew this type of horse could dangerously buck whenever it decides to eliminate the rider and run back to the barn…also called barn sour. Outlaw, would be more appropriate.

"Now for you my lady, we have Biscuit."

Of course Movie-Star-Gorgeous quickly mounts a beautiful white mane and tale Palomino. Pete stood there a moment too long combing its forelock of beautiful white. Did I hear him purring?

In the constant drizzle, I looked at my watch. "We need to start out in ten minutes."

Everyone quickly helped the sissies---new riders---get in their saddles. Two freshman boys straddled Hurricane and Torpedo. They were pleased.

The last few were selected: Rodeo for Roy, Lolita for Jamie Mink, Magic for Kim Rose and Sugar for Catora.

The Wranglers showed everyone how to roll their extra jackets and tie them to the saddle straps attached near the seats.

Since all thirty of us were in the saddle, twenty-one students and nine adults, plus the three Wranglers…Dixie was anxiously ready to leave. Before she and Cloud jovially walked off, she sarcastically yelled, "Ya'll have fun now, ya hear." That's the last I saw of them for a too long time. Coop had left ten minutes ago to warm the bus.

We began.

Leading the first group was Wrangler Dick. Nancy and I were in front with Heleena in the rear. In between were six students, Kim Rose, Roy, Jamie Mink, Catora Bell and two novices. The expert Coyotee was missing. I purposely mixed the experienced with novices. Heleena was definitely a novice, but I expected the senior Catora Bell to help her if necessary.

Wrangler Jack was chosen to lead Line Two followed by Rick Del Rio on Bullet with seven students in the middle. At the tail were Delilah and Dr. Shieter. She, the expert, had offered to ride tail, but Shieter insisted on it. He enjoyed the sight of her in the saddle. He was sitting straight and tall. Exactly what I warned him not to do.

"Lean back, relax your shoulders and let your body rock with the horse." He forgot.

Line Three was different. Highly experienced Colt was selected to lead on Pokey a fast paced, sure footed Missouri Fox Trotter. Becky Painter and Guy Wagner were at the very back of the long string. Surprisingly, Pete stayed back a good twenty yards. I realized why as I watched him in the distance while we were riding an incline. He took a can of Bull Durham from his back pocket and with two fingers poked some chew back along the side of his mouth.

And, as I looked back at the long string of riders, Eggs at the end began slowly following the pack as Guy's loud athletic voice echoed in the wind, "Hi Ho Eggs, Away."

CHAPTER 24

10:00 AM

Spirits are high as always at the beginning of a ride. My group was chatty with both Jamie Mink and Kim Rose flirting with Roy for attention. Riding between them, he loved it. "One good thing about the hooded slickers," he said, "I don't have to retrieve hats!" Nancy and I wore our Australian canvas tie-downs with wide brims that curled slightly at rounded edges. Our large hooded slickers fit over them perfectly. We were dry, not worrying as the slow drizzle now became a slow rain.

Catora Bell rode Sugar between the two freshman boys on Hurricane and Torpedo so she could help give pointers. They were pleased with the attention from a senior girl. Nevertheless, she complained, "I miss Coyotee."

"We'll find him; I'm sure of it." Concentrate, concentrate like Butch taught me. Maybe I can learn to be a Sensitive, another name for a Psychic.

Keeping with our slow pace, the four hikers babbled and flexed their vocal chords for solving problems. This start of a trail was two wagons wide and they had room to join us for a short distance. I heard:

"Let's all take mental notes to compare later," said Bob always an organizer.

"I'll take pictures. Who wants to type a short narrative about our adventures?" Blake asked.

They all shook heads a negative.

Brad began, "Hate the computer. Something always goes wrong. Trying to write a document is like driving in NASCAR with one flat tire."

"Or watering flowers with a hole in the bucket," Bing offered.

"Or like trimming a Mesquite tree with toenail clippers." Bob finished with the best comparison as we rode away and soon left them behind. Nothing like having too much fun!

Trails in the Superstitions are numerous and rock cairns marking trails are everywhere. Most hikers follow a map and the small rock pillars that lead to a destination of some kind. Those who don't pay attention, soon become lost and meet with a disastrous fate, their bones usually devoured by ravenous desert creatures. A map is needed or experienced guide familiar with the trails and where they lead. Looking around, I can see how a person can get lost. Roads and trails frequently crisscross at junctions and a rider or hiker can easily make the wrong turn.

Our ride will be moderate with some stream crossings and narrow trails through boulders and trees. Topping ridges over low canyons can be frightful, but the horses are accustomed to these narrow trails. "No bouldering please," I had begged when planning this adventure months ago with the Wranglers.

"We wouldn't think of it," they had said back in August.

Bouldering, is dangerously riding off marked trails and winging it. This is why so many get lost and ultimately die.

I pulled out my small camera that fit deep in my jacket pocket, wrapped the cord around my wrist and began taking shots of the line behind. Since we were riding in the foothills of mountains, our gradual ascent towards the Superstition Mountain allowed the visibility above the others for a good shot of the long string of three lines. Many colorful scarves waved in the wind, dampened slightly by the slow rain. Blake and I will compare pictures later. "Close-ups, close-ups, close-ups!" We reminded each other earlier. Rule of thumb: three close-ups for each wide angle.

Twisting around in the saddle, I searched for my mystery black rider. He was gone. Coming up the ridge were Rick and Line Two. I did the big arm wave and he threw one kiss in my direction. All's well on the Superstitions---or not. I expect a problem per hour. I looked at my watch---10:30. Too early. Yet, is that Delilah breaking away from the line and heading toward Rick?

I stood in my stirrups and twisted around. Now what? She and Shieter are supposed to stay at the end of Line Two of riders with Rick in the front. My horse kept pace regardless of my twisting around, but my waist was being stretched.

She pointed to Shieter; Rick pointed to Colt and kept riding. She rode back to the end of her line and waited for Colt the leader of Line Three. Shieter was the problem. His legs were dangling below the stirrups and Colt had to re-adjust them for comfort. Line Three decided to stop and wait as they watched intrigued and entertained with his speed and expertise.

Next, I saw Delilah and Shieter in a slow cantor to get back to their place in line---she rode as one with the horse like a total piece of molded plastic toy; he flopped and bounced so hard up and down in the saddle that all of us could hear the noise of his butt slapping hard leather. Shieter was leaning forward which I had told him not to do unless he was standing in the stirrups. Butter, AKA Outlaw, was being cantankerous and decided not to cantor and slowed to a hard-stiff-legged trot. Ouch! Shieter had both hands on the saddle horn as the horse finally slowed to a walk.

Rain was sparse but steady and every small wash crossing our trail was streaming with inches of it. Horses loved making considerably loud splashes while playfully walking through and a few always wanted to lie down with rider in tow. We were ready for this with reins drawn. Heavy rain and thunderbolts are to the east of us and we hope it continues in that direction.

We left the First Water Trailhead behind and are now on a do-able abandoned trail. Craggy peaks are to the southeast of us and we are surrounded by rocky hills. As we head up the north slope of Superstition Mountain, small waterfalls are cascading from its majestic sides. What mysteries it could reveal from its lopsided top, and cropped off pillars called hoodoos!

This hulk of a mountain changes colors according to various painters' palettes. To me it is a purplish gray most of the time, adding stripes of scarlet on sunny days.

It's called the Rock of Arizona with stories of bygone crazy prospectors losing their lives, searching for gold……and the thousands of Indians who lived in the area when it supported life with its abundance of animals and water; its pillar can be seen for long distances away and used as a focal point on trips. I looked around thinking about all the history that has vanished. Or has it?

Then there are stories of robbers who lived off those unsuspecting weary travelers exhausted from heat, dust and jostling from a coach. Hacksaw Tom robbed wagons and stagecoaches with a twelve gauge double-barreled shotgun in 1905 for five years.

I was day dreaming about the earlier, short lived cowboy days with the big cattle drives that existed from the 1860's through the 1880's when someone yelled me out of my reverie.

"Miss Mac, we need help!"

Potato chip girl was standing, still holding on the reins of Tornado who decided to sit and rest.

CHAPTER 25

My line of riders stopped as we all turned and looked back at Rick Del Rio's line, led by Wrangler Jack. Jack on Big Boy and Rick on Bullet, turned their horses facing Line Two. Wrangler Jack quickly got off his horse and laughed. "Tornado likes to fall asleep when following others at a slow pace. We need to accelerate a bit."

Tornado sat there quietly, couldn't care less, turned his head and looked about.

When Jack approached, the horse quickly arose, shook and began to chew his bit. The rider re-mounted, amused by it all…especially the attention.

"Chips anyone?" She pulled out a large bag of barbeque flavor, mouth-watering crispies and passed it to the rider behind her who reached in for a handful before passing the bag back to the next in line. Food—contentment for teens!

Wrangler Jack's voice loudly echoed in the steady slow rain to our leader. "Pick-up the pace!"

Dick, in the very front of my line, clicked his heels and simultaneously made a loud clicking noise with the corner of his mouth as we now began to walk faster.

"Let's Boogie!" I said to my horse as "Woogie" was pushing from behind.

I am now worried as streams and rivulets snaking across the trail are deepening. The storm is getting closer and darker as we head toward it. Thickening foliage brushed our trail as we head south-east on a long switchback—an incline ridged with Saguaros, Hedge-Hog, and thick marine green Jojoba.

Boulders are in an abundance of sizes as the terrain becomes a washboard of deep washes and mini canyons whose ledges are dangerously soft. A horse and rider edging too closely could go rolling down. Hopefully, the horse could slide down on its haunches unless the mini-canyon is vertically deep, which is normally the case.

An eerie peaceful silence accompanied the slightly demanding trail as the quickening of horses' hooves clicked along the rocks. This, and the steady rain, were the only sounds for at least thirty minutes.

Sight of the long string of thirty riders was long gone when the trail wound through washes, ravines and flat ridges. Rounding ridges, however, allowed for intermittent sight of the tail of horses coming behind us as we waved at each other occasionally. No problems yet.

I read that there was a niche in a cliff, a small wedge of an overhang at Massacre Grounds under which we could hover. This thought occupied my mind profusely as I was getting tired of the slow rhythm of the rain and its monotony.

"A chiseled niche of a cave," are the exact words from the "Guide to Superstition Trails", a pamphlet I had from a year ago. Also, we looked forward to the chow wagon brought there by some other route then this narrow trail, which forbids motorized vehicles. Prepared for rain, canopied tables are supposed to welcome us, arranged ahead.

Conical Butte is to the west of us, a treasure of a landmark if one gets lost—it resembles a mini Weavers' Needle, another important tall conical piece and famous reference for mountain climbers who ascend it easily.

Thunder cracked and a horse whinnied ahead somewhere. Tired of the rain, I was ready for cover, figuring the rain would hit hard for twenty minutes and then dwindle to nothing. An all day desert rain was rare and un-seen by many. Once we get to our site, we can settle in, devour our sandwiches and watch it pour. The ride back most likely will be dry and safe considering we have no big washes to cross.

"How much farther?" I yelled at Wrangler Dick who I could not see while I adjusted the chin strap to my Australian canvas. Looking back at Nancy with "Woogie" riding my tail, I saw that she had her head ducked while rain splattered off the top of her slicker which covered her similar hat.

No answer from Dick. Did he disappear?

I checked the time. We had been riding for two hours when my horse suddenly raised its head, ears forward and began a slow trot up a low incline, a trail between two large boulders.

Thundering out of a draw lined with Desert Broom to my left, came the black rider—the mystery man covered in a long black coat, knee high riding boots, black gloves and hat. His face in the now heavy rain was concealed.

His horse stopped yards away, reared on cue, than pirouetted on hind legs a slight turn.

I gasped and held tightly to the reins of my now overly excited Strawberry Roan. What happened next was a blur. The black gloved rider rode forward, grabbed the lead rope attached to the halter that was under Boogie's bridle, and took off with a jerk.

Our horses complied and seemed to know the terrain that I thought was treacherous. Not having done this trail before, I was really in the dark as I held my breath and grabbed the saddle horn with both hands hanging on for my life.

I tried to look behind but could not. Considering our speed, I knew the dangers from this weird happening. Horses behind trotted noisily over crushed rock here and there, an assurance we were together.

"Where we going?" Yelling did no good; my voice was easily drowned by the pounding rain and steady beat of hooves now in a slow gallop.

Putting my head down to keep my hat from tipping back, I yelled again. "Slow down; we have new riders." I worried about my two student freshman novices, not to mention Heleena Dunkin on Donut. I assumed that Rick's Line Two and Colt's Line Three were quite a distance back. Wrangler Jack would hold back the pace for their groups…if he was still around.

And where in the heck is our leader, Wrangler Dick?

Here and there in our speed I was able to see sporadic groups of cairns stacked near our trail. Good!

Thinking of the four B's hiking along, they would not get lost…but would be unable to stay with us at this pace.

We now galloped in a sandy wash with steady streams running on both sides. Heading up the north slope of Superstition Mountain towards a series of boulders, I saw the rounded tops of Hoodoos ahead, tops peaking above low rain clouds.

With both hands on the saddle horn, I held on and hoped that others were doing the same. I was helpless and kept trying to see the face of the man who was leading my horse with an iron grip.

Finally, we slowed to a walk and passed through a narrow ravine sided with Catsclaw, a dangerous bush that mimics the thick foliage of Blackberries so prevalent in the wet environments of the Pacific Northwest.

His back was turned.

To my relief, our ravine opened to a flat area of about an acre. On the left was a ledge—an overhang that seemed to be chiseled from the rock behind—a refuge from the pouring rain.

The black rider suddenly threw my horse's lead rope over its head and back to me before taking off in a blur---to somewhere.

"Holy cow! Are we in a movie or what?" Leave it to Kim Rose to always find the right touch of sarcasm to brighten a frightening event.

Other riders came bumping into us, the end of my Line One, and were speechless.

Nancy was loud. "Everybody ok?"

Astounding! Everyone in our group was thrilled with the speed, not recognizing the danger. All the better.

"That's our chow wagon over there. This must be Massacre Grounds." I nodded toward the boarded shut wooded wagon and its flimsily staked covering of light plastic, not heavy canvas which was necessary for this wind and rain.

The camp looked abandoned. We expected some kind of covered camp fire for our s'mores which would accompany our own bring along lunches. Also, there were no covered tables.

Nancy asked, "What is this place? We've never run into this before. No one is here!"

The tie line for the horses looked sturdy as I counted four wooden posts securing horizontal ropes.

Quickly, we helped each other dismount, grab our sandwiches, and tie the horses by their halter ropes. Our mounts hung their heads and shook as the rain poured a cloudburst this time.

"Follow me," I yelled as we sloshed our way to the shallow ledge Pete had told us about and hugged our backs to the rock behind—now out of the rain. It was a hand chiseled notch of a cave, an alcove with enough over-hang to protect its occupants.

Wrangler Dick, our leader, was gone and so was the black rider. Ten of us hovered and shook while watching the curtain of rain fall about ten feet in front as it ran off the overhang.

Shouting to be heard, we were happy to have made it to our destination and to be now out of the rain.

"I wonder what's happening with the others," Heleena yelled.

"They better get out of the washes and ravines," Nancy warned.

"We have one near our home," Jamie Mink added. "We just wait about twenty minutes for the water to run out and then we can cross."

Lightning flashed and three seconds later, thunder cracked.

"Let's hope it's a fast moving storm," I said.

We all agreed to eat our sandwiches and other snacks.

It was a quiet peacefulness, so contrasting after what we had been through. We looked out at the forlorn-abandoned camp. Where were the leaders? The tied horses were quiet with heaving sides due to the speed.

I looked at my water proof watch which I decided to wear in case I dropped my cell---which happens on every ride to someone.

One-thirty. We settled in and expected the riders to join us at any time. The earlier cloudburst now became a slow steady rain again, but we could hear water cascading down cliffs and fast running washes nearby.

Everyone was quietly eating.

Nancy and I settled down, opened our rainproof bags and joined them. We were all in a sharing mood passing around cut-up vegetables trying to get rid of them. Robust Heleena devoured most of them where she sat with a lap filled with sandwich bags of carrots, celery, radishes and peppers.

We hoarded our cookies and chocolate….no sharing.

Then, "I hear a harmonica," said one of the boys.

"Shhh, it's faint. I hear it too," this from Nancy.

I looked around. "In a minute we'll probably see some old prospector come around the bend over there, leading a donkey." I hoped. We all stopped chewing and listened.

I worked my ESP. Nothing!

"I know who the black rider was," said Catora.

CHAPTER 26

APACHE CAMP
Massacre Grounds
December 22, 1848

All eyes watched APACHE who gingerly reached for the valise from GAMBLER MOODY. First, a feather touch, then a sudden grab at the handle of the large canvas bag. In a squat, he hopped and shuffled away to the end of the cave just inside the ledge and faced everyone with the contented look of a gift receiver. Eagerly as a child would, he opened it wide and stared inside without moving. Putting his hand in slowly, he removed the contents, one by one with each deserving of a long examination.

GAMBLER MOODY walked away and sat on a flat boulder where he had been before. Like the other five, he too had his place of comfort.

Eagerly, everyone watched APACHE. Each stopped his previous motion to stare and wonder at this new entertainment. What were his gifts that perhaps could bring appeasement from vicious actions of malcontent?

CHINA ROSE looked admirably towards GAMBLER MOODY after absorbing his intentions and clung affectionately to FOOT SOLDIER DAVY'S arm. He had stopped rocking to stare.

DAVY unfolded his arm and clasped one of her hands in both of his, a gesture of hopeful peace as he stared at APACHE.

MEXICAN MANO sneered but had to watch from where he tended his beans, stirring with a piece of Arizona Rosewood in his one hand.

DUTCHY, hovering over his cache of recently acquired goods, watched with a squinty displeasure from where he sat wedged in a corner of the shallow cave, away from others. His thoughts were of more possessions which he could add to his collection, now hidden in a well---a six inches deep area covered with a little pile of rocks. His cache was in a treasure box of a hole, more little stones than sand. He selected a twelve inch rock as a cover for the hollow place where he hid GAMBLER MOODY'S watch, a weird rubber wedge, and a pearl bracelet. Now, his eagle eyes were hunting for more riches.

Snatching a nearby long piece of straight Mesquite, he began whittling the end to fashion a piercing spear.

APACHE lay the valise between his legs where he sat squat, harboring it with his feet. No one would take this from him. First item held at eye level was a hand crocheted doily of intricate flower design, a white twelve inch by six inch piece. Sticking his fingers through the threads carefully, he held it high for examination.

Tear drops welled from GAMBLER MOODY.

APACHE stood in place and with great pleasure tucked the shorter end of the rectangular doily under his leather belt, just over his front loin cloth---a decoration.

Fast, he sat down where he had been before, harbored his valise and looked around suspiciously. None had moved from where each sat, staring, mesmerized.

Soft snow flakes scattered about as he pulled out two small draw string bags and held them towards the sky, one in each hand. A canvas bag contained loose tobacco while the larger leather one held pemmican, his favorite dried meat pound to a powder. APACHE recognized both, having smoked tobacco in a pipe as a young boy with his tribesmen, and once tasting the powder-meat from fur trappers who had come often during his childhood. He closed the bags, held them to his chest with eyes closed and faced the sky. Again, raising them high one in each hand, he looked toward the sky and chanted a short song.

For the first time, it was a long peaceful afternoon as none had seen before. The magical valise delivered over-whelming entertainment for all.

Only GAMBLER had trouble watching as he ducked his head more crookedly now because of advance twisting of his neck. With contorted shoulders and by moving his upper body, he watched intermittently. Contentment was still his as he alone knew where his guns and Cuban long nine cigars were securely hidden, tucked away for future use. He hoped not to use his guns but planned a special occasion for the Cuban long nines.

As APACHE'S pile grew larger, he decided to share with the others whom he noticed were drooling with excitement.

To CHINA ROSE he tossed a contoured tin cup that folded down within itself. He had played with it enough turning it upside down then right side up watching it collapse and open.

She brightened!

A stack of unusually large meaningless cards with strange markings, he quietly handed to GAMBLER, placing them on his rock-table. GAMBLER nodded upon acceptance but didn't touch them.

After opening a jar of tainted bear grease, APACHE grimaced and threw the jar to MEXICAN MANO'S eager hand.

MEXICAN MANO began immediately rubbing the grease on his stump of a hand, then on his dried boots before rubbing the remaining on his whiskered face.

All the while, APACHE never took eyes off DUTCHY.

Biggest oddity was the cigar cutter and APACHE played with it the longest. Pressing the edges, he saw the sharp inner pieces close tightly. After putting his finger in the hole, he yelped, realizing that this could be a weapon. He inserted one of his arrows and discovered that he could cut off the end swiftly. "Hah"—he muttered to himself not realizing he became an apparition of peace and wonder to the others.

Wrapped in a piece of canvas were four colorfully dyed feathers. APACHE looked toward the sky wondering from what bird were these strangely colored things. Happily, he tucked the quills under the back of his rawhide head band and stood chanting, dancing around the valise.

DUTCHY whittled feverishly on his long piece of wood sharpening the point ever so perfect. Now and then he pricked his finger testing its perfection.

After finding a leather string necklace with firmly attached bear teeth, APACHE held it high, chanting more loudly and running the circle of leather around and again between all his fingers.

Scanning the quiet group and noticing their vigilance, he walked over to DAVY and gestured for him to take it while he held it at arm's length.

DAVY morosely accepted, than brooded while studying the necklace of leather twine. He rubbed his open wound. The one on the left side of his chest. The one that will never heal.

CHINA ROSE quickly took it from his loose fingers and gaily put it around his neck, after which she hugged his broad bony shoulders and smiled.

GAMBLER MOODY now raised his head sideways and noted the renewed activities with sparkling eyes for the first time. Even the corner of his mouth tilted in a half smile, a measure that took an enormous amount of effort.

APACHE cantankerously threw DUTCHY a hollow part of a pistol he had unwrapped from a rectangular piece of cowhide and laughed as only an APACHE youth knew---a combo of tease and bitterness.

DUTCHY kicked it away hatefully and whittled faster.

APACHE continued, this time with adornments. A lady's lacy garter he put around his ankle while a pair of suspenders hung from his neck.

Coveting a brass tinder box with a flintlock attached, APACHE played with the trigger over and over, before turning the valise upside down to empty the last of its contents. He shook it over and over until a teeny-tiny bell fell to the ground.

GAMBLER MOODY'S gasp swiftly elevated everyone's attention to his direction. A hand covered his mouth as he stared stunned, gaping.

APACHE jumped on top of a rectangular-purplish boulder and flung the tiny bell as hard as he could within GAMBLER'S grasp.

GAMBLER held the little bell to his chest, bent his crooked neck down as far as it would go and wept silently.

No one moved.

Snowflakes ceased.

P-E-A-C-E was too short to be embraced.

A raging DUTCHY scrambled from where he was sitting, clutched his sharply pointed spear tightly in his right hand, aimed toward the rectangular-purplish boulder and sprang forward like a lightning bolt.

CHAPTER 27

SUPERSTITION MOUNTAINS

MASSACRE GROUNDS
December 22, 2014

I looked at Catora where she sat crunching a carrot from her rain proof lunch bag. With the hood of her slicker back, her green cross-country cap looked as dry as her long straight brown hair which she had smartly tucked into her ski jacket. Rounded eyes of green softened the seriousness of her expression.

Speechless and still shaking, I looked at her and continued eating my ham on rye.

"I'm sure I know who the black rider is," she repeated.

Everyone stopped from moving around and listened. The two boys had been comparing the contents of their lunch bags, while Heleena was still finding a flat, dry place to settle. Since she was wobbling strangely, I knew that I needed to tend to her. But, I too was overwhelmed by the previous race. The wind and rain slapping hard in my face had left me numb.

Roy helped her settle on a rectangular-purplish boulder, then joined Jamie Mink and Kim Rose.

We were all secure under the overhang of the shallow cave as the cold rain changed to rolling puffs of light snow falling slowly.

Out front, the horses stood in a steaming cloud of fog from their sweaty bodies and hovered close silently wheezing. For them, it had been a mad dash.

"I'm sure it was Coyotee!" Catora began.

"How do you know?"

"That was his horse!"

"How could you tell?" Amazed, I wanted to believe her.

"Its tail was extra long and I saw how it picked-up its feet, very sure-footed like the Missouri Trotter he always rode in the Cave Creek Mountains." She continued un-interrupted. "I couldn't see much because of the rain and speed, but I could hear the sound of quick hooves at the lead. Plus, he taught his horse how to rear on cue."

We were all impressed.

Roy was first. "Where did he go? Does he know this place---these mountains?"

"We came here in October. I wanted to show him where we would be trail riding with the school. He said it was the land of the Apache and seemed extra concerned about the entire area." Catora spoke slowly as if she was trying to determine his overall intentions.

An unspoken quietness radiated from each of us as we continued eating while watching the slow falling snow roll and tumble with the wind a few yards in front of our hovel. Sounds of water cascading down Superstition Mountain loudly joined fast flowing rain water streaming over rocks and boulders to fill washes below. We were Westerners hypnotized by the beauty of snow---the rare sound of rain.

Looking at the time, I realized that forty minutes had passed without hearing from the others.

Heleena began, looking wild eyed and restless. "We've been abandoned!"

"This is eerie," said Nancy. "Those last two washes we rode in are probably wildly flowing by now and the next two lines of riders have to wait it out on a side bank."

"That includes us," said an unworried Kim Rose.

"Washes run fast." Jamie added. "We'll wait it out on this side and join them soon."

No one was worried. Entertainment was the beautiful snow and our bags of food.

"We could stay here all night," said one of the freshman boys.

"Yeah, we're dressed for it," said the other.

"Tell that to your parents. Remember, this place is supposed to be haunted."

"What is the history of this place? I forgot." It was Catora's turn.

Roy was the big brother to the girls. "The Apaches and Mexicans fought over a gold mine that is supposed to be in this area…the Lost Dutchman Mine." He spun slowly and made a circle with his arm.

I joined him. "Books have been written and bones have been found by the hundreds…right here." I sounded dramatic even to myself. This prompted the nine of us to eye the place with scrutiny.

"Indians honor the dead and believe their spirits exist where they died." This was offered by Heleena who stood with folded arms and looked puffy and unstable. Her sigh was unnaturally loud.

"What's wrong with you?" I asked.

"Nothing." She wavered.

I squinted one eye at her. She was frowning too much---abnormal.

"We need to go back in an hour." I looked at my watch. "At three, we need to find our way back—Wrangler Dick or not!"

I was pissed and couldn't believe we were alone. Actually the nine of us didn't feel worried…yet.

The snow and drizzle had stopped. Roy and the two freshman boys were out and about scouting for bones or other mementos. Picking up rocks, they had a throwing contest at a distant large boulder while laughing noisily. They climbed, jumped and scouted like little kids.

The three girls, Jamie Mink, Kim Rose, and Catora Bell, happily decided to join them.

I looked at Nancy and Heleena. "Should we be worried?"

"Not yet," shrugged Nancy as she stood and shook her yellow slicker free of rain. We all did the same. Like Pioneer women, we cleared our shelter of any loose paper bags and piled them neatly to be placed in our saddle bags for taking out.

Roy came running to us. "Someone is playing a harmonica."

"Where?" We were in unison.

"I don't know. It's coming from different places."

"Did any of our group have one?" I considered the possibility that they had scoffed at the washes and circled around.

"Not that we know," said Kim who had joined us.

Catora said, "Coyotee's out there hiding from us; I know it. But, he doesn't play the harmonica. I clearly heard it too."

Time for my ESP tune in. "It's ghost," I said matter-of-factly. "Let's walk around."

Despite the previous torrent, it was a beautiful afternoon, weather wise. A speck of sun shone through the ascending clouds, flashing sparks of diamonds in the troughs of snow, and to our dry desert eyes, it looked heavenly. "I wish Del Rio was here," I whispered to Nancy.

"I miss Colt."

The six students were combing around all the perimeters listening for the harmonica, waving their arms at each other to walk softly.

"Did you hear something?"

Nancy didn't answer because she had been studying the horses.

Heleena, who had been unusually quiet all this time answered with a negative shake of her head, still wild-eyed.

"Something's wrong!" Nancy was the first to notice the horses' anxiety of unusual prancing in place with ears twitching forward, listening. Watching them jerking their heads around in great expectation of an oncoming scare, caused my heart to race.

"Hey," I yelled to the six. "Look at the horses. We need to grab them by their halters and settle them down."

"They're spooked by this place," Nancy murmured.

"Don't start," I said.

"Remember my neighbor's cousin? Butch the psychic told us that horses have an uncanny sense of the unknown."

They pursued back and forth rapidly, kicking and bucking in place. Sugar, Catora's horse reared then fell back on her haunches causing the horizontal tie rope to almost snap.

"Whoa, whoa, whoa," we all yelled. Using every technique to calm them, we got in front to avoid flying hooves. Five were tied to one rope and four in another area close. They whinnied and pranced in place violently showing the whites of their eyes.

"No snakes anywhere," I yelled which could have been the probable cause.

We all grabbed a halter rope while speaking as calmly and loudly as possible. Only the two boy novices and Heleena stayed back out of range from trauma. "No one needs to get hurt," I yelled.

Everyone had an offering.

"Could be a mountain lion somewhere."

"Or a bear."

I looked at Heleena who was as green as a desert bush. "What's wrong with you?"

Too late. She walked back about twenty yards and vomited. "I'm better now! I'm better."

"It's that tobacco she's been chewing," said Kim. At this point each of them had to discuss the con's of chewing tobacco while we held tightly to our horses who were moving like tornadoes.

"Let's walk them around," said Roy who was quite the pro. "Otherwise, we'll have a major catastrophe with a pole or two coming loose out of the wet ground and the horses dragging poles and ropes in a tangled mess."

This we did. Catora held Sugar and Donut for the weak Heleena who was slightly bent over. Roy held two horses as did Kim. Jamie grabbed Magic. We walked around the wet, slippery area thankful it had stopped snowing and that we were warmly dressed.

"The horses still act as if they hear something!" I worried aloud.

"Maybe it's our two groups joining us---coming through the washes." Jamie Mink sounded hopeful

Suddenly, the frightened horses stopped and would not budge while staring ahead to the east towards a slight incline.

"Someone is banging rocks together," said Catora. "Or a horse is walking this way."

CHAPTER 28

"Wrangler Jack," I whispered hopefully.

"Or a Mountain Lion," someone added.

"Too loud," interrupted Jamie.

"Plus, it has a rhythmic beat." Kim's analysis was correct.

As the rat-a-tat pounding of two rocks together intensified, the nine horses reared, bucked, and tried to run in a circle, almost on cue. Spooked would have been a mild assessment as the whites of their eyes revealed a mad rage. Flying mud from racing hooves went everywhere---on our arms, faces, legs---not missing a spot.

"Un-hook the lead ropes from their bridles and turn them loose," I shouted, noticing that Catora, Jamie, Kim, and Roy had already attempted to do so. Soon, all horses were freely running down the slippery slope, sliding away from us full speed into the ravine we had ridden out of earlier, heading back to their camp.

I thought about Cloud's statement this morning that horses have an extra sensory perception and become unruly in places designated as haunted....or was it the noise?

We stood there stunned, awkwardly looking at nine vacant tie downs while listening to pounding hooves splashing through the washes. Since their bridle reins had been tied earlier to the saddle horns, we knew the group of runners would not trip over them. Being herders, real creatures of companionship, they would soon find the other two groups---who might find us.

"Yippee Ki Yo Ki Yaye," from Kim Rose halfheartedly.

"Now what do we do?" Heleena looked pink again re-awakened from the escapade, but one eye kept blinking.

"Everyone OK?" I asked, looking around holding my breath hoping that no one got nipped by a crazy hoof. Everyone shook their heads a positive, too stunned yet to verbalize our dilemma after watching the crazed nine.

We stacked our lead ropes under the ledge near the wall of the cave where the two freshman boys were digging at something with sticks.

"What's going on?" I was glad they were away from the previous excitement.

"This area has been inhabited by other people," said one of the boys.

"There seems to be lumps of uneven dirt here like someone's been digging or burying things," said the other.

They were calm and could care less that we were on foot.

Behind a boulder from the area of the previous noises, came the same rhythmic pounding of rocks, much closer and louder.

We bunched together and looked to the east towards the noise. The two senior girls grabbed Roy, the freshman boys jumped up from where they had been digging and grabbed Heleena who still looked a little tipsy. Catora, Nancy and I were angry rather than frightened, so we stood and glared toward the noise.

"Who is pounding rocks together?" I yelled to all of us but not to the 'whatever' that was beyond the boulder…checking my watch—three O'clock—as if that would give me an answer.

To make matters more frightening, a fast moving mist descended the majestic Superstition Mountain that rose before us and in minutes we were surrounded. The unclear vision contributed to our feelings of helplessness, tormented by something or someone.

The pounding abruptly stopped.

When something fell at our feet, we screamed. Roy grabbed the stick like object and said loudly, “A kid’s tomahawk.”

Now I was really pissed and facing the boulders shouted. “Who’s playing games?”

Nancy and I looked at each other disgustedly since we knew now that Coyotee was being creepy and he needs to be told that the horses could have killed us.

Fat-rubber-cupped arrows that hurt like thrown stones began to strike next, hurdling towards us, hitting accurately.

“Hey!”

“Stop!”

Everyone was ducking the way-ward arrows and gathering them at the same time.

Since this was Heleena’s first time here, she said, “Whoever planned this entertainment had better re-write the script.” What the heck? She pulled a small flask from her deep skirt pocket and sipped long and hard on a liquid. “For my throat,” she said to me noticing my astonishment.

Wow! What happened next was totally unexpected.

Out of the mist and from a plateau, jumped an unsightly Coyotee yelling and yipping, dressed as an ancient Apache with a wig and all. He was a ghostly presentation, very original with his brightly painted white face and garish adornments around ankles and wrists.

Startled, we jumped away from him and screamed, stumbling over our feet in an attempt to get out of the way.

Heleena's boot got caught in the hem of her long denim skirt and down she went face first in the mud. Nancy helped her up while I ran to my lunch bag to gather a bunch of handy wipes.

We gathered around gawking, keeping Coyotee's ghostly presence in the center, wary of his intentions. Wide black circles surrounded his eyes. Other unfamiliar markings were painted a licorice black on his bare arms and legs. Barefooted, and wearing only a loin cloth over his Blakely High green running shorts, he looked odd and I imagined, cold.

He carried no knife or gun; only an empty bow in his left hand joined him in contorted gyrations as he began chanting and wailing. With knees held high, he danced in a circle, periodically bouncing on one foot and then another. Always he ducked his head up and down paying homage to the sky and earth.

We elbowed each other and whispered:

"This is very authentic!"

"Like what I've seen in the movies."

"He's really good!"

Catora's, "He is singing his heart out," made me realize the seriousness of the situation.

"What is he trying to accomplish?" I wondered aloud to Nancy standing beside me.

Before she could answer, he stopped the loud, wild gyrations and slowed into another dance. Trancelike, and with arms stretched wide he spun a slow circle while looking at the sky.

Silence. The only noise was the soft beat of Roy slapping his palm with a rubber cupped arrow.

We were all speechless but innately decided to let it play out---his entire scene---whatever his intentions, both serious and sad. Uninterrupted, he danced slowly and sang softly to the heavens, the rocks, the mountains—down on his knees—back standing again.

Soon after about thirty minutes, his demonstration--his showmanship turned to pity. He sang and danced quietly now, a serenely peaceful song—so original sounding that we stood there spellbound and drawn to tears. Totally Apache.

I looked at my watch and worried.

We circled around him, close. How do we stop him? What do we say? His appearance of an ancient mythical character from an old black and white movie was un-approachable.

"Coyotee!" Catora hollered, her voice more like a pitiful whine, a coaxing out of his reverie.

He stopped, weaved and wavered, about to fall. Four of us stepped quickly forward to grab him. He was already on his knees when Roy and I grabbed one arm, Catora and Nancy his other.

We sat him near the dry cave where he crossed his legs Indian style ducked his head without looking at us and began to speak.

His previous perfect English became ridiculous. "This—dangerous place." Panting from his rapid dance, he rolled his eyes as he looked around. "Many bad and lost spirits here. I turn them loose."

Heleena became wild eyed. "Is this place haunted? I know it's called Massacre Grounds where many fights took place between Apaches and Mexicans." She spoke loudly, with a matter-of-fact attitude while looking around scared out of her wits. "Holy Moley!"

"Spirits here." Coyotee stood and pointed all around us. "Young Apaches died here. There is ghostly presence."

When he slurred the last important sentence, we all spun around, searching and intently listening.

"Coyotee, what is your mission here? Your goal?" Time to get the show on the road before we have a real crisis. "And, where are the others?" I looked at my watch again for help.

"My ancestors here—their spirits caught in web of violence—I release spirits to follow ancestors in the heavens."

"Ah, like a psychic," I quickly interrupted and looked at Nancy. "We needed Butch on this trail ride."

Interest was enormous on this subject bringing chatter from the girls and Heleena of the paranormal shows they had seen from television. Roy's mom was greatly interested in the guest speakers who came to the Valley of the Sun to demonstrate their encounters with the supernatural, so he related some stories of audience participation.

My turn. "I think it's ESP. People knowingly and unknowingly connecting to others without words." Everyone looked at me speechless. "Ok, like right now you're worried about the presence of ghosts and how we're going to get out of here." I waved my fingers at them.

"Doesn't count!" laughed Kim Rose.

I tried.

Nancy's turn. "Butch told me the other night there are three kinds of hauntings and one is residual like this place—where spirits are stuck in a certain area and stay there. What releases them?" She pointed her hands upward towards the sky with her last question. "No one knows."

There was no rain, no snow, only a misty fog. Coyotee now sat and closed his eyes while slightly nodding.

"Are you in a trance?" Practical Kim Rose wanted to know and almost giggled while Jamie Mink, quite mystified by the sequence of events, elbowed her to be quiet.

"My turn," said Jamie Mink. "I saw a show where spirits can react with the living. Now that's really spooky!" She was a motionless speaker; only her mouth moved as eyes enlarged.

"That's the second kind of Haunting," Nancy added.

Catora was looking around like the others. "This could get scary." She sat next to Coyotee holding one of his arms to comfort him—or herself. He was drooping now and looked spent like he had just played a five hour grand slam tennis match.

Nancy and I ESP'D about the old prospector I saw the other night when I was the last to leave Tumbleweeds. Since we did the funny looking face with eyebrows raised I knew our telepathy-communication was working. Especially when she whispered, "No one else had seen that old prospector."

"My dad's favorite movie is Poltergeist." Roy began. "That's where things fly around at you for no reason.

"Hey!" Nancy was excited. "That's the third kind of Haunting."

Now that we were really nervous and worried, we spoke rapidly like historians. Plus, it was getting late.

The two freshman boys didn't care, happily digging for treasure with their sticks.

"Over a hundred people lost their lives right here where we stand!" I started the chit chat.

"Massacre Grounds."

"Bones were scattered everywhere—found in 1862."

"Whose bones? Who found them?"

"Mexicans and Apaches ---found by foot soldiers from Camp McDowell about the same time it became Fort McDowell."

The chit chat prompted Coyotee to jump up and climb on the rectangular- purplish boulder nearby. Raising his hands to the sky, he began a peaceful chant, with arms outstretched, eyes closed.

Catora and all of us stood restlessly back and watched with remorse and helplessness.

Suddenly, a swirling mist, a lone vortex surrounded him and the rock. We were at its edge, watching an ordinary dust devil become a cold swirl of rain and sleet encircling a lone Coyotee.

What in the hell is this!

"Enough of this!" I needed to intervene and reconnoiter with our group for a plan. But, as I began to take a step toward Coyotee, two shocking events stopped my intervention.

A long sharply pointed home-made spear suddenly came flying towards us, landing at Coyotee's feet, hitting the boulder, missing him by inches.

Simultaneously, the two boys ran forward screaming, "Look what we found!"

CHAPTER 29

APACHE CAMP
Massacre Grounds
December 22, 1848

DUTCHY sprang forward with the sharply pointed spear whittled out of a long piece of Mesquite—aimed for APACHE who stood on top of the rectangular-purplish boulder peacefully chanting with eyes closed and arms outstretched.

With right arm back and elbow cocked, DUTCHY thrust the piercing spear at APACHE'S heart.

DUTCHY was fast, but FOOT SOLDIER DAVY, in youthful prime, was faster. While earlier watching DUTCHY'S every move whittling the spear, DAVY foresaw his raging evil hate and prepped for action. So impressed was he with APACHE'S desire to share his gifts, he vowed to protect the youth, so similar in age. Also, the loving attention from CHINA ROSE renewed his strength and courageous drive.

In the position of a Jamaican sprinter at the starting block, he leaped toward DUTCHY and grabbed his arm as the spear sailed into a whirl of cold wind---a strange funnel-shaped-mass dense with mist and rain drops---a small tornado circling round and round.

The spear descended with fury into the maelstrom.

With astonishment and eyes a syrupy pool of hate, everyone watched DUTCHY who simply flopped down again in his hovel with back turned. He knew their demise---that the spear would travel through APACHE---a haunting spirit like all of them. Were they not aware they were stuck, caught in this trap---this web of inconceivable transparency?

The violent circle of wind evaporated as quickly as it had begun, and before them---a bare purplish-boulder, damp from the mist, reached out to them---empty.

The five of them gawked for a long time before each became aware of this new happening. A spiritual awakening re-kindled with aspiration, and like a quick snap, each dreamed of change.

Each reminisced and dreamed a personal reality.

GAMBLER MOODY stared, squinting intensely down the narrow road for a return wagon like the new four wheeled mule-drawn hardwood he remembered.

FOOT SOLDIER DAVY searched for the return trail back to Camp McDowell---if he could only walk back. Taking off his woolen cap, he dusted it on his pants, shook his head to release the long blond straggly locks tangled in his collar, stood and circled about anew.

CHINA ROSE twirled in a circle like the one she left behind at the Bird Cage Saloon---the last dance she could remember. Hiking her long faded green velvet skirt above her boots---she danced---hoping to dance herself back, a combination of Can-Can and Irish Jig. She toned a cheery song with her rhythm. "WHEN YOU'RE FEELING SAD AND YOU'RE ALL ALONE---GIVE YOUR DOG A BONE---YES, GIVE YOUR DOG A BONE."

MEXICAN MANO and DUTCHY wanted to stay and tumble through the rocks near the area APACHE left behind.

They knew they would find the gold in the cave, hidden by the Indians and guarded by APACHE.

Throwing rocks right and left, they feverishly searched for the entrance to the cave of gold. They would surely find it now that he was gone. It was a large pile of small boulders that he always guarded with tenacity, so the two of them joined forces, lifting and heaving, removing each, one by one. Gold would bring them a new life and perhaps they too could escape.

CHAPTER 30

SUPERSTITION MOUNTAINS
MASSACRE GROUNDS
December 22, 2014

Out of the mist, standing next to, and facing Coyotee, stood an Apache youth, similar in age, dissimilar in looks. On the boulder they stood in a trance, chanting with arms raised and eyes closed, singing the same song, two different tones, not noticing each other.

APACHE was thinner, skin darker and cheek bones sharper. The twin concept could almost apply.

Abruptly they stopped, opened their eyes and nearly teetered off the narrow boulder from shock. Speechless, they stared.

Our group was silent as we held our breaths for almost too long sending me in a weak daze grabbing at Nancy.

Then:

APACHE jabbered in Spanish.

Coyotee in English. “Who are you?”

Nancy Lopez stepped forward quickly and with meager Spanish spoke to APACHE.

“*Who are you? Where are you from?*”

"*Me Apache. This my land!*" He thumped his thin chest hard and gritted his teeth in fright causing his lower lip to quiver. Astonished, he stared around at us strangely dressed people who came close hugging each other---gawking.

"*This Apache land,*"---in Spanish again, but louder. He extended one arm out sweeping the area all around him.

Catora spoke breathlessly as if she had just run a mile, an explanation to hopefully appease our panic. All the while she was still clinging to our group.

"Coyotee knows the body language of the ancient Apaches and signs of peace and friendship taught to him by his great uncles in northern Arizona. I went there with him for a festival." She grabbed my arm for steadiness and I felt like the three of us were doing The Wave like I've done at football games; I was in the middle of Catora and Nancy being pulled this way and that.

Coyotee began chanting again, the song of the ancients, the one APACHE knew---asking for guidance from the spirits. We could tell that he did not want to lose this apparition before him, a phenomenon like no other. He had earlier told us that making Peace at Massacre Grounds was his lifetime intention. A connection here, now, was imperative to his goal.

Together they sang and danced loudly---one once fed by wild life of elk, deer and grain cakes---one currently on fast food.

I looked at my watch again for sanity. Holy cow! Still three o'clock! I had an uncanny feeling that I was in some kind of past re-enactment as they harmonized and danced as one.

Our huddled group was a spectacle and a great excuse for Jamie Mink and Kim Rose to hang on to Roy. Each of us whispered a comment unknowingly…all except Heleena who was passed out on the ground from the contents of her flask, or from fright. I decided not to disturb her because I might miss the action before me.

Startled whisperings escaped our lips.

"A time warp!"

"Ghostly!"

"My next prom date!" This from Kim Rose, of course.

"Supernatural!"

The two freshman boys couldn't close their mouths. They stood there holding treasures tightly against their chests like security blankets, to show me when possible.

Catora caught me checking my watch, and looking around for others. Hah! There it is. ESP. She made a move toward this aura, this strange apparition and called out, "Coyotee!"

APACHE suddenly began to weave and waver like a fading television screen. His face was turned upward toward the heavens and his body was motionless except for the fading. He turned toward the frozen Coyotee and said *Peace. Brother!* Before our eyes he began to disappear slowly.

"Wait! Wait!" We all yelled wanting more answers. He simply disappeared leaving Coyotee standing alone.

We gasped! "WHAT! WHAT! WHAT!"

"Nancy, what is this called---this happening?" Standing next to her I grabbed her arm again to steady myself and waved the other hand at the apparition. I found it difficult to speak; my mouth was dry and my heart was thumping.

"We have to ask Butch. It's either a transmutation or a metamorphosis." She spoke softly with wonder at what we had experienced. "I'm only guessing." She seemed in a daze.

Roy's turn. "It's simply a transfer in time. Sweet! Where's my camera when I need it. Did anyone use their cameras?"

"Duh!" Started Jamie Mink. "They left with the horses!"

"Right! What's next?" He pounded a fist into his hand while Jamie and Kim held on to his arms for dear life.

Catora was now helping the slumping Coyotee down from the boulder. Not able to walk, he simply crumbled at the foot of the huge rock and looked up at us standing there starring at him with fascination and admiration anew.

"You did it buddy!" Roy grabbed Coyotee by one arm while Catora the other, and they lifted him from the ground to a sitting position on the edge of the purplish-boulder from where he once stood, chanting for so long.

Coyotee sighed over and over, his hands on his knees.

"There is peace now---here---at this place." Drained from the before actions, he didn't move as he spoke with disbelief.

"You did so well," said Catora admirably. "Your people will be so proud."

Nobody noticed a re-awakened but dazed Heleena crawl over to the wooden spear that lay near the boulder.

"Look what we dug from over there." The two freshman boys nodded towards our shallow cave where we had huddled hours ago during the rain.

We crowded close again, now a team of one, having experienced the paranormal. We were ready for anything---except for this.

The first item placed in my open hands was my modern rubber door wedge.

CHAPTER 31

"This doesn't make sense. How did my door wedge get to this place?" No one looked guilty.

"This was mine. There's a little smudge of permanent black marker under it where I wrote my room number on the back." Hurriedly turning it around, I showed everyone the remaining blur of ink and the faded number "two" which was the beginning of my room number, 220.

Awestruck, we gasped and began to look around, half excited about our discovery…or not, yet fearful of the unknowing. My heart beat wildly.

"Show me where you found this."

Eagerly, the freshman boys took me to the dig at the far end of the shallow cave. "It was buried down about six inches."

"How did you know to dig at this spot?" My curiosity and doubtfulness mixed together.

"There was a small mound in the dirt, like a hump, meaning something had been covered," he said.

Turning it over and over in my hands, I noticed thick dirt had been embedded in the creases of the bottom. It lost its newness, but I was positive that it was mine.

"WE ARE SURROUNDED BY DEAD GHOSTS." This came from Heleena, spoken in a wavy-drunken voice as she sat straddled like a toddler, toes of boots facing upward towards the sky, in the mud, carelessly moving her fingers in its wetness. In a trance-like stupor, she stared at us and continued. "*Wwha---what was that?"* She now pointed a muddy finger at the empty purplish boulder while clinging to the long Mesquite wood spear in her other hand. This, we should have paid attention to, but didn't until too late.

Far away, a lightning strike brought a distant clap of thunder. Not good for our raw nerves.

Jumping and shaking, we each looked around sheepishly. My heart continued thumping with disbelief of what I had previously witnessed. A misty drizzle began again.

"*They are here---listening---watching."* Heleena was spooking us in an undulating weird tone. Up and down went her voice. I was ready to slap her out of it.

"Your door at the meeting kept slamming shut." Pragmatic Nancy brought me to my senses and out of my bewilderment for a moment. What she said next, threw me into a worse dilemma.

"It was an entity from this place."

"Huh?"

"Butch calls spirits entities," she added in a loud whisper, spooked out of her wits. Scanning around, she turned a slow circle and breathed out of her mouth puffs of fog…in and out for steadiness, like an athlete…..or out of fear of fainting.

We were believers.

"Did all of you see what I saw?" I looked in each face separately for answers. AGAIN.

All were the same. Thoroughly intoxicated with fright; there were multiple positive nods.

"And he saw us!" This from Jamie Mink.

"Where did he go?" I was a broken record, still in a stupor. I waved my arms up in the air then pointed in every direction.

"Back in time," said Roy with authority. "Like he was released from the bondage of death." The two clinging girls looked at him respectfully, as if he knew what had taken place before our eyes, like he was the expert now.

"Sounds good! Remind me to give you an "A" for the semester." I had to admit, it was a credible announcement.

"Wait till I tell"-----this came from each of us. Myself included. I needed to set Pop straight. And Rick Del Rio too, wherever he is.

AGAIN! "Coyotee, what just happened? Explain." This came from Nancy. We gathered very close to him.

AGAIN! Sighing From his emotional drain, "It was a dance of the spirits, taking the dead to the peaceful lands of the ancients…a release." He looked at us with happiness for the first time, smiling from his accomplishment. His English was back and so was the old Coyotee.

"I feared he would grab you and take you back with him." Catora had taken off her colorful yellow cowboy neck scarf and was wiping smudges from Coyotee's wet face…wet from the mist and dance frenzy.

"Impossible! I think!" I had to try and say something smart. What did he know? He was as shocked as we were at the outcome.

AGAIN! A lone harmonica played somewhere in the distance…in the silence of mist and haze.

"We're not alone." What was my tone? Fear? Anger?

Kim Rose to the rescue. "Maybe this is a joke played on us by the stupid Wrangler, Dick."

"Yeah," added Jamie Mink. "Maybe what we saw was a "hooligram" from a hidden movie camera somewhere to make us look like idiots." She put her hands on her hips and looking all around, tried to appear functional.

"Hooligram?" I'll have to research that!

"Eerie," said Kim Rose and Roy simultaneously.

"Where's the harmonica?"

"Are we hearing things out of fear?"

Amazingly, we had not let go of each other—a hand—an arm—a tug of shirt.

The two speechless freshman boys were scared stiff with one still clinging to his treasure from the dig, tightly holding it close to his chest for security of some sort.

"What did you find?" I realized that he had been standing there stunned like all of us and unmovable.

A tarnished, dirty, small one-cup silver tea pot was in the palms of both shaking hands as he held them together.

Handing it to me, he blew dust from the crevices of its little joints as everyone gathered around, curious about another enigma.

"MINE," screamed Heleena moving rapidly from a sitting position, mud splattering around. Holding the Mesquite wood spear tightly in her right fist, she grabbed the tea pot faster than we could move.

Grasping both close to her chest, while cradling the tea pot lovingly she began to spin around slowly, dancing in a circle, then spinning faster and faster---lifting one foot then the other. The red-ribboned whistle twirled around her neck moving from front to side. She can-canned a jig! The combo was as awkward as her funny song. *"When you're feeling sad and you're all alone---give your dog a bone, yes, give your dog a bone!"*

She danced wildly like a crazy woman, faster and faster, louder and louder, until into a vortex she went—a swirling mist of rapid wind and rain surrounded her.

"It's happening again!" Someone screamed. Maybe it was me.

We crushed together so tightly, my hands became numb from holding on to another's wrist too tensely.

"Breathe," yelled Coyotee, the only sane one now of the bunch.

Didn't work. We almost toppled over from holding our breaths before...............POOF! Heleena was gone!

We stood there gaping with our mouths hanging open.

Now I was getting annoyed as I looked at the empty rock, the empty trampled mud where she had been twirling, and all the spaces in between.

We stealthily searched around us, behind boulders and bushy Hackberry in total disbelief.

"Heleena," I screamed.

"Miss Duncan," shouted the kids.

GONE.

"Ok, ok, ok, this is too much! This is too much!" We rambled and ranted repetitively while stomping around.

"Hmmm," murmured the cool Coyotee. "I have to get her back." He rubbed his chin in thought, unafraid like us. He was the only motionless person, totally sane.

Catora asked, "Where's the small silver tea pot?" She was now holding Coyotee's arm for steadiness.

"Heleena," I yelled some more.

"The ghosts are grabbing us---trading places!" This from Jamie Mink as her baby blues got rounder and her face whiter.

The two freshman boys wiped away tears and held both hands tight to Roy's elbows, a popular space vacated by the two girls momentarily. He now stood a lot taller.

"Tell me." I looked at the group. "Was she ever herself after awakening from her faint?"

No answer. Just pursed lips in thought.

"Coyotee," I heard my shaky voice lament. "We need you!"

CHAPTER 32

MEANWHILE, Rick was having a difficult time with the pace of his group. Bullet, the Missouri Fox Trotter, was one of the best he had ever ridden---fast, sure footed, hardy with stamina, facing the constant, unrelenting drizzle of a rain, all with steadfast eagerness. “You’re a trooper,” he said numerously, petting its neck with his gloved hand and thankful the Wranglers had done something right. But, where are they?

Yet, his main concern was the group following his lead. They poked along. Periodically, he turned Bullet back around to wait for the others who had slower horses, except for Delilah on Biscuit at the end of the line next to Shieter riding Butter.

She rode all over the place on her fast horse oblivious of Shieter and his mounting anger. He wanted her next to him. When the trail widened, she rode next to students to gab. Shieter’s bullheaded Mustang, Butter, bucked every time he heeled him with his boots to move faster. Rick could tell that he was both angry and afraid when he had to stay back at the end of the line. However, Colt would be there soon as leader of the third group to keep him company and help with the Mustang.

Although Wrangler Jack was no longer in sight, Rick thought he knew the trail heading to Massacre Grounds and took the lead eagerly. He questioned why Wrangler Jack would simply gallop away without looking back, acting like he had another pre-planned destination.

Twisting around after standing in the saddle, he saw a yellow swirl of riders resembling a giant puffy caterpillar, slickers in tack, swirling through ravines, down and around small canyons and rocky cliffs. Although in anticipation of problems, amazingly none has occurred since potato-chip girl's horse had fallen asleep on the trail and went down on its knees. Tornado was an unfitting name. Unscathed, the girl good naturedly passed around chips.

Clouds hovered like billows of sheets on a clothes line floating and flopping with the wind, opening a visage here and there, a kind of day that happened only about three times a year for the territory. Eagerly he kept on the lookout for the first group, now and then checking his tracker like the one he had secretly implanted on the bell Gina wore around her neck. The tracker was located in the distance about where Group One should now be riding. Nevertheless, he wondered if Dick the head Wrangler had deserted them too.

The trail narrowed as the foliage thickened. Homed next to, or under bushy Tomatillo were thorny Prickly Pear and Staghorn; all edged the trail too closely now as the horses headed upward through boulders, always in sight of the grounds sloping uphill, footing the base of the Superstitions.

Thankfully, Scouts had removed the stiff arms of Teddy Bear Chollas that had edged too closely last year. Yet, Rick worried about the puff balls of stuff that were still around, inanimate balls of creatures, ready to be blown with the wind, waiting to fish-hook on something moving. Always, he eyed the trail closely for the devils and knew exactly where the wide tooth comb tucked into his saddle bag next to the small pliers for any emergency. Hooves kicked the jumping balls under bellies too easily, and this was the problem.

Where was the first group? Looking at the time, one hour had passed since he last saw their tail, and they were supposed to be only ten minutes ahead. His recent main concern of worry was the loud galloping group of horses he heard a while back, a swift desperation of hooves pounding on rounded rocks in unnecessary hurriedness that he recognized as a sign of danger.

Each of the riders following behind was contently gabbing, back and forth, warmly covered and enjoying the ride, a holiday show of happiness. This was good!

Yet, something was wrong, and Del Rio had the uneasy feeling of a tragedy in the works before the day was over. It was an uncanny feeling that evolves with experience.

He felt alone. Wrangler Jack had disappeared in a low moving cloud up ahead…had he ditched them altogether? It was to be an easy three hours one way to the Massacre Grounds. Now, with one hour to go, and the low cloud cover, he was not sure of the trail---the correct route. Reminders of tragedies in the area filled his head with worry. *If you get lost in the Superstitions, you will never be found.* Statistics for this year alone were staggering.

Checking with the Sheriff's Office in Apache Junction last week, he learned that of searches for sixty lost hikers, eight were never recovered…no bodies, no other detail.

Cairns, the rock pillars necessary as route markers, were gone, washed away by the rain and mud….or was he simply off the trail. Switchbacks were numerous now and he didn't remember the zig-zags from last April when he rode the same trail with Gina. Then, they had not gone the full distance but had taken another route through Dutchman's Trail and First Water Creek. It was spring time, and they rode to the waterfall at the end.

From his phone, he punched Colt's number.

"How's your line? I don't see you guys anywhere."

"We're headin' up a ridge. My horse is fast but this group is slow. We stop for pictures….that's important you know. I caught a glimpse of Shieter at your tail but now we're too far back."

They both agreed that because of the dangers of the low cloud cover, and overall wetness, they should close the gap. Rick stopped his line to wait.

Repeatedly he dialed Gina. No answer. He believed she had dropped the phone or was out of a service area. While stopped, he saw Shieter decide to get off his horse and stretch so he rode over to check on him.

""I'm walking for awhile. My legs are cramping." Starting to take a step, he immediately fell to his knees---"easily done when the legs are used to sitting for a couple hours." said Delilah as she rode over, grabbed the lead rope and led Butter a short distance away while Shieter brushed the mud off his knees.

"You'll have trouble keeping up," she said.

"Stay with me."

"Not happening!" She rode back to him, and gave him the lead rope to his horse. "There's a group coming around the bend soon, or you could join the four hikers….you know, the Family Farm."

"Hhmph!" Shieter pulled Butter off the trail near a side space, marched in place for leg circulation and decided to wait.

Rick called Colt again to ask if Wrangler Pete was still around.

"Negative. He lagged behind for about thirty minutes, then disappeared."

"Same for Wrangler Jack. Something weird is happening on this ride. Our two guides have disappeared, and the first group is nowhere in sight. Are we being jerked around?" He had distanced himself from the line, out of ear-shot so no one knew his fears.

"Hey Del Rio! What would be the reason? I don't know. This is my first trail ride in the Superstitions and first with kids. You tell me!"

"Why the guns? Those three Wranglers were loaded."

Soon, three students decided to get off their horses and walk, complaining about sore bums, tired legs and loudly complaining, "Bathroom time!"

"Hey," said Rick, "take turns, and give your lead rope to someone else to hold" Nothing worse than a loose horse, Rick thought as he took the rope of one. "Go to that hide-away," he pointed in the direction of a clump of trees in a low ravine, "and watch out for snakes." That would hurry them. This hadn't happened on previous rides, but they had never made a breakfast stop either, like this morning's when the kids re-boarded with thirty-two ounce drinks.

Colt still on the line, "I can see your group about a quarter mile up the canyon. We'll be their shortly; wait for us!"

Rick asked, "Have you talked to our walkers---the four B's?"

"Yep! The old buzzards are happily moving forward."

All accounts of what happened next were different as each person's five senses recorded in short circuit, hearing a bit here, seeing some shadows there. Thundering upon them were the horses of Group One, heading to the home barn rapidly, spreading out but running full speed down the trail or next to it, hurdling over low rocks and scrambling through thorny bushes.

"Hold tight to your horses," Rick shouted as his own stead reared with excitement. "Stand your ground; the horses will go around us." He had a few seconds of control. "Hold them back. You can do it!"

Shieter and two others let go of their lead ropes leaping out of the way of the stampede and jumping on boulders.

Rick held tight to the rope on the horse he was holding and dallied the braid around his saddle horn a couple times, ready to let go if the other horse pulled his down.

"Hang on! Hang on!" Horses were bucking rearing and circling around with fear that only a stampede can cause, splattering mud, peppering clothes and faces as the passing mob flew by. Two horses from Rick's group joined them.

He buzzed Colt again, "Look out! Horse stampede coming your way."

Colt had seen them ahead and rapidly moved his group far off the trail as about a dozen saddled horses ran rapidly passed, all knowledgeable of the terrain, heading for home base.

Fearing a domino effect, Colt radioed the walkers to seek higher ground immediately and what to expect.

Recognizing the two lead horses as Gina's and Nancy's Strawberry Roans, Rick was now more worried than ever. The horses contained everyone's saddle bags of necessary equipment, first aide, and emergency phones. Checking the tracker that he hid earlier in the Christmas whistle that had been around Gina's neck, he saw movement and clamored ahead a different route towards the tracker with Shieter and the three students on foot.

"Let's keep our two groups together now." Amazed that no one was hurt, Rick and Colt were relieved---- until they heard the loud echoing "zing" of a bullet ricocheting too closely.

CHAPTER 33

AGAIN the pop of a gun whined in the distance resonating in the remaining silence from the first shot, echoing louder, a cracking sound Del Rio recognized as coming from a gun like the Wranglers displayed in their showmanship when readying the stock for riders.

"You hear that?!" Colt's radioed voice was loud and sharp.

"Yep, and I don't like it! You're about two hundred yards from me. Can you stay with the group while I check it out? Don't move em!"

"Got it!"

The group gathered now out of sync, waiting for news, chatting about the bullets. A few more dismounted and joined the two students and Shieter on foot. Colt heard mumbling of:

"Could've been a rattlesnake!"

"Naw! Too cold."

"Is deer hunting allowed here?"

Del Rio edged the narrow canyon, moving Bullet slowly through groves of thick Hackberry and dormant Tomatillo not wanting to be totally conspicuous. Weaving the horse in and out of bushes, he moved toward a cluster of Mesquites heading for the origins of the shootings.

Pulling off his right leather glove, he tucked it into a front jacket pocket and subconsciously stretched his hand a couple times. After unsnapping the button that secured the pistol, he felt its iced coldness then questioned the reason for shooters here on this heavily hiked mountain. Signs of 'No Hunting Allowed' were everywhere.

Bullets of any kind are a danger to the multitude of hikers and riders. Purpose of a gun on a ride is protection from what? Others? Attacking animals? Rattlesnakes? None fit the reasoning or current situation and Del Rio's curiosity became more entranced as he spurred the horse faster.

Fortunately, the mountain was bare of people due to the rain and the timing. The closeness of Christmas meant shoppers were in malls, not mountains.

Pulling his hat back, he then patted the heavy Kevlar vest fitting warm and tightly against his chest under his large camel color rain slicker.

The rain had stopped for the moment and he thought about the beauty of this cool-misty day, one for pleasurable riding with friends and loved ones. Not terror!! Where are Gina and her group? Hopefully, nowhere near the shooters.

Missing Gina's companionship, his thoughts drifted to a late evening's warmth at his house, and among all else, they would reminisce about today's happenings. Patience for all her school-time escapades....like this one.....riding in the rain to a dangerous place just before the holidays, were spurred by passion. He always questioned why he did what he did.....for her. Tonight, he'll know.

Hearing voices and muted laughter coming from the trees ahead, he slowed the horse and reined it into a sandy wash muffling the hooves. Hiding behind edged Jojobas, he watched the three Wranglers from their group standing around a campfire in a clearing, their backs turned to him and his lookout. Before them was a large boulder with marked holes from bullets…their target.

One half-empty Jim Beam whiskey bottle stuck upright in the sand near a rock close by. Water trickled around a cottonwood, dormant for the winter, a few yellowed leaves waving at top.

As Rick watched Dick, Jack and Pete handle their guns, he realized that these three were no ordinary Wranglers but real shooters, pros on horseback for whatever reason.

Smooth and experienced they were now and not the corny guys they pretended to be at the corrals. Who were they? Why the act? Most urgently, why the desertion?

Their conversations were crisp and clear in the stillness that follows the cleanliness after a roaring storm.

"I don't know Dick; it doesn't seem right just riding off and leaving those kids!" Jack put a metal coffee cup to his lips after adding a splash of whiskey to the steam.

Dick played with his gun, twirling it about, shoving it in and out of the holster pretending to shoot and draw.

"Hell," he mumbled, "there were plenty of adults. A few looked like they know more about horses and riding trails than we do."

"And the big guy," interrupted Pete filling his cup from a thermos. "I seen him fingerin' a device that looked like a GPS or tracker. He's no novice."

Jack continued. "We can leave. Why are we still here? The Senator and his group hired us to keep trail riders away from the gold mine he claims to be digging over near Massacre Grounds. How threatening is a group of teenagers anyway?"

Dick said, "I was leading them astray like we planned, even through the heavy storm, until the rider dressed in black on an all black horse galloped over like a mirage and grabbed the reins of the lead teacher's horse. I wasn't ready for that. I'm a city dude."

"You sure proved yourself worthy of that title today," Jack moaned. "When I saw you high-tail it out a there, I took off to join you. I'm just glad our mountain man friend here mentioned this escape place earlier if needed." He looked at Pete.

"Ain't no ways-in-hell I'm goin' near that haunted place. That's why I rode way back just planning my escape route the whole first hour. Hell's fire! I told you boys when ya' contacted me last week that I wasn't goin' near Massacre Grounds! Too many deaths. Too many lives lost." He slid his gun into the holster, took off his belt and hung it over a tree branch. "It's haunted. Someone's always playing a harmonica."

"What's wrong with that?" Dick asked.

"Ain't nobody in sight! I don't want no hostile spirit takin' possession of me!"

Sipping coffee, all three men had their guns out of their hands: ----on a rock

----on top of a gear bag

----in the holster hanging from a tree branch

Then the piercing whinny of Del Rio's horse almost shook him out of the saddle.

CHAPTER 34

"Hold it!" Rick pulled out his gun and reined his horse to the men's open space, watching their movements. "What in the hell are you three doing here in a no shooting zone? There are youngsters not too far away. Back away from your guns and put your hands behind your heads until we get this straightened out!"

He pulled back his slicker to reveal his beige official sheriff's shirt and badge.

Startled, they did as they were told and didn't move.

"Ain't causing no harm," said Pete. "We was hired by an Arizona politician to keep riders away from the Massacre Grounds site because of a mining claim in progress!"

"This doesn't make sense!" He pointed to their shooting spree. "You need to be arrested for misrepresentation---faking to be real Wranglers!"

"Sir," Dick began, "we didn't mean any harm. I was gonna lead everyone there until I got spooked by the mysterious black rider."

Looking at Dick, "Where you from?" Del Rio was more than curious.

"Detroit! Never had ridden mountains before yesterday, when we came to study the route to bring the chuck wagon."

Keeping his gun pointed at them, Del Rio said, "You can put your hands down and step this way while we talk, away from your guns. Where are the original Wranglers that were paid to lead?"

Jack's turn. "We were told to pay them off---double as a matter-of-fact with no explanation."

"But, you told them a story!"

"We said that a group of school friends wanted to lead! So, they were paid plenty for any inconvenience."

Dick regurgitated his story about planning to lead them to Massacre Grounds anyway, even though he had been paid not to, until spooked by the black rider on a rearing black horse.

"Sorry, we didn't mean to cause any trouble," said Jack innocently. "If you want, we'll go back with you now and help out."

"'Cept me!" Pete was adamant. "I ain't goin' near that haunted place! How 'bout I ride back and accompany the hiking group for a short ways? I won't leave this time….until they git close to the Grounds."

The coolness of the cloudy day with accompanying mist lightened the negative spirit of the episode. Del Rio took a deep breath and sighed as he continued.

"How'd you boys learn to handle those guns?"

"Marines, Afghanistan."

"Army, Iraq."

"Detroit neighborhoods---the wild ones."

"Give me your I.D's until the end of the day. Mount-up and be helpful. No more shooting of any kind."

Del Rio knew the type. Squirrely, but innocent. Not waiting for them, he whirled Bullet around and took off as fast as possible in the now treacherous terrain of switch-backs, thinking about the herd of swiftly moving horses that had passed by earlier. Is Group One in trouble?

The tracker on the whistle had now faded out.

CHAPTER 35

APACHE CAMP
Massacre Grounds
December 22, 1848

Glee and elation were replaced with astonishment and indecision as the five transients wandered around re-living the revelation that had occurred instantaneously with APACHE'S chant.

"Where is he?"

"What was the chant?"

Each was stupefied.

Each was a Zombie seeking an answer.

They searched the five acre area individually, standing on tops of boulders, investigating under and behind large bushes of Arizona Rosewood, Jojoba and the powerful Catsclaw----calling, calling, calling. Scanning the deep ravine in the canyon nearby each listened for any recognizable sounds.

Nothing. No APACHE.

FOOT SOLDIER DAVY wondered if he transcended to another place. "Where would he be?" He stood taller in his grass lined boots while staring around; mixed shock and admiration shone from his face. "What power enabled him to leave?"

Whining now in frustration with no answers, he looked at the façade of the other puzzled four trying to read their empty faces for answers. His mumbling was joined by others.

MEXICAN MANO kept repeating in Spanish, "*Holy Shit! I don't know---I don't know.*" Drool escaped from his mouth as he stumbled about mumbling incoherently "*He vanished in a bubble! Evaporated!*" In a stupor after knocking over his pot of beans that was simmering forever on low---forever cooking on the round rock campfire, he cried.

CHINA ROSE quickly shuffled over to DAVY worried about his ranting, and looping her fingers under the top of one drooping suspender, gently righted it and pulled him next to her. After massaging the tops of his slanted, forlorn shoulders, she combed his long dirty blond locks behind his ears with her ivory fingers, and kissed him on the cheek. White, young chubby hands formed the short pony tail she softly smoothed forever between her fingers.

Too transfixed to move now, GAMBLER MOODY rocked in place up and down from heel to toe, again and again thinking, mumbling----"Where is his body? Where is his soul?" Momentarily, he walked gingerly to the shallow enclave where APACHE had dwelled and retrieved his valise; taking it to his own spot he slowly arranged and re-arranged its contents left behind by APACHE. He too felt like the others, tall with new hope, still calling and searching in a quest for answers---how did he do it---how did he escape? He put his valise near his other hidden treasures, opened it and added the Long Nines, the expensive cigars saved for THE special occasion that he alone would decide when and where. Retrieving his special Colt Dragoon from its cache, he added it to the valise.

Three of the four stopped searching and stared at the otherwise placid man who spoke so rarely. Looking at the stunned group, he said, "We need to decode APACHE'S chant if we want to vacate this prison."

Three grouped with GAMBLER MOODY. Only DUTCHY sat alone, his back to them so they didn't see the sneer, the contorted look of craziness that accompanies a maniac. "There is no getting out!" His incoherent mumbling was almost silent. Contented he was with the sojourns into town for small tokens of thievery at night when the others were inactive; he wanted to continue, uninterrupted. Enjoyment of this kind was known only to him, tricks he had learned ages ago in Germany---the magic of transitory movement. Now he moved with the wind where he wanted to be and transformed into a human body, an old man, a replica of himself when he worked his transactions. *It was a magic he learned and would never share.* Though temporary and impermanent, it was his only enjoyment, a gift given to him provided he returned to this location---this site of no redemption. He worked with the sky's darkness reading the moon and stars for his transformation.

With APACHE gone, DUTCHY'S one goal of pursuing the gold in the hidden mine was reachable. Gold in his past brought popularity and power; he imagined again all the things he could buy; this recognition could be his again. He looked over at the other four fools with heads together and arms entwined chanting like APACHE---trying to remember the chant. "Idiots!" He laughed fiendishly. "They will never do it"!! The ridiculous happening reminded him of his second goal; it was to eliminate the other four. Poor devils stuck here with him. There would be no sharing of his gold, his magic. He had to plan!

Suddenly, a swirling vortex of loose sand, wind, misty rain drops, all circling round and round noisily to a pinnacle produced an image---a blur, a shadow immersing from static to reality.

Three chanters stood back still holding hands and gawked at what they thought they had accomplished.

Before them stood a strange woman embracing a silver tea pot to her chest with one hand and a long recognizable spear in the other.

To GAMBLER, she was the most beautiful Goddess he had ever seen.

CHAPTER 36

SUPERSTITION MOUNTAINS
MASSACRE GROUNDS
December 22, 2014

"Coyotee," I asked, feeling dizzy and dimwitted. "What just happened?" We all looked at him for answers.

Raising his hands in the air as a sign of puzzlement did nothing to elevate our confidence in him….unfortunately.

We needed answers for the impossible.

"Where'd the Apache go?"

"Where's Heleena?"

"Hmmmm," he repeated rubbing his chin in thought while adding a facial squint too difficult to read. "We had two different reversals. The Apache Kid was sent back to his ancestry….I'm sure of it after reciting all the proper language and dance sequence opening the channels for his reversal."

"And Heleena?" I asked in desperation.

"Don't know yet."

Nancy spoke. "This is Massacre Grounds where many Apaches, Mexicans and others died. Coyotee's spiritual recitation and dance helped to release one dead soul from this place sending him home!" When she spoke, everyone listened. She was so finite with explanations. Must be the red hair.

"One?" Jamie Mink asked.

"Miss Lopez, you think there are others?" Roy turned in a stationary circle looking around the place, bug eyed like the rest of us.

We tightened our circle.

"Of course! And one of them is a dangerous reactor….an entity that appears among us thieving for one reason or another."

Suddenly she's the expert. Nancy's explanation seemed plausible. Why else would my door wedge be here. And the late night mystery man who grabbed my wrist when I walked out of Tumbleweed's the other night…..after which my bracelet was missing. What's up with that?

And where's Del Rio? I punched the face plate of my cell so many times the tip of my finger was sore. Obviously, we were out of range, I thought, until I received a loud ring.

We all jumped ten feet high. It was Dixie in Apache Junction shopping. "Do I look better in red lipstick or pink? There's a super sale going on….." My phone was in speaker mode.

"PINK!" We simultaneously yelled too hyper-extended for the moment as I quickly punched the 'off' button wondering how she got thru and Rick couldn't.

My turn. "Hey! The silver tea pot and the spear that Heleena clung to were possible remnants from this place---from the past that caused some kind of an inversion---like a suction---like a black hole in the galaxy." LIKE, I was a scientist all of a sudden.

"You just said there were two different reversals. Explain!" Catora, awe struck by Coyotee's talent, enamored by his dance and song, now massaged one arm affectionately while hanging on in ownership.

"I think that Miss Mac is correct in thinking that the silver tea pot and spear are tools of the past. Openers of some sort," said

Coyotee. Plainly spoken as his language exploded with fervor anew, a feeling of great accomplishment.

"But," Kim Rose's turn, "how can someone throw a spear from the past to the present." Now a student of Roy, she looked at the two seniors for answers.

Again, it was Nancy's dynamic explanation that was the thunderbolt. "Well, Butch would tell us that it's a form of Poltergeist---when a spirit can move an object in the physical world. Remember that powerful science fiction movie years ago?"

She removed her slicker as she spoke, shook off drops still clinging, than spread it out on a bushy branch to dry.

Perspiring profusely from the previous spooky trauma, we all followed her lead unsnapping our slickers and hanging them nearby. The misty weather cooled my skin with new vigor.

"Yes, but we have a physical world from the past reacting with the present physical world," Roy questioned.

"Confusing, confusing." I shook my head while looking at the time on my watch again for answers. "What! It's still three."

"Your watch stopped," said Jamie Mink.

"No," I held out my wrist for all to see. "The minute hand is still moving." Next, we checked my cell. "Same time!"

"But, it was three o'clock one hour ago!" An astonished Catora continually clung to Coyotee.

"We're stuck in a time warp!" I spun around searching for answers from the hostile environment. I started pacing while pounding a fist in an open palm, wanting to take charge of the situation before we panicked and could no longer think clearly.

When all fails, give orders! I paced back and forth aware of those eyes I could see and worried about those I couldn't.

"Boys," I pointed to the two freshmen. "Go dig for some more treasures." This would occupy them, plus fill my curiosity.

They rushed to get busy, poking again in the same area.

"Coyotee, get up on that rock and chant again. Maybe Heleena and the spear will re-appear!"

Coyotee eagerly mounted the large rectangular purplish-red rock while the six of us locked arms at the elbows tightly. With Nancy and me at the ends, Jamie, Roy, Kim and Catora in the middle, NO one wanted to be transported anywhere.

He began a recitation, different in rhythm, more like a S.O.S transmission.

Up went my eyelids in question as I glanced at all the others for answers. Dumbfounded, they too were speechless and beyond ideas as we listened to his tongue-clicking sounds, very much a replica of the old Western telegraph staccato.

Nancy mumbled, "Where's Butch when we need him?"

CHAPTER 37

APACHE CAMP
Massacre Grounds
December 22, 1848

Static twirling in the mist blurred the image for a long while until the wind stopped churning. Then, before them stood a strange looking woman holding a spear---the spear DUTCHY had thrown at APACHE. Standing there in bright yellow, they believed she was an Angel of Redemption. Come to rescue them---take them home.

Heleena's hood had fallen down to the nape of the neck, exposing a face white in fear, pale as the clouds above and very much like the white quartz under her feet. Confusion awakened the old Heleena. Eyeballs rolled side to side, head in a stiffness she could not explain brought on by the fear of this place as she looked for the recognition of others. None.

Surroundings looked familiar, but the people now shuffling toward her didn't. The tawdry group in strange clothes, replicas of the Old West, stared back duplicating her expressions of fear. Thinking the people were wild Old-West originals, she dared not speak. Or, were they actors here on the mountain for everyone's entertainment?

Sad, sullen, worn looks stared---unreadable. Ghostly faces gawked, frightening her into a paralyzed state unable to speak. Afraid to move from this spot, she clutched the now shiny silver tea pot, no longer dull, close to her chest for security and squeezed the freshly made spear tightly in her right hand, afraid to let go.

Silence---no one moved.

While clutching her security items in tight fists, she slowly moved one hand next to the other to pinch her skin for a reality check.

"Ouch," she yelled as blood trickled.

They jumped back a few steps.

"Gina, Nancy," she called while barely moving, turning her rigid neck only a few inches from side to side, afraid to lose sight of her new gangly company.

Nothing!

Fearing the pale, lifeless and strangely dressed group would advance toward her, she decided to start chatting. What else could she do?

"Hello, anybody home?"

Setting the butt of the spear in the ground and the pointed head upward towards the sky, she held on for steadiness. She was shaking and trembling, to afraid to take a step. Aware now of her tight grasp of the new silver pot, she looked at her white knuckled fist and released the pot, unintentionally sending it falling to her booted feet.

"Oh!" cried CHINA ROSE. "My lost tea pot." She could not let go of FOOT SOLDIER DAVY'S arm out of fear. Who was the strange woman who came through to this place, from where? She wanted to touch the shiny yellow coat. Was it tangible or a mirage on a woman like a cloud of some kind standing there stationary? Tugging a stunned and hesitant DAVY by the arm, she minced over to Heleena, staring all the while like a child out of wonder. What was there to fear?

Heleena's neck length permed hair had kinked from the wetness. Straggly brown pieces now pasted around her face, framing rosy cheeks, blue-green eyes, and emphasizing her larger than normal dominating nose.

CHINA ROSE compared their boots, hers of rough-out leather for stomping on muddy streets, and those of the strange woman's shiny black pointed toes with white leather insets of flowers.

Near the boots was her shiny silver tea pot which she hurriedly scooped in her hands all the while staring at the strange woman and clutching DAVY'S arm. She stepped back slowly.

"Hello," said Heleena raising the pitch of her tone a couple octaves. Now with her empty left hand, she played with the silver whistle around her neck, fingering its red ribbon. "Where am I? How did I get here?"

The popping eyeball stare of the group, and their ridiculous attire from another century caused her heart to palpitate rapidly. Swooning, she grasped the spear with both hands for steadiness.

"Ok, where's the film crew? Hey, you can stop filming now---come out where ever you're hiding!" Turning in every direction, she stared, stunned.

Silence!

No action. Only a deep stillness. Even the wildlife was in hiding.

Looking down at the circle of mud, the rivulets of slowly moving rain water into the cracks and crevices of rocks and boulders, she realized this was the same place she had left a few minutes ago. The swirl of mud next to the rectangular purplish boulder was definitely her signature. Now she remembered.

"An Apache was here?" She had to ask the tawdry group who had been staring at her fearfully too long.

Noticing a few took a step back with breath intake, she knew that she made a hit.

"Apache!" Again she blatantly threw the word out searching for responses.

DUTCHY and MEXICAN MANO, fearing his return and the retaliation for their messing around with his gold mine, were now all ears. Each threw down armfuls of large rocks they had pulled away from the entrance of a cave, certain that it could be the mine, the one APACHE protected; each then worriedly walked toward her.

"Yeah, what about him?"

"*Que passa?*"

Gruffly they approached.

Fearing their evilness, Heleena stepped back while taking an attack stance and began swinging the spear right and left.

"Enough!" GAMBLER MOODY had pulled a Derringer from the valise and walked toward the two antique gold-mongers.

Suddenly, DUTCHY'S heinous laugh rattled the nerves of all those present. Even MEXICAN MANO distanced himself and slapped the dust off his hands. "*Mucho loco!*"

"Shoot away you ignoramus son-of-a-bitch!" He threw back his head and laughed again sending black Phenol-Peplin flying out of Grey Thorns and Jack Rabbits scurrying into ravines looking for shelter.

"We're dead!" He yelled loudly. "Dead, dead, dead, you damned-dumb incorrigible fools." Eyeing each with an evil squint and clenched teeth he drooled at the mouth like a mad dog.

Helleena, as a long time high school department head, had seen worse behavior and didn't step back. Instead, she pinched the tender skin of her under arm again harder this time. "Ouch," she screamed. "I'm not dead!" But, no one noticed her; they were too hell bent on attacking DUTCHY.

And so began a wretched torrent of loud-mouthed jabber, ramblings and accusations.

GAMBLER MOODY faced him with the Derringer. "Your tone does not augur well in front of the ladies." Slant eyed hate smoked from his face as he advanced toward him.

"Baleful egoist," roared CHINA ROSE at DUTCHY as she let go of DAVY and poked a fat pink finger a few inches from DUTCHY'S face.

"What in tarnation are you saying, you rattle brained old prospector." FOOT SOLDIER DAVY rubbed the cavernous bullet hole below his left shoulder, then accused him of chewing on the phosphorous match heads which are poisonous and used for suicides. "Chew on some more Lucifers and git outa here!" He waved an arm in anger pointing to the road.

MEXICAN MANO feared DUTCHY'S hateful rage the most though he realized he himself was now impenetrable. Running fingers over the never mending wounds to his chest, sustained from DUTCHY the devil, one heart breaking day while mining on these grounds, he cursed at him now in Spanish, using every word he remembered.

"Time for the whistle!" Heleena blew the whistle staccato style sending the shrill sound bouncing along the canyon walls, stunning all who heard.

Stepping up on the dark-purple-rectangular boulder for the noticeable attention she needed, she started: "You sound like a warpath of anger! Why the convulsive behavior?" She stabbed the spear up and down with each blow of the red-ribboned whistle. Not letting go of it was important somehow as she grabbed it with both hands for steadiness. Somehow it had real meaning. The Apache had appeared with it.

DAVY, ROSE, GAMBLER and MANO stared at her with empty faces, enthralled by the shrill sound of the whistle with the tiny red bow. GAMBLER, especially, had never seen such action from such a beautiful lady in a long, long time.

Giving them a hand flip of boredom, DUTCHY, the unimpressed worldly vagabond from Germany, stomped over to GAMBLER MOODY, grabbed the harmonica out of the valise that sat rumpled on a nearby boulder, turned his back to the crew and began playing it while marching back to the cave of gold---certain now that the nuggets were there due to his and MEXICAN'S digging. In haste to grab the harmonica, his hand also found a large gun which he pocketed for later.

The four stepped closer now to the strangely dressed woman in the daring knee length denim skirt---stopping at the knees. GAMBLER had seen nothing like this before. Each wanted to befriend her, a living person able to communicate with them for the first time.

How?

APACHE had been their magical source of spiritual prowess and this brought them renewed courage, courage of acceptance for their dilemma.

What was this magic to appear and disappear?

Each began speaking, which she likened to gobbledygook of antiquated speech. "Huh?"

"I say," began GAMBLER MOODY. "What is this mode of dress?" A half smile lifted his lips a bit as he stared at Heleena, smitten by her looks---the button on her chin, a real beauty mark. Her equine nose was similar to his which he now touched the tip in subliminal thought. He wanted to touch hers.

Before she could answer, each intervened, all enamored by her intrusion like a spiritual Goddess.

"Can I touch you?" Innocently, CHINA ROSE extended her chubby short fingers to feel the slickness of the yellow slicker which was opened wide to reveal the knee length denim skirt above her boots. All the while she clung to DAVY who had nothing to say.

MEXICAN MANO came close to examine the multi-colored pointy toed fashion boots with leather insets of red and white flowered figurines.

He mumbled in Spanish, *"Que bonito!"*

From his pocket, GAMBLER MOODY found the tiny little bell thrown to him by APACHE. Holding it out in an offering to Heleena, his long slender fingers uncurled from his fist slowly.

Heleena hesitantly touched the bell feeling its solid coldness. His positive nod and pooling brown eyes prompted her to oblige; taking the tiny bell, she placed it in the pocket of her denim skirt.

He stared in wonder and content.

All watched motionless in noisy silence. The soft playing of the harmonica in the background added tranquility.

Heleena took the whistle from around her neck and placed it over GAMBLER'S head. "From my world to yours." She thought him to be a handsome man, a mystery person she needed to know.

Taking off his beaver-fur high hat, he placed it over his heart, totally excited for the first time in his eternity. His long brown locks cascaded over his shoulders.

MEXICAN MANO and DAVY stepped forward with pieces of tobacco whittled from a plug; their only offering.

The placid moment was short lived as DUTCHY, wanting some wild excitement, ran from the cave entrance with the large gun in his hand shooting indiscriminately.

The four stood there in surprised anger as the bullets transcended through them to the boulders, Mesquite bushes, thickets of Prickly Pear and beyond.

It was only Heleena who felt a sting at her chest.

CHAPTER 38

SUPERSTITION MOUNTAINS

MASSACRE GROUNDS

December 22, 2014

Coyotee's staccato clicking tongue, a different chant of S.O.S., mesmerized us standing there too stunned to think of another solution.

Continually, we locked elbows then moved ten yards away from where Coyotee stood on the now magical purple-boulder, or so we assumed.

A misty rain began again as clouds from the top of the Superstitions descended low, sweeping like smoke swirling around us, almost blocking our visibility. Surreal? I had never seen such desert weather as this foggy day which dampened the reality of the situation. We chatted and mumbled our feelings of what was happening to keep our brains on task.

"Reality check," I said. "Everyone holding on?" Of course we were too scared to do otherwise as we stood shaking, staring, worrying.

"Call out your names," said Nancy twisting forward surveying the short string of us, all six.

We did. Roy was in the middle with Jamie and Kim glued to his side; Catora and I were on one end and Nancy on the far left.

"Don't anyone move!" I looked over at the two freshman boys digging away for more treasure.

They complied by shaking their heads in acknowledgment and continued. Each had a stick of hard Mesquite in his fist plundering the wet earth carefully. Dampness from the rain had seeped under the edge of the shallow cave facilitating their efforts.

Holy cow, we were all bouncing at the knees and swaying to the right, then left, to the sound of Coyote's regiment. My arms were getting numb!

"Heleee—NA, Heleee---NA, Helleee---NA!!" I started a chant that was more of a cheer. Everyone followed my lead. I had no clue what would happen next, just kept busy…guessing.

"Everybody saw Heleena disappear, correct?"

"CORRECT!" Even the two freshmen boys tuned in from the background and yelled with us."

Sighing, we kept swaying and chanting for Heleena under our breaths.

Any moment I kept expecting Groups Two and Three to arrive. Where are they?

Help? I looked down at my watch where my fingers were entwined, clasped together rigidly, afraid to let go, glued together at the elbows with others.

"Three o'clock," I gasped. "The minute hand is ticking, but time is still stationary."

"My cell phone's stuck on one-thirty!" Nancy had pulled her phone out of her vest pocket while still holding on at the elbows, and this was not a good idea. Nerves, slippery wet dew, whatever, sent the cell phone down in the mud. Hastily trying retrieval, she stepped on it---twice.

"You have a cell phone?" Kim Rose asked. "Not fair. Ours disappeared in the saddle bags."

Suddenly, Coyotee's large magnificent black gelding's ears shot forward as it raised its head in fear. Instantly it reared in a rage, broke loose and thundered away, mud splattering everywhere.

"They have a sixth-sense," Nancy said quietly after the noise.

When Roy added, "It heard something from beyond," we shivered. Even Coyotee took notice while still chanting.

Minutes seemed like hours; a small funnel of wind began dancing here and there around the slurry of mud that remained from Heleena's sit down.

At the same time---"We're finding another treasure," yelled the two boys bent over a dirt pile, ecstatically working away not paying attention to the new small funnel twirling wider and faster ten yards in front of them.

CHAPTER 39

MEANWHILE, Del Rio hurried his horse to his string of riders who had now doubled in size. Colt's group of nine had joined them and everyone was joyfully milling about, some on horseback, others off. For sure, they were drinking, eating, and sharing snacks of chocolates, chips, and trail-mix.

The few on foot who had lost their horses were contently chatting. But, everyone had questions.

"How far are we from Massacre Grounds?"

"What was the shooting about?"

"Where are the Wranglers?"

Rick threw his shoulders back and calmly took charge. "Listen-up!"

"Quiet," someone yelled.

He began. "We are approximately one mile away from our destination." From his pocket he eyed the list of riders received earlier from Gina.

"In our combined groups, we now have fourteen students and six adults. Ride or walk with whomever you wish. Share horses. The adults can help with the mounting and dismounting."

"And," added Guy Wagner always the coach, "we need to speed-up or it'll be dark before we know it!" He looked at his watch.

"So," Dr. Shieter asked, "where are the Wranglers?"

"They're coming behind us." Del Rio gave no other information to the students but to the adults he added, "They left earlier to chase down the loose horses from Group One. Also, Pete has volunteered to stay back with those on foot."

He lied---somewhat, and tried the tracker again.

Nothing. No contact.

It didn't make sense to him. If the whistle had come off Gina's neck and been stomped in the mud by the loose horse pack, it should still be working.

Now he worried. The darkening of the day, the low clouds and misty rain seemed more like an omen than a delight.

The crisscrossing of old prospector routes and abandoned roads from bygone wagon days could easily throw him off his destination. Unofficial trails were everywhere spiking in different directions like crooked spokes from a wheel. *If you get lost in the Superstitions, you will never be found* played on his subconscious again.

Colt rode over to him at the lead. "What's going on?"

"I have an uncanny feeling about all this until we meet with Group One." Checking his GPS brought new confidence. Then….

"What the HELL!" Rick was louder now and impatient. "EVERYONE OFF THE TRAIL; WE HAVE ANOTHER LOOSE HORSE COMING. LOOK OUT!"

Thundering down the mountain side, leaping over small boulders and bushes came Coyotee's big black gelding toward them, mane and tail flying like a comet with white lather foaming under the saddle blanket.

Guy Wagner grabbed Becky Painter's horse. "Hold on," he yelled.

Rick, Colt and Delilah helped steady the other horses that were ready to stampede.

"Catastrophe's not happening on my watch," Rick called out to everyone. "Steady the horses!"

"Whose horse was that," asked one of the senior girls keeping too close to Del Rio every chance she got.

"I don't know. Everyone ok?" He watched the horse running down in the distance a short way until it rounded a bend and out of sight.

No one answered from the stunned crowd. Rick took off his hat and readjusted short strands of hair that had fallen forward in his eyes. Others did the same. It was a pause, a reflection of the task at hand---to move out and find their destination.

"That's Coyotee's big black gelding," a student offered.

"Are you sure?" Rick wanted a clear affirmation to the day's craziness.

"Yep! And I bet Coyotee's up ahead somewhere!" Same student.

From the center of the long group now riding in pairs came a cry of "help". A girl's saddle was turning and she was about to fall off the side of the horse.

"Help!" Again.

Clinging to the saddle horn with both hands, she now dragged her right foot on the ground.

"Whoa," Delilah grabbed the horse's lead rope as a male student walker put two arms around the girl and helped her off the saddle.

Fortunately, the seasoned trail horse stood still as the saddle twisted almost under its belly.

The line of riders now had to stop and eliminate another possible dilemma like the girl's.

Loudly Rick explained. "When there's a loose cinch, the saddle turns. This is common on a long ride with loss of a horse's body fluids. The middle girth gets narrower until the saddle turns." He circled Bullet around the edges of the line facing the group. The horse was quickly sure footed, climbing up and down small ridges following Rick's lead.

"Everyone off to re-tighten cinches."

Puffing a heavy sigh of discontent due to loss of timing, he hurriedly helped others tighten cinches. Two of the Wranglers had arrived and were helpful with the situation.

"Thanks!" He called out to Dick and Jack knowing that there were eleven students on horses that needed tending.

Remounting, the group took off again. Jack volunteered to stay with the walkers who were lagging a bit due to tiredness.

"We're almost there!" Rick's comment was passed back among the riders and walkers like an echo. "Fifteen more minutes."

Now he worried again about Gina's group ahead and the four retired walkers far behind, although he was thankful for Pete staying with them.

Sure of the trail leading to Massacre Grounds, he spurred Bullet onward faster.

****

The four retired walkers, Bing, Bob, Brad and Blake were not too far behind, continuing their steady pace while telling spooky stories, real legends they "knew" to be true. Considering they had heard that Massacre Grounds was haunted, they were in the mood and hurried their pace to get there.

Each tried to compete with horrific stories that they were sure to be true. But, Bob's story from Indiana took the prize.

"My great-grandma was walking home from a barn dance late at night with a few friends when all of them heard a scream coming from the cemetery. She said a girl in a coffin had awakened from a coma and tried to claw her way out of the box. By the time they opened the coffin, it was too late and her fingers were all bloodied from trying to escape."

This brought on a debate about standards for undertakers in the nineteenth century.

"How deep was the coffin in the ground?" Bing asked.

"Grandma didn't say."

While discussing a belief in ghosts, Pete rode over and spooked them more with his stories from the haunted area of Massacre Grounds. "They're there all right. They're real! I ain't goin' too close. I'll watch ya'll from a distance. There's a harmonica that's always playing in the area."

Brad asked, "Have you heard it?"

"Dang right. A couple a days ago we had to do a quick set-up for this school ride, chuck wagon and all, and I got off my horse to take a leek. Music was so loud I couldn't even pee straight."

This prompted Brad with his Marine sense of action to get excited. "I can hardly wait to get there. Let's move a little faster."

Blake, the heaviest of the group was puffing the hardest. "Not me. I'll stay back with Pete. You three go on ahead. Follow the fresh horse manure on the trail and you won't get lost."

Bing said, "I have a GPS co-ordinate like Del Rio's, plus a compass. We'll be fine. We're close. I hear voices."

CHAPTER 40

SUPERSTITION MOUNTAINS
MASSACRE GROUNDS
December 22, 2014

The hours were actually minutes when I kept checking my watch for security measures. Time was something I could control, or so I thought. We knew that something bigger than life, something deathly dramatic, would be coming our way soon.

"We need to think positive!" My exclamation was too thunderous, more like a yell echoing in the misty silence. We were all noisily spooked as a matter of fact from fearing the lore of lost bodies….ours!

As the small funnel of wind danced around circling the mud slough that Heleena had disappeared from, we delved into nonsensical communication, still clinging to each other, now in a half moon line. Coyotee stood on the rock and the funnel spun in the middle yet a short distance away.

We still kept our distance fearing we could be swept away in the fury of the maelstrom. Closeness was our measure of fear.

"Why'd the horse go wild?" asked Jamie Mink.

"And stampede away!" added Kim Rose.

"Like it heard something from beyond!" Roy echoed.

This thought scared us the most as we glued our sights at the spinning swirl of vortex getting wider and wider. Our knee caps rattled against each other as we held ourselves upright.

Coyotee's eyes were closed as he continued a low toned staccato S.O.S. with palms towards the sky.

"Careful you don't fall!" Yelled Catora.

"Horses have an extra sensory perception!" There it was again. Nancy reminded us of what we feared the most---the unknown.

Remembering the two boys digging beyond in the sheltered overhang and what they had last said about finding another treasure, my attention focused in their direction a quick snap. I didn't want to miss what was happening in front of us.

"Be sure to carefully remove the new treasure so as not to break or tear anything!" My statement was robotic: hard, quick and precise.

"Uh huh!" They said while not looking our way.

Now, the muddy space produced an aura of wavy grain---a spectrum of activity trying to complete an image right there, within our sight.

It wavered, flattened and disappeared like blinking lights out at sea in slow motion---off and on again.

Coyotee now opened his eyes, looked toward the image and quickened his S.O.S. with heightened sounds, louder and faster. He too was frightened beyond his wits.

Blended colors began to melt into specific images of a solid figure, like globs of molten metal taking shape.

Locked at the elbows, we had not quit our swaying movement and my hands became clammy, useless appendages.

I was in a kaleidoscope of changing motifs. Boys digging on my left, Coyotee raging on a boulder, and our group swaying and chanting; the affair brought forth a change in the image slowly.

The aura of a person began to appear, than slowly shape in the form of a solid.

Soon, Heleena stood before us dressed in her colorful boots and short denim skirt, covered with mud as before. Her expression of a shocking white stare scared us beyond belief. She looked like an incandescent villain from the bygone days of earliest black and white movie films.

Coyotee stared.

We held our breaths which contributed to our dizziness. I could tell by the way we faltered in our line and grasped at each other to stay upright, that the shock of what appeared before us was real.

Crouching low, she held the Mesquite wood spear between her two hands and waved it to and fro fighting something. Her frizzy hair ascending in all directions completed the shocking image of an attack mode.

Soon while gasping for breath, her head bent forward than back again in quick repetitions.

We didn't dare move, afraid to be transferred somewhere in the surreal scene.

She fell forward face down splattering wet mud.

"Heleena!" I found my voice, though it was weak and sick sounding.

From her back, a wet thick smudge began spilling from a hole in her yellow slicker.

"Heleena," I called again. My heart beat uncontrollably and my head began to throb.

Immobile and sinking, her body fully relaxed quit moving as red blood gushed out of the hole in the torn yellow slicker.

We gasped!

"Everybody breathe," I reminded the group in desperation.

"Nobody faint!" Nancy reminded us.

Our line took a few steps closer to her. Jamie and Kim dared not let go of the astute Roy who stood tall and stout. After all, he was the clever one who indicated that the spooked horse had heard something from beyond, validated by Nancy who said earlier that horses have an extra sensory perception.

Where's my ESP? "Rick, where are you," I whispered.

Catora had now grabbed Coyotee and they squeezed each other tightly, shaking uncontrollably.

Screaming, we all called for help. Twisting around, we searched for anyone close by.

"Heleena, Heleena!" Skeptically we called out her name.

Was this real?

"Nancy, your phone!" Looking at her I realized she was more helplessly stunned than I as she was turning a translucent white, a chalky appearance contrasting with her red hair.

"Snap out of it. Don't go in to shock!" Slapping her face, I realized that I needed help here.

"Give me the phone! I bet that it still works." This from Kim Rose a teen always in control. She swiftly wiped away mud, slush and debris, then ran it over her jeans for further cleansing.

After quickly giving her Rick Del Rio's cell phone number, I crossed my fingers. We all did. Was this witchcraft? Were we sane?

Loud, clear, and very nearby, Rick's cell rang. Actually, it sounded like it was just over my shoulder---or echoing up the hill. My brain was awash in dis-connect.

"What's going on here? What's been happening?"

I grabbed the cell from Kim and started to explain. "Heleena's been shot!"

"I can see that." Rick's voice was loud and clear.

"What?"

Turning around now, we saw Rick riding in on his fast paced Missouri Fox Trotter, Bullet. He looked taller and handsomer than I last remembered. I ached to grab him and sink into his chest.

Behind him a large group of gawking riders descended down the small cliff.

Stuttering, we rambled in unison.

I rapidly explained everything that had taken place while talking to the cell phone glued in my hand.

Rick immediately got off his horse, handed the reins to *D*ick, and kneeled next to Heleena to check her demise.

"Everybody back to that space." Rick pointed to a bushy area lined with rocks from previous cookouts. "Nobody cross over."

"Is she d-dead?" Stuttering, I asked the cell.

Now everyone jabbered in a whisper as more riders joined Group Two. Gawking heads stared at us, each standing in stirrups for a better view.

"You can circle round, but don't get close!"

Everyone obeyed Rick's orders except Delilah. She was now in her field of expertise as she handed the reins to Guy Wagner after dismounting.

Looking like she had just walked out of a beauty parlor instead of riding for most of the day, she asked, "What happened here? Everybody stay back. Nobody touch the body!"

She bossed. We obeyed. I heard many riders gasp after hearing the words, "the body".

Stepping away, Rick was now on his cell transmitting orders for help with all the professional connections.

Then back to us, "I can't believe what I thought I saw." He frowned his manly look and squinted the greenest eyes ever. He stared at us, then her, then us again in puzzlement.

“”It’s true! It’s true!” The seven of us were right on top of the scene, not having moved for the past hour, still shaking, stuttering and shivering from fright.

“This is a dangerous crime scene,” he added as Delilah milled around surveying the area like a forensic judge. Colt, Guy, Becky Painter and Dr. Shieter stayed in the background to control the scene and keep the riders from coming too close.

“From where did the shots come? Who heard them?” Puzzled, Rick assumed we knew all the pieces.

“Well, she appeared like this out of nowhere!” I shouted to the now dead cell phone heating the side of my face.

“We heard nothing.” Each of the students chimed in with Nancy adding, “The horse spooked and bolted just before she appeared.”

Somehow, we could not let go of each other at the elbows while I still kept the cell glued to my ear.

Surrounding us but a short distance away in sight of the drama, were all the riders listening to our loud explanations echoing in the dead silence.

Girls started softly crying.

Boys sat in their saddles numb from the trauma.

I felt sorry for Coyotee who was silently moping with his head hanging low while moving it from side to side. Was he feeling guilty for the happening? I nudged Catora to pay attention to him and blinked an eye in her direction.

“What do you mean she appeared like this?” Delilah sanely eyeballed each of us waiting for an answer, hands firmly on her teeny tiny waist, a vanity gesture I was getting tired of by now.

Rick stepped away again to talk on his cell and on another device he magically pulled out of a pocket.

“She disappeared, than re-appeared,” I said as each in my little group echoed the same words. Some more descriptive than others.

Nancy began her rendition. "She went into a trance, acting weird, and sang a strange song about giving a dog a bone. Next, she grabbed this Mesquite wood spear that an Apache kid brought here, and disappeared from that mud slurry!" She pointed to where Heleena lay.

"This Mesquite spear? What spear? Where is it?" Delilah was being a skeptical snot. I could see it coming.

It was gone.

We were stunned. This prompted a repeat of our individual explanations about Coyotee's chant, the Apaches arrival and disappearance, Heleena's weird trance, than Coyotee's S.O.S attempt to bring her back. We jabbered, pranced around, un-clung and threw our hands in the air to emphasize our explanations as theatrically as possible for every listener to hear….except for me; the damned cell phone was still stuck to my ear.

"STOP!" Rick called out to us all. "I arrived before the group and I'm sure that I saw Heleena crouched low with a stick of some sort."

He walked over to me, pried the cell out of my white fist, and hugged me tightly. I closed my eyes and felt faint.

The sound of choppers coming from over the mountain awoke my senses. Looking in their direction I saw the four retirees standing back at a distance. I hope they heard everything so they can re-tell it to Pop the unbeliever.

Delilah yelled over the din. "OK, where's the Apache Kid?"

"Hey! Look what we finally dug out from over there. Took a while." The two forgotten boys who had been diligent treasure hunters, came hurriedly toward Rick and me, their hands laced with clinging dirt, holding a piece of jewelry. They had our full attention as I reached out to them noticing that my hands were still shaking. It was an interruption, a surprise that fit well with today's un-explainables.

In my cupped hands they placed a soiled pearl bracelet on a gold chain with an attached minute butterfly amulet. On its wings were the initials GM.

A harmonica played softly in the distance.

CHAPTER 41

APACHE CAMP
Massacre Grounds
December 22, 1848

"Oh my!" DUTCHY'S reaction to Heleena's bullet wound was a very sarcastic "Oops" before he laughed heinously, slapped his thigh sending dirt cascading off his nankeen cloth pantaloons and threw the pistol to the ground. "This gun does not work. You are all still here!!" Arms extended and snickering loudly, he turned around and headed back to Apache's cave where he had been gold digging….laughing all the way there.

Doom and gloom set in among the small group of four as they stood with heads downcast, too dumbfounded to react. A cloud of black death hovered above and around each, collectively draining positive emotions in one sweep.

Sirens of moans and cries waved among the bushes, boulders and down into the canyons from discontented spirits. Each of the group now feeling flattened, dissolved from the wholeness of before, dropped to the ground in remorse.

APACHE was gone, his spirit disappearing in a funnel of wind, not to be seen again. "He's home with his village people;" the four had whispered in agreement and felt an elevation of spiritual renewal, a connection of some sort, a positive aura that could be transferrable. That was then, earlier after his disappearance. At that time, each wished for an out, dreaming of the big disappearance, a chance to return to the comfort of once was. It had been admirable, what APACHE had accomplished.

That was then…..

NOW, CHINA ROSE cried a whimpering sob riveting from her bosom. Her large frame rose and shook with each newly formed loud sob that whined down to a whimpering siren. She carried on for hours. The earthly lady she admired was gone. She had appeared out of nowhere like an angel, a savior, and just as quickly, disappeared.

FOOT SOLDIER DAVY could not stop her because he too wallowed in defeat. He had been a youngster, a fifteen year old child when he left the greens of home to go West with friends seeking adventure. When he met tragedy, they moved on. Now, he started rocking forward and back, head hung low as he moved away from CHINA ROSE to sit in the small shelter, one hand in his lap, the other covering the terminal hole in his left chest. He had been an innocent victim, just passing through on a scouting mission from Camp McDowell for Captain Cook when DUTCHY shot him.

Her bellowing pierced his heart. It was hopeless. They were doomed from ever finding peace and happiness, and he wished he knew how to help her.

MEXICAN MANO blessed himself with the sign of the cross continuously. Then falling down on his knees and putting his one hand and stub together, he looked up at the heavens and prayed as he had never done before. A December drizzle beaded his face, slithered through his wrinkles and dripped from his chin. Aware of their dilemma now more than ever, he prayed aloud for contentment of some kind. He found a short, wet stick nearby, and pretending it was the beaded rosary so familiar to him in his youth, recited the "Our Father" and "Hail Mary" over and over with his eyes closed knowing that every small space on the stick was a prayer. He wanted peace.

GAMBLER MOODY no longer stood tall. Shoulders slumped while standing there looking down at the circle of mud from whence the beautiful lady appeared. The reality of her live appearance was genuine and became even more so when she acknowledged their existence. This had not been done before in their many previous encounters with other people who rode horses or carriages nearby.

"How did she do it? Where did she go?" He whispered low as he pondered about her appearance, then just as quickly, her disappearance.

The spear…the spear was there at the site. Yet, looking around, he saw she had taken it with her…but it came back.

Convinced that all the happenings were brought on by APACHE'S magic, he felt hopeless. APACHE was gone, never to return. Yet, as his hand went to his chest in remorse, he felt the gift of the red-ribboned whistle that the Goddess had slipped over his head. It would hang around his neck forever. He felt better as he picked up his valise and walked over to console his three friends and perhaps meditate peaceful solutions. As he put his arms over the shoulders of the young boy and girl, the harmonica hummed loudly from inside the cave, this time becoming an annoying disturbance.

CHAPTER 42

SUPERSTITION MOUNTAINS
MASSACRE GROUNDS
December 22, 2014

"There has to be a sound explanation for this," said Rick as he fingered the soiled pearl bracelet that sat like a dead bird in my cupped hands. Hard soil clung to the pieces of chain between the pearls.

"This was my bracelet, the one you gave me Thursday, two nights ago." I too offered no solution to the mystery but waited for Rick's.

He said nothing.

We were stunned.

"It was REALLY buried deep in some hardened clay," said one of the freshman boys standing next to us.

"And, we REALLY had to take our time getting it loose," said the other proudly. "Can we keep it?"

"Not yet," sighed Rick turning the treasure over in his palm for examination. Holding the miniature butterfly amulet containing my initials between his thumb and fore-finger, he rubbed the delicate figurine to a shine. He was unreadable, the usual hidden nondescript expression that I found annoying. Then finally, "This is a mystery!"

The boys enthusiastically hurried back to their dig.

A brown Apache Junction chopper had landed on a flat surface nearby and a group of uniformed police surrounded the area.

"What happened here?" A huge man with 'Sheriff' emblazoned on a badge attached to his thick vest sauntered over. No enthusiasm here! With his cap low I couldn't see his eyes but his clamped mouth showed tiredness. He reaked of a cynical attitude…been here, done that before. Disgust was evident as he probably suspected foul play. Tom Mix was the name on his cap. Fitting! Rider's pants were tucked in knee high boots. Unusual for this time of year since rattlesnakes are dormant. Most amazing were his legs, as long as Nancy was tall. I'll bet if she stood next to him, she would reach the height of his waist. His face was handsomely in proportion with his height. One inch of brown wavy hair descended from the bottom of his cap circling the back of his neck. For sure, he was a lady killer!

I could not believe that we were so totally tongue tied.

No one spoke.

The silence was deafening.

What could we say?

Ruby red blood still oozed softly from Heleena's back as she lay exactly where she had fallen.

Prominent horse noises voided the stillness as the two moved about and blew profusely through their muzzles one after another in copy cat tradition.

"She's been shot!" Offered Rick after showing his credentials to the sheriff.

In an undertone, "And she's dead," said Delilah. She identified herself before adding, "I checked for a heart beat!"

More silence.

"Where's the shooter? Where's the gun?" His questions were directed towards no one as Tom Mix seemed to be talking to himself. Walking around the area keeping a distance from the crime scene, he watched the cops cordon the area in bright yellow and motioned for us to step back. His steps were as long as his legs.

Bending with creaking knees, he stooped next to the body and studied it. After taking a small yellow note pad from a zippered vest pocket, he began to write. He wore a huge clunk of a ring on one of his fingers. A gold nugget was stuck in the middle.

"Anybody see the shooter?" Now he tilted his cap back and looked at us long and hard with squinting sky blue eyes.

We shook our heads negative.

He stared at us for too long before asking, "Where did the bullet sound seem to originate?" His thumb played a tune on his ball point pushing the end tab in and out.

I gagged an answer from my dry throat. "We heard nothing."

"Well," confronting me in a grizzled mood he asked, "how did she get here?"

"Uhmm." I was not fast enough for him.

"How long have you and your group been here?" He turned around slowly waiting for an answer from someone. I noticed that Delilah was standing next to him with folded arms supporting his authority.

"Uhmm." Nancy and I repeated about four of these.

"Who was the first to find her like this?" Much louder and expecting an answer, he gripped his yellow tablet firmly and circled the pen in the air.

"Wait!" Rick waved his gloved hands, and I hoped he wouldn't mimic our dumbness. "From a distance I heard chanting, then saw a blurred swirl of fog, after which she appeared….standing." He spoke as one asking a question rather than making a statement. He was slow, precise, and threatening. No one better question him.

He repeated and counted the three items with the side slice of his hand. "I saw a swirling funnel; she was standing; she fell on her face." And then the finale, "I heard no gun shot."

A distant clasp of thunder foretold a circling renewal of rain from the darkening sky. It was that kind of a December day.

Nevertheless, the never stopping showers compounded our demise over and beyond the devastating present circumstances. "We need to start back to the bus," I suggested after comparing the time with Nancy's cell. "We now have four-thirty." My watch was no longer stuck on three. We were moving on. Confident that the sheriff's group would handle the situation with Delilah's help, my main concern was to get the students back safely to the bus.

The sheriff bellowed, "All of you can leave," waving at our huge circle of gawking riders and walkers who had been inching forward to see and hear.

"You people," pointing to my little group of seven, minus the two boys he hadn't noticed digging in the dirt, "stay and give me your names for later questioning."

Nancy, Coyotee, Catora, Jamie Mink, Roy, Kim Rose and I stood alone absorbing the catastrophe. Although we felt important, I had a gut feeling that we would not be taken seriously. Or does the sheriff know more than we about Massacre Grounds? He himself looked strange.

Becky Painter, Coach Guy Wagner, and Colt, guided the riders and walkers back to the path from where they came. The slow pokes, Shieter and Blake had not arrived, so I suspected Pete had the upper hand with his spooky stories and as promised, would not arrive at Massacre Grounds. I was beginning to know why.

Rick rode over to the Wranglers Dick and Jack to ask for their help. "They all need to make it to the bus in one piece." Next, he asked Bing, Brad and Bob who had been standing quietly on a mound in full view of the haunting scene, to radio in for a truck to gather the small group who had lost their horses in the stampede, "when you have cell service. Our group of nine will start back as soon as possible and among us we have only two horses, so get the trucks ready to gather us when we get close."

I looked over at the two horses of Rick's and Delilah's and didn't like the way Bullet and Biscuit nestled together.

Delilah was talking shop to the sheriff who was all 'eyes and eyes' absorbing her every word…her teeny waist, skinny jeans, suave silky brown long hair.

Rick came over to me and I started whining. "I'm bad Rick! I could have saved her when she started acting strangely and singing that weird song…like she was somebody else. Not herself at all!"

He took my yellow slicker that I had just retrieved from a branch, helped me into it, pulled the hood over my head and snapped the button under my chin. I noticed that the others in my group had already done so. After pushing my tiresome cascading curls from around my face back into the hood he said, "I have to take care of you." He pulled the hood over my ears.

"And, I need answers later to what I thought I saw." Rick stared at me for the longest time without blinking. With a hand on each shoulder he pulled me closer and whispered, "I can't believe what I saw."

Was this a positive? That he saw her appear out of the mist like a Sci Fi movie?

Surrounding us now was my little mystified group, coming to life with individual thoughts.

"It's unbelievable!"

"What really happened?"

"Did I see what I thought I saw?"

"It's all my fault." Coyotee hung his head, slid his hands into his back pockets and walked nervously in a circle.

"No!" Nancy was loud and clear. "Your spiritual dance had meaning for only the Apache. There is something else going on here. There must be ghosts all around us…here in this very area." She held out her hands and moved around signaling, searching for an answer.

I expected the sheriff's rebuff to Nancy's shocking torrent of words, but Tom Mix cocked his head left and right in analyses and said nothing. Next, he took out a pair of binoculars from a back pack he carried, walked away about thirty feet and started an assessment of the area.

I tried to read him. Was he annoyed with us, bored, or wiser than we expected?

Delilah's turn. "How could you not hear a gunshot ricochet through the canyons?" Pause. "I know! It could have happened during a lightning strike." Before we could answer negatively, she answered her own question.

She finished with "There's a shooter on the loose out here."

Rick walked over to the sheriff for a discussion of some sort. The sheriff came over to us and said we could leave but needed to be available for further questioning. He double checked his list of names.

"Thanks," I mumbled but felt a terrible emptiness for the tragedy as I started to walk toward the two freshman boys to include them.

It was decided that Rick would walk us back to an area where the pickup would gather us and haul us to the bus. And, since Delilah's professional expertise was needed at the death scene, she would stay behind with the sheriff and get a ride back later.

Rick now led both Bullet and Biscuit over to the shallow cave where the two boys were still digging.

"Come on boys. We're finished here. Get on the horses and I'll lead them so they'll stay with us walkers."

"Wait! We are finding something else."

Both boys excitedly jumped up from their muddy dig and showed us two metal pieces of a gun, both easily distinguishable. One part revealed a small handle with a trigger attached. The other piece was a short narrow barrel that attached to the handle.

"Let me see those." Tom Mix anxiously looked at the two pieces and cleaned them further with his gloved hands. "I'm a collector of old guns," he said admirably. "This is a vest-pocket-pistol made famous before the civil war." His voice became a curious whisper. "A derringer from the famous arms maker of Philadelphia."

Intrigued, I had to feel the funny handle. As a matter of fact, we all did. "The hook handle was the real mark of the derringer," he continued as he took out his phone and snapped several pictures turning the pieces in different angles.

"These are yours boys. Treasure them as real antiques. There were many gun battles here at Massacre Grounds. Show these to your parents and tell them that they are from the 1840's, before stage coaches…when Fort McDowell was only a Camp."

Wow! I was soooo impressed.

"Hey. We need to double time," interrupted Rick looking more serious than ever. Was he jealous?

As the ten of us hurried away, two more helicopters logoed "Pinal County Sheriff's Department" flew in from the distance.

CHAPTER 43

Stunned, we scurried towards our destination, the trucks that would carry all of us back to the bus. A cheery event turned dark as we each silently absorbed the death scene in our own way and the devastating loss of Heleena.

Later I would learn from Rick the procedures taken for the removal of the body. For now, there were other worries.

The encroaching darkness interrupted our sadness to embrace the seriousness of the present situation…getting back to the bus in due time. We were dampened by the non-stop sprinkles, and the fact that Tom Mix interrogated our group too long didn't help our discomfort. We would be at least one hour behind the others being led by the Wranglers.

This was huge. No explanation surfaced among us as we shook our heads and re-lived the afternoon's events---over and over as we hurried along, spurred with an adrenalin rush that nixed exhaustion.

"But---?"

"But---?"

"But---?"

"All who didn't witness the event will be asking us a boat load of questions. I just hope that Bing, Brad and Bob arrived at the same time as Rick," I told Nancy as we all started on our trek.

"We'll find out on the bus," replied Nancy.

Nancy and I were the only two adults among the teens at the scene of the death spiral. Would our credibility by challenged later? Has this ever happened before in this place? The cynicism from Tom Mix could not be dismissed. He knew something. And his chunk of a gold ring---- on which hand did he wear it? Delilah would be the first to know.

"Nancy, call Butch as soon as possible. Let's get him together with us for a helpful explanation!" I was desperate.

Otherwise silent, Rick shook his head and whispered, "I want to be there." I'm speculating that his arrival at the death scene was timely, and he needs to question what he saw.

Whew, was I glad! Support was necessary here and Pop's "malarkey" may easily be dismissed to his favorite saying, "The hell you say!" I could hardly wait to prove him wrong. I felt we had consolidated an innocent rapport with Butch the other night and knew in my mind the medium would work with us in a positive manner.

A creep of some kind was haunting our home and stealing things. But why the pitchfork throw? And the shadows outside my bedroom window. I saw them but refused to believe they were real, dismissing them as dry weeds blowing about in the night wind.

And most importantly, there were the stolen goods. I had to make a list for Butch ASAP while things weighed heavily on my mind.

"Rick. I found the door wedge that was missing from my room. Remember how the door slammed shut during my meeting?" Because he was ahead leading the two horses, I was loud.

He looked my way but did not answer.

I rattled on. “But where’s my whistle? Did you see it on Heleena? She had it around her neck while twirling before her disappearance.”

“Why did she have it?” Now he was interested and turned Bullet around to face me.

“She wanted it badly, so I gave it to her but told her that I needed it back. It was a gift to me from Coach Guy Wagner.” Oops!

Rick made a loud throat noise but didn’t look at me as he turned the horse back to the trail.

Clanging horse shoes over trail rocks muffled sounds of teen chatter. The sounds reminded us that we were lucky not to have met Heleena’s fate. But why her? Why did she become enchanted with Coyotee’s incantations and not us? This would be a good Butch question.

A low fog sliding down the mountain ridge began to hinder what little view we had of the distance ahead.

“”Hey, everyone stay close. No one get lost in this fog.” I couldn’t help but be a bit worried. One catastrophe was plenty for the day.

“We’re holding on to a rope,” said Kim Rose always the most vocal of the group, but the best team player.

I turned around to look at our crew. In single file and holding on to a rope, kindergarten style, were Kim, Roy, Jamie, Catora and Coyotee at the end.

“Very smart!”

“Rick’s idea,” said Roy, then referring to the rope and cracking a half smile, “from his saddle.”

Sad but exuberant, they were feeling extra special having seen what no one does on a daily basis….or in a lifetime.

Much later when questioned separately by all the local television stations, their stories were exactly the same, punctuated here and there with exciting adjectives. Popular 'ghosts' stories on the networks honed in on all of it and made celebrities of them from this horrific experience.

Nancy and I clung closely while following Rick who was leading the two horses with the chatty boys in the saddle. When questioned later, they declared to have seen nothing but only heard 'stuff' as they dug treasures from the mysterious shelter of a small cave.

In the low lying cloud, I looked over at Rick who was near Nancy and me and regardless of all we experienced today, decided there was no one handsomer. Tingling with thoughts of later tonight, he and I…alone in the warmth of my bed…or his, I whispered to get his attention. "Hey, is it Gin and Tonic or White Russian tonight?"

He gave me a blank non-committal expression then stared ahead at the trail.

Hhmmm..What was that all about? Did I read a worry?

"We'll have red wine tomorrow night with Butch at your house." Thank you Nancy. What a friend.

Far, far away horns honked from maybe two trucks giving directions for our destination. The circling sounds echoed around careening off boulders and low canyon walls. I was in a stupor with a lost sense of direction and couldn't tell from where they came.

"Rick, are we on the right trail?"

No answer.

After ten minutes and as the sounds faded away I became worried. Momentarily, we all stopped following his lead as he pulled out his Global Positioning System and studied it with a small flashlight.

So this was the reasoning behind his mental anguish.

"We're going in circles," he said.

What a bomb! And if that wasn't enough….
"Hear that!" This from Coyotee as we stood stark still.

A harmonica hummed a slow tune close by.

CHAPTER 44

Our small group griped and stared around at the boulders checking for similarities. The sandy trail and small canyons edging our immediate location didn't give me any feeling of sameness. Sighs were heaviest from Nancy and me. Actually they were more like moans.

"What? Going in a circle? How can you tell?" I was dumfounded and feeling the tiredness that saps one's body after a day of stressful adventure. My shoulders drooped and I yawned loudly. I wanted to go to bed. Nancy too was looking terribly frayed at the edges. Her hood was crooked and one ear was sticking out. Red hair whipped around her face, stuck there by the relentless drizzle. She slouched and I started my nervous giggle. What other problems await us before the day is over?

Of course the teens were bouncing and could have danced all night if commissioned.

"How can you tell that we're going in a circle?" I was desperate.

Rick didn't answer but tried his cell again and the other contraption. Nothing. I could tell by his blank stare.

Because of tiredness, I was too loud and whiney. It was a challenge for Rick who simply pointed ahead to our right towards a group of large rocks lined prolifically with Catsclaw and shadowed by a bushy Mesquite. There was a trail, our trail that I now recognized by the shape of the double pointed boulder at its edge. No desert boulder is exactly the same. Each has a pointed wedge, a tilted round corner, a specific lean or recognizable niche…almost like a man made carving.

"That's where I rode from," said Coyotee suddenly in the know. "Down below is Massacre Grounds where I first saw all you guys."

He slipped away from our group and with great animation pointed here and there where dim noises now echoed around us sporadically. Helicopters, honking horns, distant voices and the occasional clopping of horse shoes connecting with trail rocks seemed ghostly in the misty fog and darkening day.

We discussed the fact that Wranglers Dick and Jack were way ahead of us with the major group and also familiar with the trail that led to the bus. "When they reconnoiter with the bus, they'll realize that we're not following them and will send someone for us." Again I was loud with fake bravery, losing confidence by the minute.

"This low lying cloud might soon shift and we'll have a break!" Rick said gently. And then totally out of character, "Or we'll have to bed her tonight with the ghosts." He ducked his head and did not look at me. I can read him like a book, or so I think.

"Oh no!"

"No, no, no!"

"You didn't see what we saw." Everyone talked at once.

We were one frightened bunch.

It was Roy who caused us to tremble even more when he said with a loud whisper. "There's something or someone evil at Massacre Grounds."

Silence.

"Who shot Miss Dunkin?" Jamie Mink still scared hugged Roy's entire arm.

"How did the spear disappear?" Kim would not be out done. Her voice raised a notch.

"It's Five o'clock," I said after looking at my watch, thankful for the glowing letters in the darkening night so typical for short December days. "We're supposed to be at the bus."

"Thankfully, the bus won't leave without us," Nancy added.

We bunched closely together. In the thickness of the shifting fog, visibility was only twelve feet in front. Immobile as we were, dampness began to swirl around my legs and I shivered from a combination of cold and fright.

"We need to move," I said stomping in place. This is getting serious.

Rick said nothing but kept looking upward at the dark sky and his GPS. Forget the tracker he had hidden in the whistle, or so he told me. It was a gonner! And how did he get that tracker in there in the first place? Hmmm.

"Hah! I found my mistake. Let's move out."

With confidence we started trudging ahead following his lead.

"Thank goodness the rattlesnakes are not out!" This from Nancy was a positive…which we badly need.

Still, I had my doubts. How could he lead us out of this maze in the darkness. Then….

"Flashlights anyone?" Rick had three which he retrieved from his saddle pack. He kept one and passed back the other two to the teens and especially to Coyotee who had decided to take the rear. Roy in the middle handled one.

"If someone's after us, he'll have to go through me," Coyotee said while shining the light behind him in a whirl.

The two freshman boys sitting in the saddles were too quiet.

"Hey! You boys ok?"

"We want to go back," said one.

"Yeah! There's more stuff there. I know it," said the other.

"Sign up next year," I said hiding my fear from this not so great adventure. *ONCE YOU GET LOST, YOU WILL NEVER BE FOUND,* weighed heavily on my mind this instant. Not only did I doubt Rick's expertise at this moment, but the never ending sounds of the night added to my fright. Also, thinking about the old prospector who stole my bracelet a few nights ago at Tumbleweeds, discouraged my confidence even more while trudging along. Was he a GHOST? How could the bracelet appear in the small cave matted with hard dirt?? And why didn't Heleena re-appear with the whistle that was around her neck? Where did it go? Quietly, my mind was a roaring engine seeking answers to all the details.

The trail narrowed to single-file with Rick leading the front horse. Because of the reins held loosely, the second horse followed with head lowered, occasionally bumping its muzzle on the one ahead.

I was next and almost felt like hanging on the horse's tail for guidance. "Hey Nance, shine your phone on the trail."

"Of course! Why didn't I think of that?" The bright light from the cell re-kindled our confidence as we encountered a meandering path which seemed to wave uphill and down.

Rick's confidence was back. "The trail widens ahead. When we come to the bend in the trail, we'll stop and re-access our route. We're very close." Then when he suggested that Nancy and I could ride the horses and the two boys could walk, we declined saying that walking kept us warm.

Our lights sharpened the images along the trail as we tried to keep Jojoba and Brittle Bushes from scratching against our legs. Sounds of lizards, pack rats and other creatures of the night kept us entertained and Roy and Coyotee tried to find them with their lights.

The sky was never so black…no hint of a moon or stars. Because of this, we over stepped, occasionally bumping the person in front. Hand held lighting became slivers of beam in the oppressive darkness.

Soon there was too much silence. I worried and said, "Everyone chatter a bit. Be responsible for the person in front of you."

Suddenly Coyotee stopped and shined the flashlight behind him on the trail and up the boulders as far as it would go in the mist. "Shhh," he shouted.

We all stopped. Even the horses raised their heads and twitched their ears in both directions listening.

Unmistakably, we heard the harmonica again but this time, close by.

"He's following us!" Roy's words were a dagger.

Of course at the same time, a mountain lion cried far-far away sounding like a child's scream.

"That's a mountain lion," Coyotee quickly assured everyone. "Sounds like a person sometimes."

"And the harmonica?" Nancy was startled.

Silence.

Now everyone waved their lights on the trail behind us…up canyon walls…through bushes and the muddy trail. The eerie beams landed short in the fog. Shining through the white puffs of low clouds was useless.

Rick assured us that the big cat wouldn't attack and we moved on, silently listening to the ever present "surround-sound" as creatures of the night became predators. We were in their territory. Nevertheless, we worried about every shuffling noise, and especially the harmonica.

Rick stopped our line, and viewed his GPS with his flashlight. "This is where we need to proceed straight ahead on the trail and not turn to the right as we did thirty minutes ago when we circled back."

Knowing we were extra touchy, his explanation was a welcoming change from his usual one word answer to everything.

All the lights searched for the trail as we stopped and gawked.

"What trail?" I could see only thickets of bushes in the landscape ahead.

Rick continued talking. "The bushes buffer the trail like a screen, especially at night. It's there and will lead us out of the mountains and down to the trucks and the others." He pointed his flashlight on a worn, very narrow path.

Hell broke out at once! Jamie Mink's blood-curdling scream joined Nancy's cell phone toning 'Silent Night'.

"My cell works."

"Someone pushed me and its pulling my hair!" Trying to pull away from a Catsclaw bush only tangled her long blond hair more until finally a piece of twig broke away from the bush knotting a smothering wad of hair, twisting knots descending dangerously down her forehead.

"Hold still!" Coyote gave his light to Catora to shine on Jamie's head while he broke a piece of the angry twig with his knife and gloved hand. "We'll get it off in a minute."

"Stop screaming! You simply brushed against a tall Catsclaw," said Kim, always so matter-of-fact.

"No!" Jamie winced as Coyotee gently pulled away at the tangled mess. "I was pushed."

"I was right behind you and saw no one near. You must have stumbled." Catora stared blankly around at the blackness now obscuring everything.

The distant harmonica was louder than usual.

"Hey," yelled Roy. "We're tired of that old tune. QUIET!"

It stopped.

"Sorry," Coyotee said to Jamie Mink. "I'm going to have to cut this twig out with a lot of hair or it'll turn your neck into mince meat." With his knife he sliced a handful of strands. "Gone," he said and raked his fingers through her hair in case more twigs remained. "Keep your hood up," he reminded her.

Our immobile line watched Rick who had not moved an inch while studying his GPS.

Although Nancy's phone rang a song a minute ago, it now had no service as she tried over and over again while illuminating Rick's hands. Shadows under his eyes presented a ghostly stare of black while he worked the GPS patiently.

"What's up?" I took the reins from the grip of one of his hands as the two boys sat quietly. One had Rick's flashlight and was playfully waving it around at distant cactus, catching the iridescent pupils of critters. A red wing hawk flew away when caught with the flash.

The two horses stood chomping on their bits with boredom, deaf ears accustomed to the noise of predators.

"Something's terribly wrong." Rick's whisper was a shout to our ears as my heart beat loudly and my mouth went dry.

"It's off and not taking any directions."

The three girls and Nancy and I were silent…more like numb with ideas while Roy and Coyotee stepped forward.

Coyotee asked, "Do these work on cloudy dark nights?"

Quietly, Rick shook his head yes while not looking up. "Should."

Roy dagger stabbed us one more time with his slow motion utterance of the un-predictable. "The GPS is being controlled by the malevolent GHOST who seems to be following us."

"What? How do you know such stuff?" I was both angry and frightened of the unbelievable.

And then here came the surprising proof. "My uncle is Butch Gardner, a Medium who lives in Cave Creek. He's a Paranormal consultant."

Nancy and I gasped.

Even Rick stopped and looked at him, silently, totally unreadable.

"He's my neighbor," Nancy blurted to all of us. "And he IS very good with the Paranormal."

Roy continued, "I'll bet you the GHOST is using one of us as a receptor, like ESP, you know, extra sensory perception. Through ONE OF US, he is controlling the GPS."

My panic attack! I was the guilty one. It had to be me! I decided to keep my mind blank, unreadable---should be a cinch. We were all dead silent. I could see Roy's clear blue eyes in the black of the night as he spoke.

Nervously, we shuffled closely and flashed our accumulated lights all around us for a full minute.

"Enough! I have a plan." Robustly loud and clear, Rick made his point. He reached up, helped the freshman boy off Bullet, and got on the horse. "Ok, come back up." He grabbed the boy's hand after he put his foot in the stirrup, and pulled him up behind the saddle. "Hold on to these leather saddle straps;" he showed him where they were located.

"If everyone can follow the lead of these two horses, we're walking out of here." He flashed his light at our feet and the trail we were to use. "Coyotee, you keep a light at the tail, and Kim, you keep one in the middle." Next, he traded his flashlight for Nancy's phone. "I'll keep trying to reach someone. In the meantime, this intelligent, well traveled horse will lead us to the others." He gave Bullet a loose reign and clicked a signal.

The harmonica played a fast irritating tune close by.

"Here, you can have a new toy." Surprisingly, Rick flung the GPS as far in the darkness as possible, its descent clattering among rocks somewhere.

CHAPTER 45

Rick loosened the reins to give the horse its head, put his hands on the saddle horn and made a clicking noise while spurring Bullet forward. Surprising all of us, the horse did a quick turn to the right which led uphill. "Hopefully, we are heading towards the trucks or horse trailers that are parked at the end of First Water Road," said Rick.

"We entered this area from the Dutchman's Trail," I said. "For sure these horses know the way."

Coyotee to the rescue. "Horses have an extra sense of smell and hearing. See his ears twitching forward and back. Those are his antennas." He flashed the light on the horses head. "And this horse is a leader, not a follower."

These facts we horse people knew, but hearing it from Coyotee, AkA the Black Rider, was the cement.

The drizzle had changed to a light rain which didn't dampen our spirits. The two horses' persistent clomping forward assured us they would rescue us from this maze. We tightened the snaps on our yellow slickers and pulled our hoods down from forehead towards noses. With eyes on the trail, we trudged forward, only occasionally looking up at the horses' tail ends before us.

"Everyone Ok?" Rick called out every ten minutes. After we answered, the glow from Nancy's phone swept over us as he checked to be sure.

Then it dawned on me. "Rick, where are your two phones, the satellite and cell?"

"Stolen from my saddle bag."

An answer I did not want to hear.

Nancy's phone rang again shutting off the light beam as it echoed sharply in the night throwing us temporarily into semi-darkness; the other two flashlights seemed dim in comparison. Soon, the light re-appeared. For the next ten minutes, this scenario repeated at intervals of thirty seconds.

"Someone is trying to connect with us," said Kim.

"And using my lost phone," said Rick.

"The GHOST is following us," said Kim as she reached for Roy's one loose hand. Jamie was now holding the other.

The damn harmonica was louder than ever.

Coyotee put his arm around Catora's waist to calm her shakiness.

Nancy and I weaved elbows together.

"He's harmless," said Roy. "He just wants us out of here. The next time the phone rings, don't answer."

"Right!" Rick's acknowledgement was quick and succinct. "Let's move."

The woodland soon changed to a bareness of desert and before we knew it, the Dutchman's Trail was before us. Walking was less cumbersome on the flat, well worn surface of the trail, wide enough for emergency vehicles. We were on the trail heading northwest to the Superstition Wilderness boundary and our ultimate destination, the First Water Horse Trailhead, when suddenly Rick's horse stopped and did a quick side step.

"He heard something," said Rick.

Bullet's head was held high and it seemed to stand motionless like a statue for at least ten seconds.

Next, Bullet did the welcoming whinny, a positive sign between these social creatures.

"Horses are coming," said Nancy.

Rick shined his light forward and waved.

Soon, around a bend in the darkness were four specks of lights about a quarter mile away and the distant clomping of horse shoes on rocks.

Bullet whinnied again and we moved forward. Soaked, tired, hungry and thoroughly spooked, we were hopeful.

CHAPTER 46

From a distance, 'chopper lights descended in and out of the canyons like flares hovering over and around the death scene at Massacre Grounds. All media from the Valley were gobbling every morsel of information they could glean from those at the scene. However, news agencies gathering info are second to the lightning bolt power of teen gossip, and by now every student at Blakely High and every person in the town of Cave Creek will have some "kind" of news before we even get to the bus.

Fortunately, we were gone from that area but knew we would be grilled extensively in the near future. For now, our rescued destination was hopefully within our grasps. This was our main issue.

Bullet whinnied with all ears forward and a strong desire to prance and move faster; this would only leave us walkers running to stay together. Rick spun the horse around in a circle every once in a while for calmness and to stay with our string.

We walked faster now carefully watching our footing. With unbelievable left-over adrenalin, we sloshed through rivulets of rain water annexing the widening trail about every twenty feet.

Mountain trails are like above ground tree roots with crooked fingers rolling and pivoting in mass directions. A tractor-bladed-smooth-trail will lasts only until the next big rain after which dirt flushes down and out from the heavier sand, sending all into deep washes. Seasonally, rock edged trails are maintained by Scouts, or there would be none.

Our mini lights hit the rain washed main trail and Rick waited for us to cross the more treacherous areas with the light from Nancy's phone.

Now the heavy rain had changed again to a drizzle and our fast pace kept us warm. Yet, this last half mile seemed to be two or three. Even under my long yellow slicker, my pants stuck to my legs and everywhere else like glue. I imagined that at any time now my soaked skin would peel away from muscle. And of course, I had to verbalize my discomfort.

"My pants are glued to my skin!"

We girls giggled in recognition.

The boys didn't.

Somehow, we still clung tightly to our lead rope for security, and I felt the occasional pull by someone stumbling behind me.

We were so ready to reconnoiter with the distant four lights coming towards us. The mystery silenced us a bit and we played guessing games as to whom they belonged.

Rick said, "It's probably the liveried staff of Wranglers. The lights tend to bobble like on a horse."

Kim Rose said it was Dixie Hoot ..."coming to show us what she bought while shopping."

"Nope! It's the GHOST multiplying to trick us!" From Roy, this was not funny.

Rapport was good considering our horrendous experience.

Nancy's phone toned "Silent Night." Finally there's cell service and the phone was on speaker mode.

"Hey, wave your lights so we can see you!" Colt's voice was enlightening. "There's so much confusion all over this mountain, we can't tell where you are."

Rick answered. "I think we're riding toward you. Are you one of four?"

"That's a positive. The three Wranglers and I are riding toward you----maybe."

Rick waved the phone in his hand a wide angle and we copied with our flashlights.

"What did he mean by 'maybe'?" My group supported the question with a tinge of insecurity.

"Yeah!"

Looking up at the lights rather than down on the trail, I stumbled and fell on my knees while still clinging to the rope. Like a roller coaster of attached cars, Nancy and Jamie went down with me. Roy had grabbed Kim and kept the tail end from tumbling. My one hand fell on a pile of loose rocks and I placed a chunky one in the vest pocket under my slicker. "I'm keeping one for a souvenir," I said trying to be jolly in my stupor. Nancy and Jamie recovered quickly and we moved on.

"Whew! That was a surprise awakening." Nancy brushed mud off Jamie's knees and all was fine due to our eagerness to meet the advancing lighted group. Muddy knees were nothing compared to our previous experiences.

The group ahead did the half circle wave in answer to ours every now and then.

Minutes seemed like hours in our anxiety; the lights reminded me of airplanes coming in for a landing---so close, but yet so far away, seemingly taking forever.

Soon we were in yelling distance.

"All of you together?" This from Colt.

"Yup, the original—minus one—and plus one," said Rick sadly while turning Bullet around to check our line again.

"What? Minus one, plus one?"

"Coyotee, our hero!" This from Catora brought forward too many questions from the new group.

"What happened?"

"Hero? How come?"

"Ya'll make it out of Massacre Grounds alive?"

Pete's words were daggers in the dreary night and no one was in the mood to explain.

"What took you so long?" Colt asked. "We expected you a couple hours ago."

Rick readjusted his hat under the yellow hood and sighed. "We took the scenic route, circling a couple times."

"Where's your GPS?"

"Long story." Rick was now the Del Rio I knew so well; abruptness was his trademark; short and commanding was his reply as he clicked his heels to hurry on.

At this, the Wranglers offered their horses to the walkers for a break, but no one wanted to change.

"How much further?" Jamie Mink asked.

"A short quarter mile," said Dick.

Colt phoned a few details to Coach Guy Wagner who had stayed back by the two trucks to set up a lead line for gathering the horses, the few that remained. They learned later that all the horses made it to the stables including Coyotee's which he needed to retrieve with his small trailer. Catora decided to travel back to Cave Creek with him when possible.

In the glow of our circle of lights, we caught sight of something arching in the sky towards us.

In a quick movement, Rick stood in the stirrups, extended an arm and grabbed a raw looking, freshly hewed spear.

"Oh my God!" We gasped in unison and spit out fearful expletives.

"Is that THE spear?" Nancy's shocking reaction spoke for all of us.

"Throw it back; it's evil." Coyotee yelled in fright. "It might draw you back into the past."

Shaking his head a negative, Rick broke the spear in half on the saddle horn and palming the two halves in his raised left fist shouted into the night, "No more!"

With the four newcomers leading us and Rick with the freshman boys now in the back riding behind Coyotee, we swiftly headed towards our destination, totally unaware of the army of people and panorama of different groups waiting for us at the end.

CHAPTER 47

The quarter mile seemed short considering our previous jaunt over crooked and winding trails that led us astray. For entertainment, the entire mountain exploded like a fourth of July fireworks---noisy, loud, and annoying. All experts looking for answers.

Who are these groups? It looked like a small town gone wild and too close for comfort. Far off in the distance a thousand lights flooded the bus arena. And, this is where we are headed.

Lucky for us the two lone trucks are near a vacant clearing some distance away from it all where a few horses had been detained on tie-down by Coach Wagner, and there wasn't a flood of people. Obviously, groups had been told to stay back by the bus at a specified area to keep from advancing on us. We were soon to learn our popularity.

As we approached, the four B's came toward us with helpful assistance. Shieter was not with Blake at this time but back at the bus bathing in popularity---or was it notoriety?

We hugged. Silence was heavy.

Horses were tied to a horizontal rope until ready to load into trailers. None shuffled about in their tiredness. Yellow slickers were taken off and thrown in the back of the truck that was to remain with the horses. I wish we could shed our worries as easily.

The teens climbed into the truck bed with sighs of relief. It had been a short journey turned long. Proud were we for survival as we sighed deeply and rested our weary bodies.

Actually, I speak for myself and possibly Nancy because the teens were still exuberant with excitement when they hopped into the truck bed in a split second like rabbits, totally refreshed.

I looked over at Nancy and whispered, "Amazing!"

She rolled her eyes and whimpered a sigh.

Guy Wagner looked drenched but more rested than our gang when he hunkered out of a double cab truck. Since coaches tend to weather all environments, he looked solid and ready to be of assistance.

We must have looked horribly be-draggled because everyone was overly helpful. Bing and Brad tied one horse to the horizontal rope while Bob and Blake hurriedly took the other from Rick and secured it. Guy checked that the teens were seated down properly in the cab and not sitting on the edge like chickens. Colt courteously opened the doors for all of us, the wearisome lot.

Never was I more content then when I slid into the back seat between Guy and Rick. Pete, Nancy and Colt sat in the front.

Our truck was un-hooked from its horse trailer for the ride back to the bus, and as previously planned, Dick and Jack would stay with the other truck trailer hook-up while Pete delivered all of us. On his return, they would hurry back to the stables.

With tail gate down and assistance from the teens, the four B's climbed into the bed of the pickup for the last ride of this glorious expedition. They had been quiet, but I knew in my own mind that the Family Farm would be at our house for many nights of margaritas, nachos, trading stories and asking questions.

Pete drove his 4-wheel truck about five miles an hour sliding and sloshing through mud and over small streams.

No one talked. We were eerily quiet and I'm sure it was from tiredness and fear of the mob ahead. What did they already know? What would we tell them? What would they believe? A slow steady rain splattered the windshield as the rhythm of the wipers filled the void.

I sat with my hands clubbed between my knees feeling totally whipped, yet content encased between two super men. Rick's arm squeezed me close and we crushed together in one ball.

Guy's worried gaze looked out the window at the encroaching lights. "What in hell?"

The broken spear lay under Rick's booted feet.

Coop the bus driver phoned Nancy's cell to relay the message that Coyotee's mom was more than half way here. "Seems the kids told her that he was here at the mountain," he said, "and he needs to wait for her."

"Good plan," said Nancy before signing off. She too hugged closely to Colt who had his arm around her shoulder and kept whispering to her concerning her comfort.

Then Pete began, ranting and raving out of his reverie. "Someone needs to tan his hide."

"Or hers," added Colt angrily.

Although we should have been content with our warm comfort and the solitude of the cab, we were still weary, emotionally spent with the unbelievable actions of the day and the sadness for the loss of Heleena. We itched for answers.

"I'm sure it was a man," I said abruptly with confidence. "I saw him twice."

Pete intervened. "I ain't never goin' there agin!" His phone rang as if on cue and he jabbered what sounded like business. "Well you owe these folks some food. Git some pizzas in Apache Junction and have them sent to the bus…a whole lot of 'em. I 'spect these kids are hungry."

"Pete," began Rick, "the I'D's. Give Jack and Dick theirs. You've been good troopers." He handed them to Nancy to give to Pete.

"Sorry 'bout earlier." Pete put the three driver's licenses in his vest pocket.

I gave Rick the look. What the heck was that all about? Before I got a word out, he shook his head for me not to go there now. O.K! I'm thinking that he has a story to tell me tonight. If we can stay awake long enough.

Guy, who had been silent this entire time said, "We need a round table discussion with just a few of us. I need to be in the know."

"With Butch," I said, " and our particular line of riders."

"Who's Butch?" Guy asked.

"A paranormal expert."

"My neighbor," added Nancy.

"Roy's uncle," I continued sporadically.

"Complicated." One word from Rick said it all.

"Nancy and I'll make a list," I said quietly.

We felt the truck bob as the seven teens jumped out. The tail gate was lowered and the four B's gently slithered off, helping each other.

"Lordy!" From Pete, this was an understatement as we surveyed the craziness that was going on in front but soon to surround us. The bus was stationed about fifty yards away with the door barely cracked for the new arrivals. The students ran for the door and entered seconds before the door was shut. This tells me a lot.

The four B's shuffled about enjoying the excitement.

Various kinds of on-lookers were stunned by the teens' swiftness out of the truck bed and became more demanding. A group of parents were kept at bay by Shieter with rules of, "No one can enter the bus. District's orders." Several were pounding on the bus while talking to their kids who had opened windows an inch. A minivan of nosy town gossipers arrived to add to the ruckus. They unloaded much too quickly.

Spot lights turned darkness into day where two local media-vans were parked close to the bus cutting off its route out of the parking lot. Coop will have to honk his way out.

I recognized fashionable media personalities reporting to cameras trying to explain the happenings. Of course there would be nothing but questions and allegations at this point. Hopefully, they did not have the gall to question students who would be quite inventive and creative about what they thought they saw. Actually, I don't really know myself how many of them saw what we witnessed. Did some of them arrive after she appeared out of nowhere? Did they see her get shot? Most of all, I need to question Rick thoroughly tonight, in the still of the bedroom; exactly what did he see?

I clicked off a count of eleven police vehicles with strobe lights turning from red to blue. Colorful uniforms were milling about in every direction.

We sat there silently with doors locked and windows slightly cracked. We winced as the rotary sounds of helicopters vibrated above our cab annoyingly close.

Soon, two reporters from different stations, one on each side of the truck, tapped their microphones on the glass windows aggressively.

We cringed.

Colt said with his hand on the door handle, "On the count of three!"

CHAPTER 48

"One-two-three!"

Our four doors swung wide too aggressively as we unwillingly stepped out to join the chaos and rabid din of noise brought on by a throng of people equal to that of a football game gone wild.

Pete's door knocked a robust, moustached man on his rear as the reporter tried to back out of the way quickly but stepped in a soft mound of unstable mud.

'You ain't supposed to tap a driver's window with that weapon." Pete wagged his finger at the muddy reporter who sat there thumping his mud soaked microphone on his chest. Pete stepped over him and tried to move away from a mob of advancing reporters right on his heels. In doing so, he slipped on a loose muddy rock and inadvertently reached out to the closest person next to him, a glamorous reporter, and pulled her down on top, chest to chest. He grinned. She didn't. Two others followed the foray and it was a cold, muddy mess.

"Cripes! I ain't had this much fun since Halloween," Pete cackled while collecting his mud covered hat and thumping it against his side; he was able to crawl out of the mess on his hands and knees. The unlucky ones were not so happy while helping each other get out of the muck but slipping back in as it became wetter.

Pete quickly got to the pickup and backed away slowly, honking all the while to disperse the crowd. He did a giant wave as he saw us bolting.

On our run to the bus, everything blurred around me, but I was thrilled to catch the carnival of events surrounding Pete.

Since Colt was in his cop uniform, no one seemed to mess with him and he was able to shuffle Nancy over to the door of the bus. Coop was ready---a swift open and shut of the handle let her in. As he tried to slam it shut, a belligerent bystander from town who was there for the excitement, had one hand in the door casing, and a foot on the step.

Coop was now the Captain of the Ship. "Out! Nobody's allowed on this bus. District's orders!"

Sounded official to me! I'll have to use it periodically to make it through the night.

Some over-protective parents had made the one hour drive to the Superstitions to see their teen in person, even though they had learned via the teen network that no student was injured. These same parents were discontent as they yelled to their teen through lowered bus windows cracked a few inches because they wanted their demands met.

"Yakkity-yak," didn't work because teens did not want to ride home with insistent parents who were deranged with the chaos. Shieter stepped in on behalf of the students and suggested that they follow the bus back to the school.

"District's orders!" His second usage made it official.

Cops of two different suits from two different counties due to the colossal acreage of the Superstitions, were moving traffic. Maricopa and Pinal Sheriffs' Departments supported each other because of the popularity of the massive mountain and the blunders of loonies wandering around lost while looking for gold.

I locked elbows with Guy and Rick as we ducked low hoping no sharp eye would comment about the broken spear Rick clutched. They hadn't heard that part. Rick didn't even know it all; he just knew it was an important piece of the larger puzzle.

Bright lights hurt my eyes as a microphone was shoved in my face by the same person who had been tapping on our truck window when we arrived. I cringed as a tall brunette blocked my route and shouted so everyone could hear her important question.

"How many people were shot? Do you have a count?" She wildly looked around at others as she spoke, and I realized the reason for her concern was a mini blonde wearing bright red holiday lipstick who shoved her aside with a sharp elbow to the ribs. They tangled, grabbed mics from each other and fell to their knees….not worried about the mud.

I kept Rick and Guy to myself, and as we hurried away they shouted where they now sat, "Tell us how many students were hurt by the stampede." They crawled toward us. "We heard that rider-less horses came running back to the stable."

Turning around and looking back at their mascara smeared faces I casually asked them, "Where's the Principal? Ask him! He's the authority." What an escape. I cleverly kept my voice sounding normal while being sarcastic. Takes talent. Ask any teacher.

There he was, surrounded by parents seeking his attention, all bathing in his improvised aura, touching him on the shoulder while he strutted about with fictionalized information for his audience. Re-arranging his bolo tie and flicking mud off his damp jacket, he announced with a positive air, "We heard no gun shots. We think that she slipped in the mud and fell on a stick, piercing her heart." He muffled this last part in a clandestine effort of secrecy. Believable? The group shook their heads with acceptance of this false information and sadly clicked their tongues with remorse. What a politician!

At this point, Rick and Guy lifted me off my feet to move on and I peddled wind. I was enjoying the entertainment since nobody recognized me hidden between two super men. Still hooked together at the elbows, we sandwiched our way toward the bus while ducking our heads shunning the reporters and all.

Coop opened the doors just in time as another shifting eye reporter hurried in our direction, notebook in one hand and microphone in the other. Guy jumped on a door step first and pulled me with him. Rick wasn't so lucky. The aggressive, fully bearded reporter wrestled his arm away from me and catching him off balance, physically yanked him away before he could put his foot on the step.

Rick grabbed the man by the throat just as the door closed and Colt's cell loudly rang. Through the open window Colt yelled, "Tom Mix wants to speak to the sheriff in charge of the ride!"

"Don't go away!" Rick demanded of the bearded reporter as he threw him loose. He might as well have been talking to a puppy. The guy wimped away and we never saw him the remainder of the night.

Rick walked away from the crowd as he talked to Tom Mix, the main sheriff from Apache Junction.

I settled back in my seat and realized that both Rick and Guy knew nothing about our total experience. I also knew that their doubts would equal their impatience. Rick saw some of the events and I'll have to question him tonight.

The bus was ready to roll. We were waiting for pizzas and of course Rick to get back on the bus so we could take off. Coyotee and Catora were waiting inside the bus for his mother to arrive; then the three would drive to his truck and trailer to gather his black horse and travel home.

No way in hell would we let one of the teens out of the bus in this chaos; they were content with the warmth of the humming bus, the darkness of the night, and especially the sound of rain splattering on windows for special affect. Some of the kids slept while others chatted quietly. No interior lights were on and the serenity of the scene lulled many to sleep. The brightness of outdoor lights was enough to visually read a newspaper.

We adults on the bus were quiet. All had been told that each would be included in a serious discussion with Butch when we would discuss all the details of Heleena's demise. Nancy was busy outlining the sequence of events on a note pad which she would periodically show me for approval. Reading over her shoulder as she wrote, Colt was astounded and quietly shook his head with shock of the unknown.

Dixie and Cloud were catering to our every piece of comfort.

"Do you need my pillow?" Dixie tried to hand me a soft crocheted piece that she had been cuddling next to her large chest for security.

Cloud tried to pour me a small cup of coffee from his thermos. "It's still hot, believe it or not!"

Coach Guy Wagner had sunk in his seat with Becky Painter asleep on his shoulder. They were out!

Coop, the Captain of the Ship, was busy punching and scrolling on his I-Pad. For sure, like he had said before, this was not his first rodeo.

After fifteen minutes of peace and quiet, the door was opened for Rick, Coyotee's mom, and the pizza man. The bus lights were turned on and pizza was passed around like presents under a tree. We never realized the depth of our hunger. Pizza boxes were the cue for the four B's to awaken and get busy. They were overly helpful, making sure everyone got many pieces and then helped pass around black bags for clean-up.

Rick's face looked drawn and his mouth drooped. Never had I seen him so distraught. He slunk into the aisle seat next to me where we sat in the very front behind the bus driver. Rain softly splattered on the window next to my shoulder. For now, Mrs. Raintree had joined Coyotee and Catora a few seats back for some pizza.

"Her body is still there," Rick said quietly to the few of us in the front seats. Group One riders had settled close to us and listened in. "They can't locate any next of kin in their data base and have exhausted their search."

"She should have an emergency contact person on file at the school," I said.

"The Superintendent has been checking all records. So far, nothing."

Depression set in among us as I looked around. At least two hours had passed since we had left the scene and the thought of her lying face down in rain and mud, all this time, made me shiver.

Rick continued, "Seems there is a time line for next of kin to be contacted before the body can be moved. If no one can be immediately contacted, her body will be sent to a local mortuary."

The kids in our group knew nothing about her, which was unusual since they know every detail about each person on campus.

"She never mentioned anything about her personal life," offered Jamie Mink. They mumbled and exchanged whisperings among themselves and kept shaking their heads.

After Catora got permission from her parents to ride back to the school with Coyotee and his mom, the bus was ready to leave. This had been the last detail before rolling out. They had been huddling closely, whispering. For sure, they would have much to talk about. Mrs. Raintree had been brought to the bus by a relative, so now she could ride back to the school with her son.

With the brief opening of the doors, the sound of "Deck the Halls with Boughs of Holly" filtered in as the three scooted out and swiftly disappeared to a waiting truck. An unbelievable group of Christmas carolers were singing loudly, totally unaware of what had happened out on the desert. They were intrigued with the lights and thought this was a holiday festival of some sort.

I wish it had been.

Both Dixie Hoot and Cloud bombarded us with fifty questions as they silently whispered about the happenings. Every time they looked at Guy or Rick for answers, the two shrugged a negative. "We rode in three separate groups. Their group was about one hour ahead of our middle group due to miss-haps with the students," said Rick.

Guy, who had only been resting instead of sleeping, offered more. "And our last string was stopped numerous times by Shieter who decided to get off his horse and lead it. This slowed down our group considerably. We really expected no problems with this procedure until horses got away and ran back to the stables."

Every student around us was searching for answers, and when we talked, they were all ears. I looked at them and shrugged, "We are trying to figure it out for ourselves."

Dixie and Cloud both wanted to know how the horses got away. "Weren't they secured?"

"Yes and no." I said. "But it all started when we heard gun shots coming from another area of the mountain."

This opened a new can of worms. "Wow! This really is complicated," I whined to Rick now that I remembered having heard those other shots.

"Nancy, make note of that." She had been busy writing all this time.

"Done!" she said.

Coop, who had been half listening while punching away on his I-Pad, got up from his seat and asked the question a little too loudly in the humming bus, "What really happened to Heleena?" He looked at each of us searching for an answer.

Now the bus was too quiet as eyes and ears were focused up front. I was in no mood to try and explain the unexplainable.

"Kim, your turn." I looked back and focused on her, the one with the best rapport among her comrades.

"She disappeared, than re-appeared!" Kim was loud and quick.

"How did she do that?" Someone asked.

"She disappeared in front of our eyes, than re-appeared as she got shot and fell face down." Kim continued so matter-of-fact, that no one wanted to contest it.

"We saw it. We were right there," said Jamie.

"It happened right after the Apache appeared, and then disappeared," added Roy.

"WHAT!" Everyone was annoyingly loud as they repeated the word "Apache" multiple times.

My neck started to hurt because I had been clenching my teeth together too tightly while unknowingly breathing gulps of air through them. I waved my head side to side to relieve the stress.

"Coop, start the bus. Let's get out of here!"

Dixie and Cloud had made the official count and we started to pull away with the assistance of a Sheriff's Deputy securing the area and waving us through the crowd.

I threaded my arm around Rick's and rested my head on his shoulder.

My eyes would not close.

CHAPTER 49

The bus ride back to the school was too short. The pizza, the warmth, the splattering of rain, the rocking of the bus, but most of all the tiredness, vaccinated the entirety of us occupants asleep. Not a whisper was heard.

Shock came when Coop opened the bus door and parents stomped in to awaken sleepy kids. We adults in the front sat quietly until all others stumbled out, the hardy teens clutching pillows reverting back to childhood.

Each of the four B's had a quip before dragging down the steps.

Bing pointed out, "Include us in the Butch discussion."

"Never had so much fun since my divorce thirty years ago," Bob whispered with a wink.

"Include us in your next shindig," said Brad with a smile.

"We love ghosts!" Blake jiggled his car keys in my face as he stepped out.

"See you soon!" We all mumbled practically in unison and at the same time, started planning our next date, the important one with Butch, the Medium.

****

It was at this time while driving home with Rick at one in the morning that my brain numbed, depression settled in, and I felt alone as I sat in the front seat of Rick's Ford 350, hugging myself for comfort.

"Let it go for the night!" Rick wearily glanced my way and I realized he was as fatigued as I. The slow desert rain dancing on the windshield offered the only consolation for the moment.

We had been following Dixie home. She now swiftly parked and hurried in the kitchen door where Pop stood hovering by the light, hands in the pockets of a frayed at the knees robe. She grabbed him by the shoulder and hurried him reluctantly away allowing us privacy. For our welcoming, he had thrown a web of colored lights on a Jojoba bush nearby the patio and its radiance lightened the moment.

"I suppose I'm staying here tonight?" Rick drooped a pitiful look my way with his hand on the door handle. "My place or yours?"

"Here of course."

Did he hear me? The next thing I knew he was helping me undress where we sat helping each other, both exhausted seated at the foot of my bed. We stripped to the nude with all damp and muddy belongings landing on an old sheet strategically spread on the floor.

"Where did that come from?" I asked.

"Your linen closet."

Someone should marry the guy.

Last, he hung his hat on the special horse shoe jutting out of the wall by my bed.

"My rock." I found it in my jacket pocket and placed it in the glass bowl containing my rock collection from my hikes here and there.

"Sierra Club's gonna come after you for your rock collecting." Rick followed this with his only smile of the day.

"It's only a pebble!"

We pulled back the brown soft coverlet and quickly fell between cool sheets, each hugging a pillow.

Rick babbled the last words of the lost night as I curled one leg over his.

"Someone got killed on my watch. Tom Mix wants to meet with us at noon today."

****

Sunday was a day to remember. It seems the smell of bacon floated through the walls long before we arose, and this was the good part. Our showers were quick and serious, no time for fun, after which we met Pop and Dixie at the breakfast table around nine-thirty. They had already eaten hours ago but kept a large vegetable omelet in a lidded skillet on low, waiting. A carafe of fresh hot coffee sat on a tray accompanied by a small creamer and matching bowl of sugar cubes. Pop didn't mess around.

Nobody talked much. "Pop," I started, "I'll tell you everything later." He knew when to back off with his relentless questions. Comes with being half retired and running a "screaming" bakery.

"Dixie knows nothing," he said as she handed us some hot buttered toast, shrugged her shoulders and shook her head. I knew that he had questioned her all night about happenings. Pop was one person who had to be in the know; so he sat there impatiently thumping his fingers loudly on the wooden round table and rubbing Nellie the Greyhound with his foot where she lay on her back with paws in the air.

"We're heading back out to the Superstitions to meet with Tom Mix and Delilah. It'll be a full day."

"Who's we?" Pop poured half a cup of coffee in his huge brown mug, added two lumps of sugar and while stirring looked up for an answer.

"Just Rick, Nancy and I. When we all meet with Butch Gardner the Medium, we'll include you, the few teens from Group One who saw everything, and a couple others. But, you have to think positive, have an open mind. Remember the sharp, heavy pitchfork that came flying towards you missing by a hair?"

He raised his cup to his lips hiding a recurring fright.

Rick noted that our group meeting with Butch is getting too large.

"I know. But everyone wants to be included as to what exactly happened. This is better than listening to wasted gossip later."

"What about the media?"

"NONE!" I was adamant.

CHAPTER 50

December 23, 2012

We met Tom Mix, Delilah and a coroner at Mix's headquarters, a stuccoed, non-descript building lined with trimmed Brittle Bush ready to flower bright yellow in a couple months. Texas Ranger brush was spotted here and there with its rose-purple flowers absent, although a few lingered from its fall show. Summer lasts forever when no freeze shortens it to winter. This is the norm. Rain from yesterday dripped from an overhang filling a strategically placed dog dish.

The coroner met us at the door because Tom Mix was busy at a filing cabinet shuffling papers. After introductions, chairs were circled close to his massive Oak desk near which two sheriff's caps and a large black western hat hung on a dried Cholla hat tree that reminded me of an old 1940's movie from Pop's massive collection. Matching this were a tall Cholla lamp against a wall and one short brightly lit piece with multiple arms sitting on the edge of his desk. This was the look of the old west.

"Before we head out to Massacre Grounds," he began, "we need to get answers on paper."

Delilah sat close by on his right, dwarfed by his size, with note pad and pen. Hah! After watching facial gestures and little touches from Delilah on his arm as we spoke, I could never have been more content. She would not be drooling over Del Rio. How could I be jealous of Movie-Star-Gorgeous anyway? Subconsciously I adjusted some curls on my head pulling them out of my face. She caught one edge of my mouth curling a piece of a smile and raised a trim eyebrow.

Nancy fetched her big Mary Poppin's bag from the floor and pulled out her bus notes from last night, now attached on a clip board. Her nails looked as raggedy as mine from yesterday's fiasco, but her gorgeous Kelly green sweater, matching long green skirt and knee high boots, stole the show.

The pale white skinny coroner, was a shrink of a man wearing a striped collared shirt that paired well with his narrow shoulders. He scooted next to Nancy, then not to be intimidated by others, he sat listening with his legs crossed at the ankles and one arm hanging over the back of his chair. Regularly, he needed to push his loose black rimmed glasses up on his thin face and spoke only a few words here and there. Considering his expertise and experience with sobbing relatives, less is more. However, since no sobbing relatives have been located, he seemed at peace with himself and liked to eyeball us with his glasses lowered, tired of anchoring them.

"For 'next of kin or other', she simply wrote, 'The English Department', which I assume includes you two." T. Rex began. Rude of me to compare him to T Rex, but it's fitting.

Nancy and I shook our heads up and down, "Yeah!"

"Her remains are at the Apache Junction Mortuary. Do you want to see the body?" He started to push away from his desk.

"Uhh, not yet."

"Uhh, maybe later." My knees became tense.

"Of course we do," said Rick. "Afterward would be fine."

T. Rex sat tall in his chair, relaxed, his two massive hands on the desk top clutching yesterday's rain-wrinkled yellow note pad. His Tom Mix name tag an inch under his sheriff's badge, rose up and down with an occasional shoulder twitch, a dead give-away of hidden secrets. At least in my book.

His chunk-of-gold topped ring looked larger then I remembered. Especially since he kept fingering it to a shine.

"Tell us all that happened. Every piece of detail and we'll share what we discovered." T. Mix added, "I'm recording our full discussion today so that later we can connect all the dots." He pushed a button on a small contraption.

Dumbfounded, I looked at Nancy Lopez who rolled her eyes and ran her fingers through her red hair. Pulling back a long swath behind her left ear for comfort, she than referred to her notebook, the one we worked on last night....seems a week ago.

"Where to start," she began.

"How about Coyotee grabbing the lead rope and hauling our horses behind him extremely fast," I said unemotionally. I was determined to be a matter-of-fact speaker today, especially when we get to the part of the unknown. The less drama, the better.

"Coyotee? Who's that?" T. Mix's quick reaction alerted Nancy and me to put our spurs on because T. Mix wanted facts and he wanted them now as he leaned toward us behind his desk, his voice as heavy and huge as he is tall. T. Rex!!!

The only relaxed person in the room at the moment was the coroner who had shifted back in his chair with his ankles still crossed for comfort. Rick sat close with his arms folded, his recorder in his shirt pocket not missing a valuable word.

I explained about our dangerous gallop through the treacherous terrain to Massacre Grounds where Coyotee let go of the lead rope and disappeared.

"Ok, next!" Tom Mix's piercing stare rattled my nerves and I kept referring to Nancy's note pad for security.

Nancy explained the next scene when the horses tore loose and stampeded away a moment before Coyotee started shooting at us with rubber arrows."

"Very odd!" Tom Mix was the only one who interrupted periodically; since the recorder was on, no one wanted to add their voice unnecessarily.

"Well, he's Apache and planned ahead to perform a spiritual dance where he told me earlier, many Apache spirits dwell."

"He didn't want us to ride to Massacre Grounds," Nancy added. "He kept saying that it's haunted." No reaction from Tom Mix was surprising.

We continued back and forth with our explanation of the entire scene. From beginning to end, we painted an unbelievable, yet accurate picture, from rubber arrows, peaceful chanting and the strange appearance of a hand whittled spear....which by the way Del Rio kept hidden in my room for later analysis.

"In other words," T. Mix was frowning heavily, "he acted as a psychic for lost Apache souls, his mission to release them back to their ancestral heaven!"

Huh? T. Mix was well aware of hauntings in the Superstitions and probably had a bag of stories in his repertoire.

We continued listing tangible mysteries, slowly, saving the unbelievable for Butch. I started. "How can items from the past be interchangeable with the present time---like stepping in and out of a room?" I explained the rubber door stop, the exactness of my bracelet, and the disappearing whistle.

"Unexplainable!" Tom Mix was quick.

I stared him down. He was holding something back.

He clamped his jaw tightly shut, threw his pen down on the desk, leaned back in his chair and folded his arms behind his head…still staring. A shoulder twitched.

Rick intervened explaining everything he saw when he came riding in, which of course was logical because he didn't see the full picture that we witnessed.

It was stupid of me to try and explain the unbelievable of how she was shot even though I knew it sounded foolish and I would be reprimanded. "She was stuck in a transparent time-warp, from past to the present. First, she disappeared to the past. Secondly, she re-appeared and caught a bullet to the back. Then," I squinted for emphasis and spoke an octave above a whisper, "a slender film of time through which a bullet transcended from the past to the present, happened before our eyes."

"No!" Delilah spoke for the first time. She shook her head so swiftly, her brains must have twisted.

T. Mix was the authority and took the reins. "She was killed by a real live bullet from an 1848 Colt Dragoon. Collectors by the hundreds have them and come to the Superstitions to fire them where they hide out." He looked long and hard at Nancy and me. "You young school girls need to relax this theory of Heleena's death." A shoulder twitched.

"Teachers!" I interrupted.

I saw for the first time aided by the brightness of the day, grey tufts of hair beginning above his ears and circling around his neck in defiance of youth. He has to be pushing fifty.

He continued while loudly thumping the back of his hand on his wooden desk, "Didn't happen. She was currently killed, intentionally or accidentally. We'll soon know." As he stood to move us out, I was reminded again of his largeness, much like that of a Saguaro. And then the clincher,

"LADIES AND GENTLEMEN, WE HAVE A KILLLER ON THE LOOSE IN THE SUPERSTITIONS!"

CHAPTER 51

Rick, Nancy and I stood outside the building waiting for Tom Mix, Delilah and the coroner to drive up in a double cab truck for our ride to Massacre Grounds. The sun was bright with only a few clouds rolling above.

"That went over well," I said.

"It went right over their heads," added Nancy. "I don't think they even listened to what we said."

"They tuned out the minute you two mentioned the appearance of the mystery spear and the Apache kid. A large majority of people are skeptics when referencing the Paranormal. Considering what I saw when I came riding in, I don't know what to think. The found treasure is most puzzling. We need a successful meeting with Butch. Arrange it ASAP while images are fresh for all of us." Rick's no nonsense approach earlier, was now encouraging.

"Sorry I took so long." T. Mix cordially opened the back doors to his double cab Ford 350. "I had to send out awareness notices to all the deputies about a shooter in the mountains. A mounted sheriff posse from both counties will work together to find the killer."

I asked Delilah for any news on Heleena's family.

"I'm working with the Records Administration in Chicago where she was born. They're gathering as much info on her as possible considering holiday help is limited and today is Sunday. They'll be more precise then anything I find on the computer."

""Where's her family," asked Nancy. "Everybody has relatives."

"No, no, no, not true." T. Mix was quick. "In my line of business, I've learned there are many loners out there!"

The coroner quietly shook his head in acknowledgement. Perhaps he was one of them. I needed to know more about him and his conclusions about Heleena's demise. So far, there were no negative vibes. He was difficult to read and I felt the need to pump him for information. This I'll do when viewing the body.

We drove as close to Massacre Grounds as possible, before footing it a good thirty minutes. The storm was gone, the sun was out, and the desert would soon dry. Few remaining clouds floated overhead and on the ground, mirrored in tire track puddles.

Everyone split their attention in different directions, each taking pictures with cell phones and other devices. No one played follow the leader except Nancy and I clinging together reliving yesterday's horror.

Rick, joined by T. Mix and Delilah, inspected the shallow niche of cave near the diggings, each taking multiple pictures while he discussed the impossible treasures. Rick would tell us later on our drive home, their exact comments.

Nancy and I stood in the exact area where we were yesterday facing the calamity and now feeling a bit edgy. The Coroner stood close to Nancy, his hands behind his back, taking it all in quietly while we mumbled. The large, rectangular boulder on which Coyotee and Apache stood, had not moved, of course. In front of us, about ten feet away was the muddy wallow in which Heleena had lain for too long as I discovered later. To our left and a short distance away, was the shallow cave, the overhang under which we ate lunch during yesterday's down pour, the area habited by the two freshman boys all afternoon. T. Mix, Delilah and Rick were there now on their knees with sticks in hand, searching for evidence of some kind. They quit after a few minutes.

T. Mix had brought with him a long heavy stick which he used to pantomime a throw from their area to the purple boulder.

"Hey," I said, "I'm glad that he believed that part of the story and hopefully, the fact that Heleena grabbed the spear before disappearing."

"Probably not!" The Coroner's few words of the day.

His arm moved back and forth studying the flight of his stick before letting go. Then T. Rex yelled, "Move girls!"

Girls again! Obviously he didn't see the coroner standing by us.

The spear-stick landed in front of the tall purplish boulder. Not satisfied, he clownishly continued his spear throwing several more times, first from the shallow cave, then moving every five feet from this base, he heaved the stick while Delilah followed him like a kitten writing notes. He studied the area like a student writing a thesis.

Rick, now joined by the Coroner, circled around seeking clues. They both studied the beaten down area of the tie down and fake picnic wagon. For sure, we are going after the congressman who paid off the original Wrangler outfit, demand a refund, and give him hell for his irresponsibility. Rick will handle it.

"I'm tired." My watch now showed two-thirty.

"I'm hungry," said Nancy.

Nancy and I mumbled the fact that Rick did not tell all at the office an hour ago. The repeating harmonica, the control of the GPS by an unknown, his lost cell, and of course we followed his lead. Like ESP, we three clamped shut. Why tell all? We need to explore for ourselves. Save it for Butch.

Like a lightning bolt I saw something new that was not there yesterday. "Nancy, we spent half a day here yesterday walking all over the area. That pile of huge boulders and smaller rocks were not there when we left." I nodded toward the far end of the overhand about twenty yards east from where the cache of treasure was found. I tried to be as quiet and indiscrete as possible because the long legged T. Mix was examining that particular spot over and over. Undoubtedly, the pile of boulders was of an extraordinary interest to him too!

Nancy gulped air. "You're right. What is that all about? Maybe our ghost monster lives there."

She meant it. I added, "Let's not tell Rick now." I started taking pictures nonchalantly here and there, trying not to be conspicuous of my added interest in the massive new pile of rocks. I took about a dozen all around it. Special interest was on the ground in front of the new pile, looking for any sign of over-night tractor work. None! The ground in front was virgin soil, tramped only by a few boot prints and horse shoes, untouched by tire tracks for half a century.

Unfortunately, the sheriff was ultra-interested and studied the huge pile for too long. From this new exact area, he threw the spear about twenty times.

"He knows more than he's sharing," I squinted.

Delilah's phone toned 'Jingle-bells' loudly and she became pale with excitement while listening for about five minutes.

"Very strange," she said to all of us staring at her. Next, her pause caused us great discomfort thinking the worst as she dismembered the message. Looking straight at Nancy and me, she said loudly for all to hear, "Heleena was part Apache."

CHAPTER 52

The key to our mystery was handed to us in a short phone call hundreds of miles away. Vital Records and Statistics from Illinois had given us serious and shocking information about Heleena.

We stood there numbed by the news, wondering how much percentage of Apache blood.

The coroner was the first to speak. “Figures!” He walked away from us not wanting to be questioned. This we will do in the mortuary. Now handed a large chunk of the puzzle, we need to learn more about her background.

The non-believers had a renewed interest.

Delilah and Tom Mix started re-examining the area with keener attention, and while standing over the muddy wallow, she noticed a sharp glitter for a second as the sun shone brightly between two passing clouds.

“What’s this,” Delilah said bending down to pick at a tiny object half encased in drying mud. Soon, she held a small round silver object in her hand. After washing mud away with the water bottle she carried, a tiny antique silver bell lay in her palm. It was a miniscule piece that an infant might wear; and like a diamond ring on a sandy beach, it was a magical find.

Each of us had to touch it treating it like an alien piece.

"So this is what she was wearing when she disappeared the first time." Delilah tried to confirm her statement as actual knowledge while rolling the bell in her palm with her manicured nails before looking at me.

"Nope! She had a whistle on a ribbon around her neck when she disappeared and none when she re-appeared."

"Exactly," added Nancy. "We never saw this tiny bell."

Rick to our rescue added the visual of her in the vortex, spinning with the ribboned whistle swinging around with her. "I know that I saw it from where I sat on my horse." No one questioned his expertise.

"We need to screen-clean this entire muddy wallow for more clues. Maybe it's buried here somewhere." Tom Mix, waved his hand indicating the entire wallow, and supported by the Coroner, declared Heleena was clean of any trinkets when examined at the mortuary.

Delilah annoyingly continued questioning with her manicured hands around her tiny waist, not believing everything. "How can someone disappear before your eyes, and re-appear with no scientific explanation a few minutes later but with an additional catastrophe?"

She gave me an ugly stare.

"Fog." T. Mix stood tall over the site, legs looking like stilts. "It's called fog. Makes your brains fuzzy and you see things that don't exist. My thoughts are that you girls were dead tired after the fast, scary ride to this place and a loony dressed like an Apache, appeared jumping around in the fog, over rocks, yelping like a mad man, then shot the poor woman in the back before running away. We have a killer running loose. Everything else is hogwash." Steely and firm was his attitude as he stood staring us down with hands in his vest pockets.

There it was, "girls" again. I took out a tissue and blew my nose nice and loud hoping he would disappear. Nope. He was still there staring.

Rick, who had been standing close with his arms folded, twisted around and spat.

Delilah pocketed the tiny bell. "I'll have this carbon dated." Whose side is she on? I couldn't tell because of her showmanship. However, much later, when we three drove away from the mortuary, she followed right behind us in her copycat Jeep. Except mine is cobalt blue. She wasn't sticking around Apache Junction. She was on a mission.

For now, after about an hour of re-explaining what we saw, what we heard and from where, T. Mix and the Coroner were exhausted from listening to us and began walking around looking for new evidence.

No loopholes were found; no "what ifs" were made as we stuck closely to Nancy's bus notes from last night. They were bullet proof. Everything was in the exact order from when it happened, verified by Nancy, me and the five teens last night while the events were fresh and we could think clearly in the bus. The two freshman diggers were not accountable.

Tom Mix continued his inquiry from the site. "I can't believe you didn't hear the gun shot. You know that the early morning news speculated she fell on a stick and pierced her heart. Where'd that come from?"

"The Principal," said Rick. "When questioned last night, he decided to speculate rather than act un-informed."

"That's terrible." The Coroner decided to speak. "It's worse to give out false information." His cell rang. "The Medical Examiner is at the morgue and wants to meet with us."

T. Mix threw Rick his truck keys deciding that he wanted to stay on the site longer to work with the search parties for the shooter. “I’ll get a certified copy on my desk later.” He played with the ring on his finger, polishing the huge lump.

Now Delilah and the Coroner were extra enthusiastic as they climbed into the back seat. Nancy and I eyeballed each other—ESP. My heart began to thump. Did I eat enough lunch earlier? Can I see a dead body? When’s the last time I saw one? Never!

“Uh, let’s drive thru a Coffee Cup. · I need a Vanilla Latte.”

Nancy’s idea was seconded by all of us. No one argued.

The Medical Examiner didn’t know what to say when he saw us walk in slurping, and we really didn’t care.

He was easily under five feet tall, fully bearded, well rounded in the middle and wore a French beret. Hair and beard match that of a Golden Retriever but those emerald green eyes, he stole them from Del Rio. He looked like a mad escapee from a prospector’s camp until he spoke.

He gave us a friendly wave with his gold chunk of a ring and said, “Hey! Was I supposed to call in my order ahead?” His smile, those teeth…perfect for a dental poster in an office.

Another gold chunk of a ring? Hmmmm. “Sorry,” I said. “Next time.”

No one else spoke and I discovered later that I wasn’t the only one with the thumping heart, scared out of my skin, going to see a dead Heleena. Rick and Nancy stood back, slurping, while Delilah wanted to get on with the show; being a forensic medic, this was her territory.

I loudly sighed too many times and the napkin I carried with my Latte, was now shredded in bits.

"Tee hee hee---You'll be fine." The Leprechaun Medical Examiner extended his hand and told us his name which was an immediate blur to my thumping ears.

I stepped back afraid to shake hands with someone who handled dead bodies in case he didn't use soap. No worry. Rick heartedly greeted him respectfully.

"Follow me," he said.

We each dumped our empty cups in a container as we walked under an arched doorway and through a hall.

Delilah and the Coroner pranced behind him like eager pups. This was their territory, two officials eager to determine cause of death.

Nancy and I wavered. Rick took each of us by an arm and we followed slowly. Was he pushing or pulling? Soon we entered a cold, cold Frankenstein room with handles extending out of a wall, just like in the movies.

The Leprechaun pulled out a bed-like drawer and Heleena lay looking at us peacefully in alabaster white, an almost translucent skin. Her nose was longer than I remembered. Tipping my head this way and that hoping to get a better look, I tried to remember her old voice. Is this what people do? Next I looked up towards the ceiling and around the room. Was her spirit here laughing at us or lapping around us.

Sadness flowed around. My shoulders relaxed after having faced the abominable event, but my left eye began to twitch and when I looked at Nancy's super pink face, it became fuzzy. I had an eye aura and needed help.

The Leprechaun quickly pulled forward three chairs. Rick took charge by sitting in the middle. He knew we were a mess.

"Tee hee. The three of us are going to examine her for an analysis and you three can listen without watching." He pointed at us and continued. "I doubt an autopsy later is necessary."

"Now," he began quietly to the Coroner and Delilah, "see this area on her back where the bullet entered? The velocity of the bullet exploded close to the heart."

The drone of his voice put me to sleep and I nodded off hoping that Del Rio and Nancy Lopez were soaking it all in so I can ask them for bits of information later. My head shot up when he mentioned the gun.

"The gun was definitely an 1848 Colt Dragoon, a smaller size version of the original Colt Walker which was called the 'Grandpa Gun of the Wild West', and used extensively during the war with Mexico. Since the Grandpa Gun was a huge honker of a gun, Sam Walker asked Sam Colt to revise the gun to a smaller version. It was a Gambler's prized possession."

I heard Delilah's voice next. "How do you know that it was a smaller version and not the original?"

"Less black powder. The Colt Dragoon holds fifty grains of powder, less chance of explosion, and the Colt Walker holds sixty grains in each chamber. The Dragoon retained the Walker's .44 caliber ball shot. These were the bullets you know. And, the balls were pure lead." At this point he handed the bag containing the one bullet to Delilah for forensic study.

"Check this out thoroughly. I believe the bullet was an 1848 bullet and not a replica."

Wow! All of a sudden he was ten feet tall. He continued, "Someone stole an old bullet from a museum or from Grandpa's cache of antiques." Then he laughed when he said "Or, she traveled through time like a fugitive, tee-hee-hee!"

Not one of us laughed at this last part and since we acted mum, he seemed to read each of our faces and knew that something more sinister was awry.

He continued, "Apaches insist it is haunted."

No comment.

"Ok, what are you not telling me?"

CHAPTER 53

The Medical Examiner continued again. "What's the secret you're hiding?" His demeanor changed to a serious squint and I missed his humorous laugh.

The Coroner saved us from having to tell our story a multiple time. "I'll tell you later. It's too baffling."

This seemed to please the Leprechaun who had been standing on a step stool while viewing the body for the assessment which took longer than I wanted to stay.

Rick and I both looked at our watches. Nancy ESP'D with a nod of her head upward that it was time to leave. Considering yesterday's fiasco, our reserve energy was now drained.

Impatiently, we shuffled our feet and cleared our throats.

"Ok," said the Leprechaun, "we're done for now." He covered the body and the three stepped back with their individual clipboards in hand, Delilah still writing. Next, she flashed two separate sandwich bags before us, one containing the tiny bell, the other the bullet from the body.

"I'll take these to my lab in Phoenix for carbon dating." She stepped away and looked at Rick. "Now, where's the spear? We should check that too!"

So now its "we" not "I". Remembering the story about the spear, she assumed it was in Rick's possession. She was right again.

Rick decided to go with her and they agreed on "tomorrow." Knowing Del Rio, he was not giving the mystery spear too anyone.

With no next of kin, a burial date was not immediate. But since she listed the English Department as the responsible party, we would certainly agree on a few days after Christmas and not prolong the event. Because Delilah started the research and discovered that Heleena was part Apache, she agreed to keep checking for any next of kin among them and let us know "within two days." She warned us that the Apache Nation may want to be involved depending on her percentage of Apache blood. "That might cause a burial delay."

Now thinking of Mrs. Raintree and Coyotee, I mentioned that I would check with them on burial information too. And, we all agreed on "the sooner the better."

The Coroner and Leprechaun were content with "time" of death and "cause" but not a hundred percent sure of "how" she was killed.

Since Rick Del Rio mentioned "that's Sheriff Tom Mix's expertise," they signed off with their part, turning multiple pages for signatures.

Rick continued that an investigator from the Maricopa County Crime Lab would be involved with the sheriff's analyses. "They'll probably test the bullet theory with a shooting reconstruction to determine location of shooter."

"How do they do that?" My curiosity was going crazy because I knew the shooter was a ghost from the past.

"They won't believe what we saw," said Nancy.

Delilah added some knowledge for all of us. "A forensic private investigator will work with everything we throw his way. I know a guy who can work on some answers to my questions."

She had our full attention because we were wondering what she was thinking. "He's also a fire arms expert and will definitely have answers to our puzzle." She added some more notes to her clipboard.

I was starting to believe that Movie-Star-Gorgeous was leaning to our side of the story considering our rendition of Coyotee and his dance on the boulder. Plus, with her own cell, she learned that Heleena was part Apache, a thread that holds it all together.

"It's no puzzle for us," said Nancy. "We saw exactly what happened and there was no fog." She was inflexible.

The entire room was quiet.

The Coroner and Medical Examiner swallowed hard and cleared their throats.

Hah! ESP. They know the mountain is haunted.

Rick took off his hat, smoothed his wavy hair back for comfort, and re-positioned it handsomely. He had no answer.

We all walked over to the body for perhaps our last goodbye.

She was smiling.

"Hey, the corners of her mouth are turned up!" I was no longer afraid, knowing that somehow, her final destination would be a peaceful one. ESP.

"Muscle spasms," said the Leprechaun.

"Tomorrow is Monday, Christmas Eve," Delilah began, "but since I know everyone in the Phoenix Forensic Lab, I'll call them tonight and get them there early in the morning. For sure, they will be intrigued with everything I have to show and tell."

She pulled the two plastic sandwich bags out of her purse and held them again within our viewing vicinity. The bullet from the gun was simply a round lead ball, but now the bag's interior was sort of misty from a greasy film.

"What the heck?" I was first.

"Hey! Where'd that come from?" Nancy pointed to the smear in the bag.

"That was a clean sandwich bag," Rick stated tiredly.

"Of course!" Delilah had no reaction but paused a good ten seconds staring at it collectively with us.

I suppose on her job she sees everything and doesn't make any false concerns. As of now, she secured the two bags in her purse than patted it. After turning to Nancy and me she said, "I'll let you know what we find tomorrow, ASAP."

CHAPTER 54

Sunday, December 23

For our drive back, Nancy and I quizzed Del Rio about what was said at the digging site with the Coroner and Tom Mix.

"When you told them about finding the bracelet you had given me, that was stolen, how did they react?"

"They didn't! I had to mention it twice. And next, when I mentioned your rubber door jam, same thing. No reaction. Finally, I asked them what they thought about all of it and they just commented with, 'very unusual' and no more."

I threw in, "It was nice of T. Rex to let the boys keep the antique gun pieces."

Nancy added, "He seemed to know a great deal about the 1848 Colt Dragoon."

"Most unusual of all," Rick continued not to be side-tracked, "was his interest in a big pile of boulders and smaller rocks east of the alcove, about thirty yards from the dig. He examined that particular area with great interest and checked the weight of the smaller rocks by shoving them."

"Did he move any?"

"No. They've been buried there for more than half a century."

"Well, guess what!" I exclaimed too loudly.

"Yeah! Guess what!" Nancy and I both went crazy with our new discovery.

Rick smiled at our craziness and said nothing knowing we would follow with the info.

"That pile of rocks was not there yesterday." I pointed my finger so fiercely with emphasis that if I had hit the windshield, it would have cracked.

"NOPE!" Nancy was louder than I.

"Oh come on! How can you be sure with the rain, the mud, the fog, and all the distractions with the horses?"

We both pretty much talked at the same time, using precise wording and specialized visuals mapping out every piece of Massacre Grounds, finishing with the fact that we walked the entire area many times looking for the harmonica player.

"Wait a minute! The cave! There was a small cave opening exactly where the pile of rocks are now!" Nancy to the rescue.

"You're right. But how could that be?"

Rick made a weird sound through his teeth. "Another puzzle."

Nancy added this latest mystery to the small note pad she now took out of her purse. "For Butch," she said waving it in the air.

Rick agreed to let Nancy and me go with him tomorrow to meet with the forensic private investigator after we swore not to interrupt the research. "Just stand back and take notes," he said. "We meet at Ten A.M. in Phoenix.

Of course we reverted to black mail by telling him our meeting with Butch and the gang would be kept a secret if he didn't let us tag along.

"Childish prank." He laughed at my black mail idea. "You couldn't keep a secret if paid a thousand dollars. Actually, I'm afraid to let you two out of my sight. The ghost might come and get both of you. You know too much!"

After agreeing on what we would wear tomorrow, Nancy dragged out of the truck with a yawn. "I'll set the meeting date for the day after Christmas with Butch, and we need to contact our list of people for the meeting."

As we drove away I asked Rick what he thought about everything.

"I lost my cell, part of my tracker, and my GPS. Next month, let's go back to Massacre Grounds and dig for them."

It had been a frustrating two days.

I called home to tell Pop that I was staying at Rick's place tonight.

"But, but, but……"

"Pop, I have no answers for you yet! I'll be by in the morning to grab a quick change of clothes." I explained briefly where I was going and why. "In the meantime, keep the pitch fork well anchored."

As we pulled in, I turned off my cell. The patio lights softly beckoned a comfortable good night.

We took a long, long hot soapy shower together with all the trimmings.

Bed never felt so good.

CHAPTER 55

Monday, December 24

Plan was for us to meet with Delilah in downtown Phoenix at Ten in the morning and no earlier because she wanted to go over everything with her work force before we got there.

"It helps to clear my mind when there are only a few of us for preliminary presentations."

Makes sense to me! Actually, all three of us were curious as to how she would "show and tell" our material, our story.

Rick looked at the two of us in his truck on the drive to town. "Must be Christmas." We were dressed alike in matching red and green striped sweaters and denim jeans. Only our jewelry of bells and candy canes were different. On my wrist was my pearl bracelet with the butterfly amulet.

"Looks like we're going to a party rather than a forensic briefing," he said, dressed to kill in complete denim.

"We need some cheer after being spooked out of our wits," Nancy said dryly as she opened her huge Mary Poppins bag and took out the bus list of notes. "Seems a week ago when we wrote this."

We both re-checked the sequencing of events making sure to add the new pile of boulders and their significance.

Parking was no problem. Holidays have a way of emptying streets. Other than vagrants here and there, the sidewalks were vacant of town hustle and bustle.

We bounded out of the truck with enthusiasm, curious to learn the perspectives of the professionals, but also somewhat cheery since we had been told by Delilah that the meeting would be "holiday" short.

The windowless building was a two story grey square about a half mile from the center of town, in a seedy block of early twentieth century half-furbished neighborhoods. Old bungalows waiting for new paint, and yards begging for a manicure, sat among shuttered new offices, the majority being dental and attorneys.

We followed a small driveway of pavers to the left that led to a back parking lot where Delilah's Jeep was parked next to two other late model cars.

Wanting to enter from the front, we walked back to street side. The door was heavily fronted with iron re-bars over glass. An absence of pots with flowers and plants signified a serious business inside or seemed to shout, "Stay out".

Science! Where's the glamor? How did Delilah fit in?

Rick opened the unlocked door and a glamorous appeal was immediate. Magnificent leather couches and matching chestnut recliners circled a square glass coffee table that could easily handle a hundred cups. Although the glow from two standing lamps added vitality to the atmosphere, the room was brightened by a sky light. A healthy Rubber Tree plant bathed in footed lighting, stood next to the entrance to an open hallway, lined on both sides with glass cubicles. So much for the tawdry outdoor veneer! This business is definitely incognito to all outsiders.

Loud voices were coming from a lit area in the back. No one came forward until Rick knocked on the inside of the door. Delilah and three casually dressed men walked toward us. Her readable face of shooting eyebrows indicated that we two were an irritant to her plan of meeting with Rick alone. All three men wore huge wrap around white aprons. Just like in the movies.

After greetings, the team got immediately down to business. Although we arrived at Ten, they had been researching since Seven. "We met early," said one of the men, "because of the holiday. The very unusual set of circumstances Delilah presented on the phone was quite an ear full and we were anxious."

I will title him the TALKER since the other two were silent. I assumed he was the forensic private investigator or whatever. Since no one wore a name tag or title tag, and greetings had been too quick, I guessed at their expertise.

Rick handed the now bagged spear to the TALKER who gave it to the two SILENCERS who eagerly took it back for scientific investigation.

"Let's sit," he said sternly, and we followed him to the plush couches and recliners. We sat, but he didn't, opting instead to stand which I found intimidating.

Next, he pulled from his large apron pocket the plastic bag containing the bullet from Heleena's body, or I guess it was still in there. Now, it was such a greasy mess, I couldn't see the bullet until he shook the bag.

"This is a lead bullet from an 1848 Colt Dragoon Revolver manufactured between 1848 and 1860, one of the most powerful handguns of its day. Every Gambler carried one."

Delilah handed Rick a picture of the revolver which he shared with Nancy and me.

"It is a cap and ball revolver; its ammunition in three components; the percussion cap, the ball shot and the black powder, are carried in a tight fitting case with the gun." Highly animated, he put the bag back in his pocket and the way he talked, I assumed he has shot a Dragoon many times.

"Approximately seven thousand of these guns were sold in the beginning."

Rick was all ears. This was his territory. Nancy and I sank back on pillows and tried to get comfortable. I swallowed a yawn. The last few days have been tough.

He continued and I tried not to nod off. "Each gun held six chambers of black powder and unlike its predecessor the 1847 Colt Walker that held sixty grains of black powder, this one held only fifty grains. Less chance of explosion." He didn't stop for a pause and I knew he was in his territory. Some of the information was fresh, and some we had already heard from T. Mix.

"The Walker was used extensively in the 1846-1848 United States-Mexican War but was too big and heavy at fifteen inches long and weighing four and a half pounds. The military and civilians wanted something smaller." He patted the picture lovingly. "This old gun was referred to as a Horse Pistol and Grandpa Gun of the Wild West." Lowering his voice he added, "These are worth thousands of dollars, whether it's the Colt Dragoon or the hefty Colt Walker, new or old."

He paused, went to a desk nearby and pulled out a small wooden case of cigars. "For the holidays." He offered; we declined. Rick on the other hand, took one for the road.

"My great-great granddad used to peddle these in the Old West. Story goes, he got hanged for totin' guns after sundown." Laying the cigar case open on the square glass table, he continued as if he were a product of by-gone days. "My two compadres will want a smoke when they come back."

I thought this smoking bit highly unusual, but what do I know. Like he said, 'For the Holidays.' He continued after a long serious pause. "Someone out there on the mountain, shooting one of these guns, is living in the past as a hobby or is a wandering loony, one of those searching for the Lost Dutchman Mine." He blew the sweet smoke behind him and sucked on the wet end like it was candy, twirling it around in his lips.

I gagged.

Nancy coughed.

Delilah interrupted and asked if he knew of any groups of shooters in the Superstitions who belonged to an old-timers-club.

To this the TALKER said "no" and continued his historical mastery. "Most military and later, civilians, carried a couple of the guns loaded and ready in big holsters attached to their saddles. This is because it took several minutes to load each chamber properly and I might add, carefully. Each chamber was sealed with a lube of some kind, usually the popular bear grease. Currently, shooters with Dragoons use shortening."

Silence. We said nothing.

Looking eagerly at Rick for an answer, "You say Heleena was shot in the back with this bullet?" He held up the smeared mess of a bag. "You saw it happen. The medical examiner fished this bullet out of her back."

Rick re-told his view of the circumstances, what he saw from where he sat on his horse and he added the approximate distance in yardage.

"Someone's out there playing games with us." TALKER now sat, and while swinging the bag casually between his knees added, "This bullet is from about 1848 and not a replica. We analyzed the lead content. And the biggest mystery of all is the bear grease in the bag. Where does one buy bear grease these days?"

This was a spark for the three of us. We gasped and stared more closely at the grease. Delilah had no reaction, having been part of the study earlier.

Silence!

TALKER stood and carefully stamped out his cigar with an apparatus, put it back in the wooden box and closed the lid. Precision!

"Delilah told us the complete story as you had told her, about an Apache appearing and disappearing. And Heleena doing the same." Long pause as he paced the floor.

" Impossible. I am a man of science and believe there is a logical scientific explanation for everything."

Silence again.

We had no answers.

"Where can one buy bear grease?" Repeating his previous question slyly I shrugged my left shoulder, a cunning gesture and part of my smart ass attitude that was now showing signs of defiance.

Rick and Nancy tempered the moment by explaining what was logical to appease the forensic investigator.

"As I came riding in, I never heard the shot but watched her reactions before falling face down in the mud."

"And the spear she grabbed earlier, she carried it with her before she disappeared, and afterward, it was gone." Nancy sounded logical, matter of fact, and like it was an everyday occasion. "Where's the spear?"

Almost on cue, the two other men excitedly arrived from a back room carrying the bagged spear. "This piece of wood is from the 1840's. Where did you find it?"

"Amazing," said the TALKER. "This should have succumbed to decay long ago, a natural process for an inanimate piece of nature."

Holding the bagged spear he asked, "Why is it in two pieces?"

Rick explained how someone hurled it from the darkness toward them and he caught it. "Actually, I broke it in half on the saddle horn and decided to hang on to it for whatever reason."

I wanted to mention that we feared its magic as warned by Coyotee, but chickened out. These were people of science and wouldn't believe the Paranormal.

The TALKER factually finished his analyses of the three items. "All these items were from around 1848. The tiny bell, the lead bullet, the spear.... have to be from a museum. Someone stole the items from a museum and that someone out there is playing the role of an old-timer from the past. No telling what else he or she has taken to a hiding place."

On cue, Rick, Nancy and I said, "No telling!"

CHAPTER 56

As we drove away, I played with my newly found bracelet that the boys dug out of the dirt at Ghost Harbor. "Ghost Harbor, that's the new name for Massacre Grounds," I said twirling the silver piece around on my wrist wondering why I didn't mention it to the science group.

Although we lived through a mass of trauma these last few days, I couldn't help but laugh when I looked at Nancy's big bag of notes at her feet.

"Well, that went over well. I'm glad you told them ALL that happened."

"We should invite them and the box of cigars to our meeting with Butch," said Nancy. "The four B's and student eye-witnesses would promptly put them in their place."

From Rick, "Not happening."

"I'm hungry," I said.

"Triple that. Let's stop for a late lunch somewhere. We need a break," Nancy added. "And let's complete our list of who's meeting with us and Butch."

Good grief! The list again. Is it getting shorter or longer?

Since we were fifteen minutes away from the middle of Cave Creek, we decided our hunger could wait for our favorite dive, Greasy's, and the lunch bunch crowd.

Judging by the trucks and cycles in the parking lot, most of the town's shameful party goers were here and we were eager to join them. Tis the season !

Our picnic style table on the patio was two away from a group of carolers snacking, drinking and singing. Near each table was a warm heat lamp, ideal for cuddling. December nights easily dip to the low forties. "It's a dry cold," we always say.

"Nachos, the works piled high," I said to the waitress wearing Rudolph earrings glowing red at the snout and a plastic head band of Rudolph ears.

"Make that a double with a pitcher of beer," added Rick.

"Hello!" Bouncing to our table was Delilah, our Delilah who we had hoped remained behind to impress the forensic group with her scientific details.

"It's Christmas Eve and I have nowhere to go tonight. Tomorrow, my company is arriving, and look, very important stuff you three wise-men left behind." She raised her voice a couple notches in a rush of excitement. On the table she placed the bagged spear and tiny bell in its own small sandwich bag. Motioning for the waitress, she delicately, like a cat, sat next to Rick, butt to butt. Nancy and I were sitting across. "Forensics is keeping the bullet for further investigation."

"Thanks!" said Rick gratefully. "This needs to go in my truck now!" He got up. She followed.

"How could we forget those?" Nancy and I reprimanded each other with a glare.

I put the bell in my purse. "Butch needs to see both of these items."

Nancy the lister, showed me the invite for the Paranormal gathering. "Along with those who were present at the scene as it happened, we need to invite the four wise old owls, Bing, Brad, Bob and Blake. Later, they can help analyze anything we might have missed."

"Of course, Pop and Dixie will be there. Pop needs answers to the pitchfork throw; maybe he'll get them." We were both repeating ourselves. Must be nerves.

Nachos, two pitchers of beer, a tray of glasses and Rick with Delilah arrived at the same time. With fangs, we all began to devour the two big platters. The owner of Greasy's brought bowls of sour cream, salsa, guacamole, jalapenos and extra napkins to our table. "Happy Holidays," he said cheerily with a wink and hurried away to a rapidly filling patio.

"And here they come," said Rick to the sound of four arriving cycles.

We waved them over. Rick, with help from the waitress, pulled another table next to ours. With a few handshakes and hugs, they joined us.

"This comes off after the holidays," said Bing scratching his bearded face.

"Bugs or rash?" asked Rick.

"Both," they simultaneously agreed.

"What's happening?" asked Rick.

Bing began. "We have firmly decided that we're going to spend the night at the old Cave Creek Cemetery sometime this week to prove that ghosts do not exist." He slapped his hand on the wooden table with emphasis. Then smiled.

"Who's we?" I asked.

"The four of us."

"Well," I continued, "you better dress warm and carry a big stick."

"And be prepared to call 911," Rick said. "Don't call me. I've already been there."

"Take Pop with you! He's a non-believer. You might want to wait until after our meeting with Butch on the twenty-sixth. It could change your minds." I had to tease them with a squinty eyed threat.

"Good idea. We need some food from the baker," one of them said.

The afternoon got boisterous as we swayed with joined arms at the elbows and bumping shoulders to every Christmas tune the bunch of us could remember. Tables joined tables clicking mugs together with memorable thoughts of holiday presents while comparing silly happenings and cherished traditions.

"My grandmother decided she had to have the latest silver-aluminum Christmas tree that rotated on a turnstile with colored lights shining through it. Gaudy but beautiful to our eyes, we sat around it admiringly."

Others joined Brad's story with, "We had one of those too."

"How many of you ended up putting the tree inside a play pen to keep the baby from pulling it down again?" Laughter and a remarkable show of hands.

Dog and cat stories generated the most tales.

"Our big dog always had to stand next to the tree wagging his tail until it had taken off most of the tinsel."

"My two kittens chased each other up the inside to the top making it topple over."

All of us were shouting above each other with stories of holiday ridiculousness until one of the singers at another table took a harmonica from his pocket and began playing it.

We paled, recoiling from our past experiences a couple of days ago. I had hoped never to hear one again. But it was an innocent gesture as the player continued with singers joining him at his table. They had no clue as to why we had paused for a bit, and we were not about to mention anything.

It was around Four in the afternoon when Delilah received the important call about Heleena's background. She gave us the hopeful look while leaving the table's noise to talk on her cell. We needed answers to pertinent questions.

Are there any next of kin? How much Apache blood and what does this mean, if anything? When is the burial and to what extent is the English Department's involvement?

While Delilah talked on her phone, she turned her back to us and covered one ear with her other hand. We were loud.

Soon, Pop and Dixie arrived from the bakery with boxes of left-over chocolate eclairs and cranberry-orange muffins to a clapping crowd. By this time, Greasy's owner had put a carafe of coffee and a tray of cups on each table; he knew us well. Everyone split back to their original tables and talked among themselves. Rick ordered more nachos with "extra cheese and pintos."

"None!" One single word from Delilah was an unwelcome piece of information. "Searching extensively, they found that she had been orphaned at an early age, never claimed by anyone, and contained a good amount of Apache blood from a renegade tribe."

We all mauled over this while drinking coffee or beer, nachos or eclairs. We were expandable. Everyone helped explain the situation to Pop and Dixie who had no clue about all our past and current experiences. I was in no mood to relive everything at the moment. I did add, "I'll get together with the Principal Shieter and talk about a burial date."

This was a downer to our high spirits a few minutes ago; we frowned and sighed but carried on.

"What could we do for Heleena that would be special?" I asked.

"A quick burial with her favorite things," added Rick looking at us for ideas. "You all know what she liked most."

"How about an Apache chant or dance, something sentimental and appropriate?" Nancy looked at our now silent group for an answer to her idea. "Remember her dancing jig?"

"Superb!" I said quietly not waiting for others.

Dixie added that she saw Heleena daily and could easily make a list of her favorite things to place in her coffin.

We were her family and would not be swayed by school administration formalities. Our ideas alone would be enforced. After all, she listed "the English Department" as her next of kin knowing that our creative ideas would be fashionable. At this time in the early evening, I decided to call Shieter to make arrangements for the burial and also Mrs. Raintree about Coyotee's performance at the burial site. I'm thinking that his chant would be lovingly fit considering initial involvement.

"Stay put," I said. "I'll be back with decisive news." This would be the time for discussion since everyone was here.

I dialed Shieter first not worried that it was Christmas Eve and it could be a personal interruption. Our problem was urgent and Heleena was our number one priority at this time.

He was unnecessarily verbal and giddy about something. I heard background noise; but, not being distracted, I firmly explained the importance of an immediate burial. "This is what she would want," I said, "and most of the students who knew her well, would be available for the services."

No answer.

"Hello! What do think about a quick burial?" Where was he and who was he entertaining? No telling.

"I hear that some of you are meeting with a Paranormal. If this is true, I need to know when and where so that I can be there." Bribery tactic was a Shieter game.

Hmmm. Quick thinking on my part. "Well, we haven't decided yet. When we do, we'll let you know." I felt my nose to insure it had not grown longer. Mr. dillydally needs a quick thinker…ME!

"How about burial on the twenty-seventh, two days after Christmas?"

"I'll contact the District and get the orders ASAP," he loudly confirmed over the background noise of a harmonica.

"Is that a harmonica I hear?" My chest thumped loudly without my kick starting it with a jog.

"Good news. Old man here knows how to find the Lost Dutchman Mine."

CHAPTER 57

Stunned, I instantly punched off before saying goodbye in case the ghost invaded my cell phone space and came after me. Taking deep breaths in and out to clear my head, and after looking all around, up, down, left and right, really bug eyed, I inched back to the merry table where all my close family and friends sat singing…. except Rick who had left the table to check on me.

"What's the matter?" Firmly holding me at arms length while looking in my eyes, I noticed a big smudge of lipstick on the side of his mouth.

"Don't say it! I haven't seen a ghost but I know where one is." I licked my fingers and methodically wiped the smudge away.

"It's Christmas," he said without a care. "You're shivering. Let's go sit."

Slowly, I told everyone at my table about my phone call with no further explanation or drama.

"So?" Pop and Dixie asked the question simultaneously while feeling the holiday spirit and ready for an adventure.

Nancy gulped, put down her cup of coffee and poured herself a glass of beer.

Delilah wasn't impressed and showed no emotion as she wide-eyed me with eyelashes that touched her brows. Then with her cup of coffee hiding her face as she sipped, she was unreadable. But, did I catch a side glance toward Rick? A questioning look? Or was it longing?

There I go again.

The four B's were galloping excited!

"Oh boy, I'm heading over there now," said Bing, sort of the ring leader.

"Not without us." The other three were out of the picnic table and following Bing to their cycles.

While reeving-up and helmeting, Bob yelled above the din, "Don't call us. We'll call you."

Joyfully they motored off.

"Boy are they cockie!" Dixie scooted over closer to us. "Ok, now tell us everything that we don't already know." Pop joined her.

"I've got this one," said Delilah feeling important. She explained all that she knew, unemotionally from a forensic's viewpoint, minus our rendition. "And Sheriff Posse members are searching every foot of the mountain for the shooter."

Nancy and I sat quietly eating while she spoke to Pop and Dixie. No way were we going to correct her. We'll save all the commas and apostrophes for Butch who needs to follow Nancy's list of happenings in sequence.

Rick reminded me that I better call Mrs. Raintree with all the latest details. "Coyotee needs to be at our meeting on the twenty-six."

Excusing myself, I left the din to a quieter area and called Mrs. Raintree. Happy to know that she was home and in a positive, supportive mood, I discussed with her all the dates of happenings and "could Coyotee help us?"

She was excited to learn about Heleena's background and that she was part Apache.

"A quick burial, would be the Apache way," she said, then added her appreciation for Coyotee's part at the burial scene.

"He will feel honored," she added before closing. "And, I will have him call you as soon as possible for arrangements."

Next, I decided to call the mortuary on this holiday eve, connect or not, to get on with the burial plans.

"Tee Hee," the Medical Examiner, AKA Leprechaun, laughed his usual when I told him I was surprised that he was there working on Christmas Eve. "I live here," he joked, "in one of these cool beds."

He'd already had some Holiday cheer and I realized by the noisy background that he was at a party and not the mortuary. Duh!

"Thursday the twenty-seventh," sounds sooner than I expected," he said, "but actually perfect timing considering accommodations will be necessary at 'the beds' for all the deceased Holiday prospectors searching for Dutchy's Lost Gold Mine."

Was he serious? Probably.

We discussed the time and School District's involvement. I finished with, "Shieter gave me the go-ahead to secure arrangements."

"Tee Hee" was his last goodbye.

As I turned toward the tables my phone rang.

"Hey curly! I have a fresh batch of mistletoe waiting impatiently to wilt," whispered Guy Wagner.

I should have said, "Not happening," but instead, "Put it in the fridge," came out of my mouth.

"For later?"

"For later!" I whispered back and punched the off button. Why did I say that? Blame it on the smudge.

Back at the table I joined the singing festival of carolers.

Soon the four B's were back and hurried off their cycles extremely excited. Like boyish juveniles.

"We missed him!"

"Principal said he vanished…like poof."

"Explain. What did he mean vanished?" I asked. "Did he get the old man's name? Where he lived?" I ducked my head playing with the last bit of food on my plate to hide a wry, crooked smile and continued. "Did he take any photos? Did he ask what kind of music he liked?" Noting my facetious attitude, Rick gave me 'the look'---the one where I can't be an undetected smart-ass.

I continued. "You could have invited him to spend the night with you at the cemetery." Now Nancy, my partner in crime, started giggling the silly one that calls for me to join in. We slammed our heads down on the table for a full-minute-belly laugh.

Pop, Dixie and Rick just shook their heads with annoyance.

The four elderly cycle friends, members of Pop's group, the elite Family Farm…continued not missing a beat.

"Well, Shieter did give us this small gold rock that he wants back," Blake said with heightened animation. "The prospector gave it to him to keep."

We gathered around and inspected a small pebble that was wrapped in plastic for safe keeping. After opening the wrap, the small piece lay in the middle of his palm for all of us to see and feel.

"Hey! I have a duplicate of that, only mine is larger. Remember when I stumbled and fell then picked up a small rock on the trail for a souvenir?" I looked at Nancy and Rick.

They shook their heads yes, but everyone else quipped, "You're kidding?" I must have heard several sparks of excited interest.

Dixie asked, "Do you remember exactly where?"

"No, it was dark."

"Girls, we are going on a long holiday hike soon!" She rubbed her hands together, looked at us and patted a few drum beats on the table.

Sounded serious but I knew for sure that she was full of bull!

Pop kidded along. "But, you might get your painted nails dirty."

As Blake put away the gold pebble, I asked him and his group what night they were camping-out at the Cave Creek Cemetery. "So I can bring you a pot of coffee. You don't want to miss anything."

"A couple nights after Christmas," said Bob. "We'll show you the truth. Everything else is hogwash!"

"Are you tenting?" I asked. "No fair staying locked in a camping trailer."

"Doesn't matter," teased Rick. "Ghosts don't use doors."

"Pop should go with us." Bing was not joking.

"Uh, the bakery needs me. E-mail me from the cemetery…send pictures." His ear to ear smile followed.

With a yawn, Delilah was the first to leave. "See you at the funeral."

"We're going home to wait for Santa." The four B's went their separate ways.

Looking around, I noticed the other tables had emptied. We were always the last of the merry-makers and now Greasy's Manager was cleaning the place hurriedly.

"Thanks!" We said, remembering to leave a larger than normal tip.

He saluted. "Happy Holiday!"

"Big Christmas breakfast at my house," demanded Pop to Nancy, Rick and me.

"Absolutely!"

****

Seems it is always a repeat of a first date when Rick and I enter his bedroom for the same sequence. I undress, fold my clothes neatly, lay them on one arm of his large recliner while he lights one unscented candle, undresses, and lays his clothes on the other arm.

This time when I started to pull back the covers he said, "Hold it." On the bureau he had music ready to play and pushed the button for one of my favorite old-old-tunes, 'White Christmas'.

Although it was a sweet, romantic idea, we got over heated too quickly while pressed together as we danced in the dark…briefly.

Must be the candle!

CHAPTER 58

December 26

Normally, the day after Christmas has always been a downer, but today would prove to be excitingly exceptional. After taking a head count, we strategically placed chairs in a circle using every inch of the living room and decided where to place Butch.

Nancy had arrived early to help. Others were supposed to meet here at around Ten, for a couple hours of discussion before lunch is served.

Pop and Dixie offered to cook two large enchilada casseroles, a red-chili beef and a green chili chicken. "Hold the garlic and add lots of cheese," said Rick in a good mood while arranging chairs. Since our late night discussions about what happened last Saturday were non-existent, I knew he was eager to learn more today from us on-the-spot viewers, and I was anxious for details of what he had REALLY seen when he and Bullet arrived at Massacre Grounds. Knowing others had arrived later, their comments would not be highlighted as important and no one was invited.

Everyone who had been invited was told the exact meeting time and to “put-a-lid-on-it” because it would be a secret kept from Shieter and the media.

After Dixie, Nancy and I reviewed the list a couple times, we brought in a few lounge chairs from the outside patio. Dixie said she and Pop would share a bench near the entrance between the kitchen and living room to help serve coffee and tea. We needed fifteen chairs for all of us: Butch, Nancy, Rick, me, Mrs. Raintree, Coyotee, Jamie Mink, Roy, Kim Rose, Catora, the four B’s and Guy Wagner.

“Ok, I need to be invited because my gift whistle is a missing piece of evidence,” begged Guy eagerly, purring on the phone when he wished me a Merry Christmas yesterday and also asked, “When can the mistletoe and I come over?”

“Later!” I kept putting him off.

Visualizing who would sit where, I looked at the room filled with chairs and decided Guy Wagner would be with the four B’s so we could convince him to chaperone them at the cemetery Friday night, the day after the funeral. Good job for a mischievous coach. “You could coach them with your fearless attitude,” I told him later in the day.

“Well, that depends.”

“On what?”

“The mistletoe.”

Good grief!

Nancy and I discussed the reasoning for leaving the two freshmen boys out of it. “They obviously didn’t see much.”

Mrs. Raintree was the only parent invited considering she was Apache and encouraged her son, Coyotee, to take part in the funeral ceremony tomorrow, the twenty-seventh.

And it was decided when Shieter admonishes us for not inviting him to our Paranormal meeting we will tell him, “You had the important funeral to arrange out at Apache Junction.”

Cloud said that he would learn all from Dixie, Nancy and me during lunch.

Delilah said she didn't believe in the Paranormal and ghosts.

Becky Painter was not interested. "Count me out! I've had enough horsing around for awhile."

By Ten, everyone had arrived and sat where I pointed. Since Butch was Roy's cousin, Roy had the task of introducing him to all.

The girls shrank when seeing his 'almost' seven foot size but soon became enamored by his friendly attitude and humble demeanor.

"I'm anxious to hear all the circumstances," he said softly from his chair next to Roy who was feeling important.

We few in the know, the seven of us, sat close to Butch while the outsiders listened. Butch was sandwiched between Coyotee and Roy. We girls sat on both sides, then Mrs. Raintree, Rick and the others.

Nancy and I sat close reviewing every item on the note pad and decided to sequence the events chronologically. When we started with the rubber arrows, we asked Coyotee what was his intent?

"To set the mood, I guess, after listening to my uncles recall stories of the Apache and Mexican fights. These stories were handed down for generations."

Each person who talked had the floor respectfully from the bunch of us. We were the important seven.

Butch stretched out in his chair relaxing while listening to us. We, on the other hand, were tense and sitting as straight as arrows.

"It was unbelievable the way the horses acted," said Jamie Mink as she explained how they were spooked and ran away.

"They have a sixth sense," offered Butch without blinking.

Relating to Coyotee's spiritual chant with the results of the Apache appearing and disappearing, he said, "Congratulations. Your efforts were successfully rewarded. You released the spirit from bondage."

Discussion about the spear took the longest.

"It appeared out of nowhere!"

"Then disappeared with Heleena."

"But, she didn't bring it back with her again."

"Later, the spear was thrown to our small group as we traveled in the dark returning to the bus." We mentioned Rick breaking it.

Butch closed his eyes. "The spear is magic. I feel its power now, close by."

We all looked at Del Rio who gingerly stretched an arm behind him to bring out the two pieces of the spear where he had them hidden nearby.

No one spoke. My heart thumped as the seven of us came unglued due to our fearful past experience.

"Hold Tightly."

"Don't let go."

Butch pointed out that the spear "now has half the power," but after looking at its sharply pointed tip added, "I see that it can be exceptionally dangerous. Give it a good grip," he said to Rick who was showing white knuckles.

We were becoming spooked as we continued re-living the events. I noticed Guy and the four B's were sitting extra tall, intently listening. The non-reactionary was Coyotee's mom, probably wiser than all in the room except for Butch.

We filled in the blanks for Rick after hearing what he saw and missed.

"You didn't see her disappear?" Butch asked.

Rick shook his head "no" but most importantly saw her fall when hit with a "silent" bullet. Then the shocker, "Forensics insists that the bullet is from 1848 and covered in old bear grease from that time too."

The students were amazed at this fact and shook their heads with satisfaction. "Makes sense," they all agreed.

"We have a Time Warp," Butch started. "Coyotee's chant opened the door, penetrating the thin film protecting us from villains of the past." He closed his eyes. "A group of by-goners, victims of their traumatic past, have taken residence from where they might have died."

He opened his eyes. "You've heard of a Hornets' Nest, and Bee Hives. Now you know about Ghosts Clans. The lost souls are not all necessarily evil but it sounds like there is an evil one at this place; it could be in opposition to others by discovering the power to transcend from the past, to the present, and then back again. This is an old European trick from the Sixteenth Century, its base from Germany." Then turning his head looking around at all in our circled group he added, "We need to lure it back to its cage and discover how to totally contain him."

He paused for a long minute while we thought about this. Then Rick said, "He likes toys," then mentioned the GPS.

"He's a pack rat for sure," said Butch after listening to Nancy's reading of the list of items from the dig. "The entire area of Massacre Grounds is dangerous. Many wars were fought in that area over a lost gold mine somewhere. Hundreds of hollowed-out skulls were found in the 1860's by the cavalry marching through."

"And the new pile of rocks Nancy and I saw the next day, what is that all about?" The students appeared startled by this news and we explained to them the difference.

Butch continued. "Time does not necessarily co-ordinate with our time. The fact that you saw the new pile of rocks on December twenty-third our time, does not mean that they were put there on that particular date in the past. Time spectrum bounces around uncontested."

Long pause.

We all sat quietly mesmerized as if in a trance.

Nancy pulled out the bagged bell from her big bag and passed it around. "This is carbon dated to be around 1848."

"Heleena visited the past and met violence from one, and benevolence from another," added Butch to the spooked group, each in turn looking at the tiny little bell afraid to touch it.

We were the most startled when Butch closed with, "The spear and bell are from the past. These items need to be placed in Heleena's coffin."

CHAPTER 59

Butch's words "Lure him back into his cage…" resonated harshly with all of us believers. How in the heck do we do this? And who would have the nerve? We mumbled and grumbled.

We were so captivated with his expertise, we would have skipped lunch if Pop had not loudly intervened with, "Let's eat!"

When Butch sat at the table, we all hovered around him any way we could, some plates on the table, some on our laps.

"Good food!"

"Delicious!"

"Outstanding."

Pop beamed, Dixie announced, "Come get something to drink." The counter set-up consisted of a tub of soda pop and beer on ice. Two tall coffee carafes contained decaf and regular. For sure, Dixie was keen to everyone's favorite beverage. Sugar and Cream were available.

We unbelievably minced at our food, too caught up in Butch's explanations of the Paranormal.

"Why was the pitchfork thrown at Pop?" I needed to ask since Pop certainly wouldn't. At this point, I tried to read Pop, but he avoided my look.

Butch answered, "You mentioned that you were standing at the entrance waiting for wood. I believe it was meant for you…a scare tactic." He paused, sipped on a cup of coffee, and did not smile. We sat silently tense, wishing for perfect answers.

"This entity is evil and didn't want you going to Massacre Grounds where I believe he dwells…in a clan of others."

We were ghostly quiet. Whenever one person asked a question, we sat with full attention, almost in a trance, listening.

"Where's the spear?" Jamie Mink suddenly awakened us with her freight.

"Held tightly to the floor," Rick answered as a few looked toward his booted feet.

"Where are you keeping it tonight?" Bing wanted to know as the others supported his question.

"Where I kept it last night, locked in the tool chest that's on my truck." Without smiling he added, "I should break off a piece for Guy and the Family Farm to take with them for their cemetery all-nighter!"

"Not happening," said the four as Guy smiled at the idea. We needed the break as a few chuckled.

Suddenly, Nellie the Greyhound jumped up from where she had been sleeping near Pop's feet, ran over to Rick's boots and started barking sharply, her head down, her feet firmly planted near the spear in fear.

We grabbed each other by the arm.

"Sit still," said Butch. "It's harmless here around us. In a group there is strength, and I feel its weakness."

"My feet are vibrating." Rick's wide eyed look of astonishment meant trouble.

Roy and Coyotee quickly left their seats, went to Rick's side to help hold down the spear, and yelled.

"Get out!"

"Go away!"

Looking at white faces around me, I knew we were all connected to the scene, believers of whatever, definitely afraid of the unknown.

Forget my ESP. It's lost.

Everyone grabbed another person, but no one grabbed Butch, nor did he move from where he calmly sat sipping his coffee, firmly holding his cup with two hands.

As the heavy table began to gently shake, Butch yelled at us again repeating the order, "Hold still. It wallows in fright…breathe!"

In unison with someone pounding on the back door, he ordered, "Hold your forks tight in your fists!"

"Come in!" Pop hollered trying to push away from a clinging Dixie.

Barrel legged, pickle nose Pete opened the door wide and as he did so, a "woosh" of wind from around us elevated the table about an inch before slamming it down again. Traveling over to Pete, it slammed the door open wider against the wall and blew off his hat when he ducked.

"What the…I ain't seen such a thing ever. A dust devil in yer kitchen?"

"Eliminate the word dust," I cried out.

"Git out! Was the creature here?" He stumbled against the door as he gathered his hat. "Ya'll saw him here now?" He pointed down to the floor with his hat.

"Yep," said Kim Rose, "and we lived through it."

Roy said, "You arrived just in time to let him out… or let him in." Then he continued with the most solid question of the day, an answer to which we badly needed. “How do we lure him back to his cave? Or where ever he lives.”

Butch frightened us by using the term “it” instead of “he” when he said, “We will send Heleena back in time to do the work for us in eliminating ‘it’.”

We quietly pondered this awhile before Mrs. Raintree spoke, “We have a burial song of praise that Coyotee can sing at the burial. It will be special for Heleena.”

Catora leaned close to Coyotee and whispered words of encouragement.

Pete had been standing there afraid to move until Pop insisted he fill his plate then tell us about his experiences out at the mountain.

He selected a Root Beer, sat and began talking. “I ain’t goin near no burial. The Creature might claim me as part of his mountain.”

Now “it” is a “Creature”. Pete’s uninvited visit had the good intention of bringing us current about his past experiences with the harmonica player.

“I didn’t know ‘bout yer meetin’! I came fer more info ‘bout the area on account of I might continue workin’ in the Superstitions. I like excitement…the right kind.” His can of Root Beer fizzed out when he sat it down too hard while explaining the timing of the harmonica in certain areas.

“I hear more music during holidays and cold weather.”

Rick wanted to know why the ghost would still be bothering us.

Butch said that ‘its’ timing may be out of order and it is still in the scare mode. “Entities like to let their presence known when possible and the ticket to the present time for ‘it’ is the broken spear. This spear needs to go in the coffin ASAP!”

“”What?” Pete had to ask about this latest announcement from Butch. He looked under the table at Rick’s boots anchoring the spear.

“Cripes, is that ‘thing’ following me?”

Now references from ‘it’ to ‘creature’ to ‘thing’ wrung me dry emotionally. I noticed that we had squeezed together tightly.

Hey!” He continued. “I know two senators we could send out there at night time fer an adventure of their lifes.”

Rick explained the shooting episode as Pete ducked his head in shame and played with the rim of his hat.

“I ain’t got no sense tyin’ up with those buzzards.”

I looked over at the Family Farm cycle group…the old retired-pudgy-whiskered group were like Pop, all ears about the big happening at the Superstitions. At this moment Butch announced, “Pete needs to accompany the retired group to the all night cemetery party, considering ‘it’ arrived the same time as Pete.” Then looking at him, “He likes you.”

“You mean take them there?”

“And stay with them there.” Butch didn’t smile.

“Nope. Ain’t no gun big enough!”

“It’s not Massacre Grounds. You’ll be safe.”

Butch looked at his watch. “Time to go. Rick, lock those two pieces in your truck’s tool box and drive your truck to the burial site. Let’s hope nothing disappears.”

“Probably not, since we’re about twenty miles away from the Superstitions,” said Pop.

What happened to his disbelief and “malarkey”?

Before the small group parted, I informed them about the text message I received from Shieter pertaining to the burial. “A private grave side ceremony at Apache Junction Cemetery will be at Eleven A.M. tomorrow.

“District’s Orders!”

CHAPTER 60

December 27, 2014

All of us from the English Department and the few others within the school who knew her well, planned to attend. My phone rang every ten minutes concerning the directions and so forth.

A large black tent covered forty chairs ready for any sniveling rain drops. This was a private party and those rubber-neckers wandering around the cemetery, were whisked away by cops on foot patrol. Noted as part of the Superstitions' criminal scene, there were many gapers hoping to see a ghost or learn more about the drama.

The journalists were too vague, and since one mentioned the three magic words in her article, "Lost Dutchman Goldmine", the mountain was suddenly crawling with people pretending to be hikers. Those uninvited who knew about the grave side funeral services, desperately wanted in. Because of the crowd, the cemetery gate was heavily manned by four armed patrolmen and Guy Wagner who tended the list of invitees since he knew the teachers and Del Rio didn't. Del Rio's job was to co-ordinate the uniforms on duty.

Rick, Nancy and I had arrived earlier at the mortuary before the casket was sealed, to add the two broken pieces of spear and the tiny bell which we placed in Heleena's hand. We also added two other prizes from the faculty who knew her well---her clipboard with her own hand writing and the favorite pens she kept on her desk.

She was dressed in the same clothes she wore for the trail ride, having been cleaned and pressed by the mortuary crew.

Our little group that saw her killed, sat in the front row that was tied off with purple ribbon, Heleena's favorite color. Roy and the two teen diggers were dressed in suits and ties. Catora, Jamie Mink, Kim Rose, Nancy and I were in floor length winter dresses. Mrs. Raintree wore pressed slacks and a dark jacket all heavily adorned with silver Indian jewelry. Sitting next to Catora was Coyotee in formal leather beaded Indian attire. All very impressive.

Since Del Rio was regulating traffic on his walkie-talkie, Guy decided he needed to communicate with me via text messaging while he waved car loads of teachers through the gate. Made him look official.....

"Mis-Toe N fridge wating 4 u".

OK. I needed to keep extending his offer. Why? I don't know. Blame it again on the smudge. "Sve 4 Nyrs".

OFF

The last minute minister stood military erect next to the casket, hands clasped, very official. He looked at me with a faded smile and nodded.

I nodded back without smiling. After all, my text messaging was supposed to be very official.

"Lo sve me a seat-Rick"

OFF

"N yrs 4 sure-Guy"

OFF

I totally turned off my cell to set a good example for all present. It beeped, glowed, and faded away so I put it in my purse.

The Minister winked, impressed with my example of politeness and watched others do the same. Time was getting short.

What was that? A beep! Thinking it was a channeling mistake, I simply took the cell out of my purse, and turned it off again.

The Minister two feet in front, was watching me.

After one minute, it beeped, and glowed with a message;

U R NXT

"What the heck. I turned it off?" I looked at the Minister and Nancy for an explanation.

"I saw you turn it off," said the Minister in astonishment.

Oh! Oh! My heart jumped out of my chest and my ears started drumming. I turned around and looked over at Butch one row behind me and on my right. I ESP'D pointing to my cell. Otherwise speechless, this was no time for a chat.

Butch waved his fingers indicating he wanted my cell. Getting up, he took it and walked away, gesturing to Rick as he did. My heroes will take care of me. Please Guy. Do not send a text about mistletoe while Rick holds my cell in his hand. The burial needs to be quick.

Too late; he did. This will be bed time fodder.

In the meantime, what was the U R NXT all about? And there was no name for sender.

Impossible!!!

While in Rick's hands, my phone went dead and fortunately did not ring again the remainder of the day. At this point, I never wanted one again until Butch calmly said, "Don't worry about it. Scare tactics. Leave it with Rick for a few days. I sense that the ghost will be gone after the burial because it will have a new enigma to deal with…Heleena."

He was so positive in his announcement that I felt relieved and at peace with the whole episode. But still, where was the proof?

The Minister began his remorseful tone of appraisal for Heleena, listing all the positive comments and attributes written about her by faculty members that he had memorized.

This followed by prayers, softened our spirit. We whimpered and cried soft tears. Some did the sign of the cross while others clasped their hands and bowed their heads until AMEN.

Next the Minister sat with us to watch Coyotee's performance.

This time, his song and dance gig was different, and so was his costume. Fully clothed in Apache formal wear along with a colorful head-dress, he sang and chanted quietly without the powerful dance, all the while waving a leather fringed wand over the closed casket. After ten minutes, he sat in the empty chair between his mother and Catora. The three held hands prompting all of us to do so, as the casket was lowered into the ground. We sat frozen until all remaining soil piled nearby, was used. This was the unique plan initiated by Butch, and the mortuary. Who were they to argue, noting that this was a specialty event and all internments were individual.

Tom Mix, Delilah, the Coroner and Medical Examiner were first to leave. "We have paper work to file." There it was again. T Rex's shoulder twitch!

It was late in the afternoon by the time we parted. All of us hugged, cried, and went our separate ways with words like, "See you soon," and "Keep in touch."

No one wanted to plan an after funeral banquet gathering since a few days remained of the holiday vacation. Good decision. We were all sapped of energy.

For sure we would be communicating with the cemetery "all-nighters."

"We are going to the cemetery tonight to gather loose spirits from this eventful day," wise-cracked Bob.

He was the spoke person for the non-believers, all though I felt that Brad the retired Marine, was the least skeptical considering the miracles he had seen in combat.

"Six of you going?" I asked the group still milling around.

Guy said, "Wouldn't miss the fun!"

Pete shrugged with, "I 'spose, since Pop mentioned that Massacre Grounds was twenty miles away. I say, what the heck?"

Rick told them with a smirk as we now parted, "I'll keep my cell fully charged."

I was happy to go home with Pop and Dixie to crash on my bed for a never-ending late nap. Rick was un-readable anyway after the funeral. He sort of snubbed me without a goodbye.

It was pitch black when the phone rang, lighting the room.

"You coming over?" Rick's voice coaxed.

"Depends. What are you cooking?" I purred.

"Steak, baked potatoes, greens, and the beverage you asked for last Saturday, White Russians."

So he had been listening. And I cringed with thoughts of last Saturday. How will I ever forget the nightmarish events?

Feeling good after my long nap, I drove the couple miles to Rick's. Finding him tending a barbeque, I wrapped my arms around him from the back where I thought I could hide out. "Smells good."

As predicted, Rick was not happy about the mistletoe Guy thing. He turned around and faced me waving the steak thongs in the air and said, "He had to text you at a funeral."

"Maybe it was the ghost." I giggled.

He cleared his throat.

"You had lipstick on your face." I stepped back with folded arms.

"She slammed one on me in a hurry before I could pull away," he explained. "We didn't text plan anything."

"Gee. How did that happen? You're about a hundred pounds bigger…don't burn the steaks. I like mine medium rare." Someone needed to man the kitchen.

Rick turned off the barbeque, plated the steaks and we went inside to a table setting of salad and baked potatoes with all the trimmings.

Rick hugged me before we sat and pleaded, "Would you please quit being jealous of Delilah?"

"You mean skinny butt!"

His smile was huge. "If you'd quit eating those chocolate ding-a-lings, you'd lose your caboose."

"Then I'd be flat like a man."

"Oooh no! Forget it. I'll bring you a box of them tomorrow."

We cleaned the kitchen, settled on the sofa, put on my favorite movie-- Mama Mia, and drank White Russians. Rick fell asleep within two minutes with his head on my lap. I tenderly massaged his head and worried about two things: What was the meaning of the text I received on my dead cell---U R NXT---, and how are the six men managing their night at the Cave Creek Cemetery?

I reached over, found Rick's cell and turned it off.

At midnight there was a strange sound of multiple, very loud pings. We were asleep on one pillow when Rick reached over and turned off his tracker.

"Heleena has made it."

CHAPTER 61

Hurriedly, the six men prepared their camp knowing darkness would soon be upon them. Each brought something to contribute to the outing in Guy's huge tent. "I'm a camper, a hunter, and outdoorsman," he teased after smashing his thumb as they pounded down the stakes to hold the ten-by-twenty canvas piece. The flooring of an attached plastic tarp, kept critters out.

The men rolled out their thick sleeping bags along the sides leaving room for the fold-up table and camping chairs positioned in the center. Card games are planned ahead for entertainment and they decided to go "raw" which meant no electronics and no cells powered on. Flashlights are to be used for making the rounds in shifts, searching among the tombs in the old, decaying Cave Creek Cemetery.

"What if we git snake bit?" Pete worried.

"My truck's parked close. Snakes are not out in December anyway," said Guy who had gathered the group in town at Screamin' Ice Cream where they had chowed down on burgers and brought extras for midnight snacks.

"No cooking!" They had decided earlier.

Pop is supposed to bring carafes of coffee and home-made breakfast burros at Seven. For now, they decided that beer was the best sleep cocktail.

Darkness at the cemetery with no lights within a mile, invites billions of stars lighting the surroundings with a faint glow seeping over tops of tombstones.

"Turn off the light," Bob said to Bing who brought his lantern, the only planned light for card games. They stepped out of the tent flap to look around. Eyes soon became adjusted and they were aghast at the beauty. Expanding their knowledge of the stars, each contributed a school lesson pointing to different constellations, the Big Dipper the easiest to locate.

"What's that big white sheet on the ground over there on the side of the tombstones?" Blake pointed out.

"Probably white quartz," said Guy.

Everyone turned on a flashlight.

A huge mound of half buried white quartz glowed back at them. Scattered around was Rose Quartz, a pinkish translucent rock, sometimes polished for jewelry.

"Quartz is plentiful out here," said Guy to the small group, some of whom were new to the desert.

Surrounding them silently in the glow of the stars, sat about a hundred headstones, most tilted from age and soil movement.

"Below our feet is a lifetime of old stories," Brad remarked while looking around the decaying cemetery, no longer in use.

"After we play cards, let's come out here and read the inscriptions. Should be interesting." Bob led the group towards the tent, surprised at the distance they had covered.

Then: "Hidee-ho-ho! Brought my own sleeping bag." From behind the tent stepped a man they couldn't see from the distance.

The stunned six, stopped and stared.

"Hey there. The Department sent me over to make sure you guys are ok. I'm newly retired but know this area well. Did you bring any guns?"

"No," said Bing. "We were afraid we might shoot each other in fright or at some teenagers necking behind a tombstone."

"Hold on there!" Barrel legged pickle nose Pete pulled two revolvers from holsters under his thick vest. "Jist in case that there harmonica creature comes my way." Twirling the guns with expertness, he shoved them back in their holsters "These pets, I've had fer years!"

"There's no such thing as ghosts." The old sheriff beamed. "I've lived in this area all my life and ride my horse a great deal at night." He rubbed his clean shaven leather-skin face as he rambled on slowly. "The only spooks out there now are night owls, dormant rattlers, and some squirrels foraging around for food." They admired the retired Deputy's freshly pressed suit, containing local badges and insignia. He continued. "When Del Rio asked for permission from the Sheriff's Department for a one-nighter at the cemetery, we all laughed and wondered why."

"To prove there are no ghosts." Then the old Deputy looked at the group, "A-hah! This is part of that Superstition stuff I've been reading about!"

"Sort of," said Blake.

Pause.

They all looked at each other, worried about how much they should tell the old gentleman.

"Time to play cards." Brad interrupted as he pulled out two decks of cards and a pair of dice. They planned to play the easy game of Help Your Neighbor so they could have a conversation swapping stories about their pasts. The Deputy pulled up a chair. "Deal me in."

"I need to plan for baseball and track. I'm not playing." In the dim light of the one lamp, Guy wrote on his clip board.

As the night wore on, tales ranged from the impossible to everyday domestic complaints.

"Since I'm the new guy," said the Deputy, "I'll do the first hour's cemetery duty." He borrowed a flashlight, and went out to make the rounds of the silent graveyard.

The men yawned and grumbled mentioning their list of mundane everyday chores.

Bing of the NYPD started with "I hate emptying the dishwasher."

They tried to out-do each other with their lists of hates.

"Mine are taking out the garbage and wiping out the shower. These haunt me from my childhood," said Bob.

"How about folding clothes? I like to pile them on the bed and leave them there," Brad added, "but, I hate to lie on top of them when I go to bed, so this is always a last minute crappy task."

"Where are the women when we need them?" Then Blake listed vacuuming and cleaning out the dryer's lint trap.

Guy said that those last two were his also.

The Deputy never offered a problem. He lay on top of his sleeping bag, hands behind his head.

The sleepy group decided it was picture time before shutting off the lamp and calling it a night. It was past two in the morning.

Blake took a variety of silly pictures with his smart-phone making sure that all seven of them posed together, behind tombstones and other goofies. In all, he quickly shot about two dozen before quitting. After checking the photos, they all agreed they were good.

The uneventful night went fast, each making one last round checking for ghosts or whatever.

At Seven, Pop arrived with food and coffee. Burritos oozing with chorizo, eggs and cheese were washed down with coffee and bottles of water.

"So, did you see any ghosts?"

"Hell no! Aint none here," offered Pete quickly.

"Where's the Deputy?" Guy was first to notice the empty space where the old man and sleeping bag had been.

"He's probably gone home," said Brad.

"Well, how was it?" Pop asked with a mean grin.

"Basically, it was a beautiful starry night," said Guy, "and I'd do it again."

They all agreed on that and took their time eating and milling around in the cool morning.

At Eight, Rick arrived. "Ok, how many did you count?"

"Why you up so early?" Brad asked.

"Duty patrol. Besides, I heard Pop was making breakfast burritos. You have to admit, you were a bit spooked. Tell the truth."

"We were until the retired Deputy you sent showed up and settled our nerves," said Brad.

"What Deputy?" Rick's burrito was half gone as he looked at the crew while sipping hot coffee.

"The one you sent to stay with us." Bob pointed out where he had laid his bedroll to join them. "And, he said Del Rio sent him."

Next, Blake and Guy got involved describing him.

Rick took a deep breath and quietly said, "I didn't send a deputy out here. There's no such person you described."

Pop began questioning. "What was he driving?"

"Uhh!"

"Did you hear him arrive?"

"Uhh!"

"Did you hear him leave?"

The men stomped around in a kind of dizziness.

"Sit!"

Rick and Pop gave the order at the same time.

There was a long pause as the group stared at each other feeling for answers, too dumbfounded to speak.

"Wait. I have pictures. Lots of pictures." They gathered together to watch Blake's smart phone as he brought multiple pictures in the view frame.

The men were in the photos, all six, but there was a blank space where the Deputy had previously posed.

"I reviewed these pictures last night? He was in about ten or more shots…now he isn't."

Rick shook his head. "The ghost came visiting. You better make sure nothing's missing."

They went back into the tent to check around.

"My two prized pistols are gone." Pete ranted on and on rambling with anger.

"Let's see your holsters." Pete handed the belt with the two empty holsters to Rick's outstretched arm.

"There's something in the bottom of this one," and he pulled out a shiny harmonica. "Not a good trade."

"CRIPES!" Pete paled.

CHAPTER 62

APACHE CAMP
Massacre Grounds
December 29, 1848

For seven days sirens and moans from the troubled four continued through the canyons of deep arroyos, screeching to the mountain tops, crackling through brush and trees, sounds only the animals could hear. Noisy swirls of wind swept quickly up and around pillars of hoodoos, then just as quickly cascaded down in slippery swipes, wrestling resting rabbits and lizards out of habitats to scamper for other shelter. Javalinas and Bob Cats stayed their distance from the four, as did a variety of others, especially shy Black Bear and Mountain Lion, all sensing a new awareness of trouble in the area. Wild game ran farther into the Superstition Wilderness, away from the howling.

CHINA ROSE sat in the cove infant style, butt on the ground, chubby pink legs sprawled out in front, hands hiding her sobbing face. While occasionally wiping her nose on her long green velvety skirt, she continuously shined the silver tea pot, her souvenir from home, her piece of security. Glancing over at Davy increased her remorse. She would never dance and sing again.

For days, young FOOT SOLDIER DAVY sat whimpering nearby, rocking forward and back, both hands hanging down in the dirt like a puppet. A long suspender hung carelessly off his shoulder to his elbow. Doom and gloom was his. He would never find peace. An innocent young victim he was when he first walked here from Fort McDowell, and now all is lost forever. Turning his head, he watched MEXICAN MANO hoping he could find peace for all of them.

For days, MEXICAN MANO sat reciting "Our Father" and "Hail Mary" on the short stick he used as a rosary, it now shiny and warm from constant use. Every small space on the stick was a prayer and as he sometimes ducked his head with chin on chest to look at his prayer stick, an accumulative roll of skin and wrinkles reminded him of his aging body and time spent on this mountain, time forever lost. Shuffling around so his body leaned to the back of the sheltering cove, he watched the movements of GAMBLER MOODY. After a while, he arose and started a little bean pot fire.

For days, GAMBLER MOODY brooded. Not sitting still like the other three, he continuously shuffled slowly between the large purple boulder, his space near the cove, than back again to feel the wallow of dried mud. He followed the circle of the wallow with the toe of his boot, arousing vivid memories of the beautiful Goddess who acknowledged their existence. Believing the spear to be the magical tool, he became irate when DUTCHY took it with him on his last trip to town. How long had the evil one been gone? His hand went to his vest, remembering the emptiness where the chained watch had been. It was with the demon DUTCHY somewhere. Lifting the red-ribboned whistle to his lips, he kissed it lovingly in remembrance of her gift to him.

For days, the motley group of four stayed away from the evil cave, the one from which DUTCHY the demon left vacant when going to town. Large rocks and small boulders now lay nearby the tight entrance in a heap, thrown out earlier by MEXICAN MANO and him after APACHE disappeared. Now

MEXICAN MANO stayed far away, unhappy with the change of events.

MEXICAN MANO'S keen ears were the first to hear the harmonica. "Psst!" He notified the other three.

The four stood together defensively, reeking with anger, flaming with hate as they stood watching him walk toward them, and turn to his cave. Nevertheless, they were drawn to follow him to his cave to learn his secret, his magic of connecting with the living. Was it the spear? The harmonica? They mumbled among themselves for solutions. There were NONE and now they wanted answers to their destiny.

"Heidee-ho-ho." DUTCHY waved a greeting at the hopeless four. "Look, you dumb fools! Treasures! Not yours, but mine." He laughed heinously, the one they remembered so vividly from a week ago when he shot the beautiful Goddess. "Look!" Twirling two pistols he had pulled out of his pocket, he then shot at the purple boulder; no one moved as bullets ricocheted around.

His laugher echoed loudly through the nearby canyons. "Such a sad, sad group. Here crooked neck, these are for you." Laughing, he threw a pair of white opalescent dice at the statuesque GAMBLER MOODY hitting him in the chest. Not moving to catch them, they bounced off his chest and tinkled on the rocks.

DUTCHY moved closely among them taunting and laughing like a crazy demon with power, tormenting them with his new gadget, a weird compass thrown at him from a man the living called Del Rio. Laughing callously he continued, "I will now leave you to your destiny," and started walking towards his cave at the end of the cove.

Instantly, a swirl of air funneled down toward the dried wallow near the large boulder, spiraling clouds of dust and pebbles. Stunned, the group of five stood hypnotized by the occurrence before their eyes. Again! No one blinked. Soon the fuzziness disappeared with the fading swirl of dust.

THE GODDESS stood before them, shiny, fresh and free of dust, dirt and mud.

Unmoving, they gaped.

She smiled broadly.

The sun came from behind a cloud in the dimming dusk.

GAMBLER MOODY brought the whistle to his lips.

CHINA ROSE held her silver tea cup to her heart.

FOOT SOLDIER DAVY stood tall, pulled his suspender over his shoulder and held his cap to his heart.

All were silent in disbelief.

MEXICAN MANO did not move from where he sat stirring his campfire to a flaming height.

"Hah" laughed DUTCHY. "Remember this?" Before anyone could move to tackle him, he pulled his new two pistols from his pockets and started shooting at THE GODDESS. This time it was different, and he could not be more astonished. All the bullets went through her to boulders and bushes behind. Only lizards scattered as he emptied the pistols wildly of shot then heaved them in the bushes.

Gasping with fear, the four wavered with disbelief. Again!

THE GODDESS stood smiling, unmoved by the bullets.

She joined the group of four, holding hands, slowly shuffling toward DUTCHY, resentment steaming from their bones.

Unafraid, DUTCHY laughed a piercing shrill, turned his back on them and said, "I'm going to my den." Barely squeezing through the tight opening, he entered his newly acquired cave, the gold mine vacated by APACHE one week ago.

Without pre-planning, the crew immediately sprang into action placing boulder after boulder into the tight entrance, rock after rock in front of the cave until there was a space of about twelve inches wide.

"Hey, Stop!" For once, DUTCHY'S sinister laughter was replaced with demands. "Here, you can have my harmonica." Through the small crevice he flung it out to the waiting hands of CHINA ROSE.

"I have more treasures to offer!" He begged and begged until they could hear him no more. For one hour after, they piled a mountain of heavy rocks at the entrance. Heaving together they rolled one last lonely boulder at the end.

THE GODDESS was back where she belonged, next to these people who brought her so much happiness on her last short visit. "My name is Heleena," she told all of them and especially GAMBLER MOODY.

Walking over to MEXICAN MANO'S fire, she threw in the two broken pieces of spear. Sparks of many colors, a firework of explosives, flew upward.

Like the lifting flame, their spirits rose higher and they laughed for the first time in years.

GAMBLER MOODY hurriedly opened his valise and pulled out his favorite cigars, the expensive Cuban Long Nines, saved for a glorious occasion like this one.

CHINA ROSE came forward to feel the fabric of Heleena's skirt of soft denim so new to her eyes and never seen before.

MEXICAN MANO admiringly traced with his finger the figurines of colored inlays on Heleena's boots knowing he could tool the same for everyone.

Happiness had never been theirs; and here it was.

"For you," said THE GODDESS as she placed the teeny tiny bell back in GAMBLER MOODY'S hand.

The three men looked on, swaying with happiness as FOOT SOLDIER DAVY played the harmonica and the two women sang and danced.

"When you're feeling all alone, just give your dog a bone."

DUTCHY grumbled with disgust but did not panic. He sat on a pile of gold rocks playing with his toys. "I have all the time in the world. Someday, some fools will come along and dig me out."

He was right!

CHAPTER 63

Mesa, Arizona
HEAVY EQUIPMENT RENTALS
You drive---We supply

CLERK #1 at closing time. "I tell you. I've seen it all."

CLERK #2 "What happened?"

CLERK #1 "Three men of opposite sizes walked in this morning for equipment. One man looked like he was on stilts. One was skinny as a rail. And the third was a little short Leprechaun.

CLERK #2 "What did they rent?"

CLERK#1 "A bull dozer. Said they needed to clear away some storm rubbish.

CLERK #2 "Rubbish my foot! It's that Superstition stuff."

CLERK # 1 "Most interesting was the gorgeous lady that followed them in. I know I've seen her before in a movie. Name some movies for me!!"

CLERK #2 "Tomorrow. Right now, shut up, lock up, and let's get out of here."